Born in 1963 in Suzhou and now living in Nanjing with his family, Su Tong is one of China's most celebrated bestselling authors, shooting to international fame in 1993 when Zhang Yimou's film of his novella *Raise the Red Lantern* was nominated for an Oscar. *Madwoman on the Bridge* is his first collection of short stories to be published in English. It is to be followed by his latest novel, *Check*, a violent drama set in the aftermath of the Cultural Revolution, to be published by Doubleday in 2009.

Also by Su Tong

RAISE THE RED LANTERN
(a collection of three novellas)

RICE

MY LIFE AS EMPEROR

MADWOMAN ON THE BRIDGE

Su Tong

Translated from the Chinese by Josh Stenberg

BLACK SWAN

TRANSWORLD PUBLISHERS
61–63 Uxbridge Road, London W5 5SA
A Random House Group Company
www.rbooks.co.uk

MADWOMAN ON THE BRIDGE
A BLACK SWAN BOOK: 9780552774529

First publication in Great Britain
Black Swan edition published 2008

An earlier version of the translation of 'How the Ceremony Ends'
by Josh Stenberg first appeared in the Kyoto Journal #63, 2006.

This book is a work of fiction and, except in the case of
historical fact, any resemblance to actual persons,
living or dead is purely coincidental.

A CIP catalogue record for this book
is available from the British Library.

Addresses for Random House Group Ltd companies outside the UK
can be found at: www.randomhouse.co.uk
The Random House Group Ltd Reg. No. 954009

The Random House Group Limited supports The Forest Stewardship
Council (FSC), the leading international forest certification
organisation. All our titles that are printed on Greenpeace
approved FSC certified paper carry the FSC logo.
Our paper procurement policy can be found at
www.rbooks.co.uk/environment

Typeset in 11/16pt Giovanni Book by
Kestrel Data, Exeter, Devon.
Printed in the UK by
CPI Cox & Wyman, Reading, RG1 8EX.

2 4 6 8 10 9 7 5 3 1

Contents

Contents

MADWOMAN ON THE BRIDGE

MAD WOMAN ON THE BRIDGE

Madwoman on the Bridge

The madwoman was wearing a white velvet cheongsam, and in her hand she held a sandalwood fan. Standing on the bridge, she revelled in her own elegance. For those who knew her this was not at all surprising, but other passers-by assumed she was an actress here to shoot some footage. She gazed around her and raised her fan to wave at the children going past, but they ignored her. The boys stuck out their tongues and grimaced, hoping to frighten her, while the girls pointed at her cheongsam and, whispering confidentially, paid no further attention to her.

They were like lively clouds, floating one by one across the bridge, only to disperse at the slightest puff of wind. The madwoman's constant companion was a pot of chrysanthemums, which stood watch over the bridge with her. November chrysanthemums: from a distance, they seemed still to be in bloom, but up close you could see how they dropped. Just like the madwoman. At first glance she seemed beautiful, but closer scrutiny revealed that she was as faded as her flowers.

The madwoman on the bridge appeared very lonely, unbearably so in fact, for she kept twisting her head and body this way and that, looking from side to side. Her brow furrowed as she glanced over at Mahogany Street, on the near side of the bridge, then mumbled something which sounded like a complaint. What was she complaining about? Or whom? No one cared.

Besides the pot of chrysanthemums, her intimacy extended only to the sandalwood fan. All those who knew her were familiar with this article: it was dark yellow, threaded with gold and had green tassels hanging from the handle. You could smell its fragrance from far away. Although the season for using sandalwood fans was already long past, the madwoman clutched hers whenever she went out. She spread the fan so it shaded her brow; golden strips of sunlight slatted her pale countenance. At times it looked like dazzling make-up, at others like terrible scars.

Occasionally, when the figure of an acquaintance floated towards her over the bridge, the madwoman's dim eyes would glint suddenly, and her whole body would set itself in motion to strike a seductive pose. She would wave at them with her fan, slowly undulating her svelte waist in greeting. Then she would poke playfully at their hands with her fan and say, 'Oh, the heat. I'm just burning up.' At this point, whoever she addressed would avert their face and glance towards the bridge. They wore impatient expressions, for they were normal people, and normal people pay no attention to madwomen. They just waved her away unfeelingly and hurried from the bridge. To be honest, there weren't very many people on our street who embodied the warm-hearted spirit of revolutionary humanitarianism. I don't know whether the old woman from Shaoxing was one of these or not, and it doesn't much matter now either way, but I do know that the Shaoxing woman stayed on the bridge that afternoon to talk to the madwoman; she stayed for quite a long time.

The old Shaoxing woman had bound feet, but still undertook to deliver milk to the whole of Mahogany Street. Since feet were bound for aesthetic delight rather than practicality, the Shaoxing woman had trouble walking, and had to pause every few metres as she pushed her little cart. She shouted rhythmically as she walked to keep her spirits up. Her afternoon was devoted to collecting the empty bottles, and as she hobbled along, she groaned for people to bring them out. Today the Shaoxing woman had about thirty bottles as she tottered onto the bridge.

As usual, the madwoman remarked, 'Oh, the heat. I'm just burning up.'

The Shaoxing woman took a handkerchief from her bosom to wipe away the sweat and replied nonchalantly, 'Yes, I'm sweating like a pig.' Suddenly she realized who she was speaking to and cried out in surprise, 'Oh, what are you doing here? Why aren't you at home like you should be? What did you come here for?'

The madwoman opened her fan and wafted it a few times, saying, 'It was so hot, I came to the bridge for the breeze.'

The Shaoxing woman gave her a hard look and, sizing up the situation in an instant, said, 'I don't think so. It looks more like you were worried your cheongsam might go mouldy in its chest, so you thought you'd come here to show yourself off. Do you know what season this is? You must think it's still summer, coming out here wearing your cheongsam and waving that fan around. Winter's coming on, you know!'

The madwoman seemed unconvinced; she looked up at the sky, then reached out one hand to pass it over the chrysanthemums. 'Summer's over? But the chrysanthemums are still blooming. How could summer be over?' she mumbled to herself. Then, suddenly, her eyes lit up as she asked, 'When will winter start? When it does, I should wear my fox-fur coat.'

The Shaoxing woman gave a startled sound and replied, 'How can you still bother yourself with things like that? Haven't you been through enough already? Look at you, all dressed up and looking like a fright. That's what made them terrorize you in the first place – and that's what made you ill. Don't you understand?'

The madwoman did not, and remarked, 'With the

fox-fur coat I'd have to wear matching boots . . . What a shame they stole my lambskin boots.'

The thought of her lost finery caused a mournful expression to appear on her face. She walked a melancholy circle around the Shaoxing woman's cart, then another. 'No more high-heeled shoes,' she said with a glance at her feet. 'No more jade bracelets,' she said with a glance at her wrists. 'No silk stockings either,' she said, stroking her knees.

The Shaoxing woman couldn't suppress a cry of protest, 'They're gone, and rightly so! Otherwise you'd probably be dead by now! Don't you understand?'

The madwoman did not and lowered her head to study the milk bottles in the cart, or more specifically the multicoloured silk threads wound around the empty mouths of the bottles. 'Look how pretty those threads are,' she said. 'Won't you give them to me so I can weave Susu an egg cosy? At mid-autumn festival next year we can hang salted eggs in it.'

But the Shaoxing woman protested. 'You're not going to make a fool of me again. Last year I washed all those threads and gave them to you, and what happened? Before you even got home, you'd given them all away. Susu didn't get a single one, poor thing. What a shame such a sensible girl is saddled with a mother like you!'

The Shaoxing woman was old and her vision fading. She hadn't noticed at first that the madwoman was wearing a brooch. But when she bent down to put the milk bottles in order and looked up again at the madwoman, she caught sight of something on her chest: something sparkling, glistening in the sun. It was quite dazzling, and the Shaoxing woman gazed at it vacantly for a moment in disbelief. 'Oh, no! Whatever possessed you to go out with that on? A treasure like that . . . it cost your grandmother a bar of gold. Quick, take it off!'

It had taken a moment for the Shaoxing woman to realize what she was seeing. Now she rushed towards the madwoman and clutched her by shoulders. The madwoman raised her sandalwood fan and tried to fend her off, cheongsam rustling as she swayed this way and that to evade those grubby, gnarled hands. The fan was beautiful but impractical as a weapon, and the slippery white velvet cheongsam even less threatening. In the end the madwoman was no match for the Shaoxing woman, and she stood with her arms by her sides and suffered the brooch to be removed.

It was a remnant of a bygone era, a butterfly-shaped brooch executed with exquisite craftsmanship. The butterfly's wings were outlined in blue enamel and inlaid with several gemstones shaped like grains of rice. Its precious wings dominated the front of the cheongsam, secured at the back by a clasp, skilfully designed to prevent theft. No matter how hard she tried, the Shaoxing woman was unable to undo it.

'Who made this? They must have made it so difficult to undo on purpose,' she complained, then she went on to complain about the madwoman: 'And what can I say about you? I don't care how vain you are, or how much you love to wear your cheongsam, you mustn't ever wear this brooch when you go out. I know just about every stick your family owns, and the only valuable thing left is this brooch. If you lose it, it'll be too late to start wailing. Now help me take it off. I'm not going to swipe it, I'll just take care of it for you and give it to Susu tomorrow.'

Still the madwoman didn't cooperate, and the Shaoxing woman practically had to force the brooch off. Finally she tore some sealing paper off a milk bottle, wrapped the brooch in it, and concealed it in her bosom. 'There are lots of bad people about, looking to prey on people like you. Don't you understand?' The Shaoxing woman peered vigilantly all around and, finding no bad people in sight, gave a sigh of relief. Brusquely she nudged the madwoman towards the end of the bridge with the cart, saying, 'On a chilly day like this, you shouldn't stand out here and freeze. Go home now, go home.'

But the madwoman obdurately refused, saying, 'I've lost my key. I'm going to wait here for Susu and go home with her.'

The Shaoxing woman frowned at her. 'Even if you're ill, how can you just forget from one day to the next how to do the simplest things? What does it matter if you don't have the key, just go next door to Li Sannian's, and climb in through your window from their courtyard.'

But the madwoman shook her head, and said, 'I won't go to Li Sannian's. They won't let me. His wife says, "The troll! The troll's coming!" as soon as she sees me, and their youngest son starts crying and throws things at me.'

It took a moment before the Shaoxing woman understood this, but then she remarked levelly, 'You can't really blame them, not when you get yourself all dolled up like that. If a child ran into you in the dark, of course he'd think you were a troll. But grown-ups shouldn't say these things; it's wrong to bully someone like you. I'll take you home. We'll go through Li Sannian's together, and see if she dares swear at you then.'

But the madwoman persisted shaking her head, saying, 'I won't go through her house. I can't climb through the window. I'm wearing my cheongsam; I can't get through the window.'

'Well, *that*'s true enough. A thing like that is no good for anything but making an exhibition of yourself.' The Shaoxing woman glared disapprovingly at the madwoman's cheongsam. She fingered the neckline for a moment and patted the waist. Then she asked, 'Can it be comfortable to wear it that tight? It's really more than just ordinary vanity with you, isn't it? I was just remembering how, when you were young, you used to wear a cheongsam even when you went to measure out

16

the rice. Wiggling along, carrying the rice in a straw bag.'

The madwoman objected, 'It wasn't a straw bag. It was a woven craft bag. They were made for export, but I got one surplus.'

'A straw bag for export is still a straw bag – don't try and impress me with your fancy foreign garbage,' the Shaoxing woman retorted harshly, 'The reason you've had such hard luck is that your thinking is rotten through and through. If you think wrong, you act wrong, you rub people up the wrong way. It's not all your own fault that you're ill, though, half of it is your own problem and half is other people's. If I were your mother-in-law,' the Shaoxing woman ran on, lifting one hand as if to hit her, 'I would beat you. I'd beat you every day, and when I was tired I'd get my son to beat you. I might beat you half to death, but at least I'd make sure you knew how to be a good wife!'

The madwoman reacted instinctively to the Shaoxing woman's hostile tone and gesture, retreating and raising one hand as if to shield herself. The Shaoxing woman was usually so kind: why would she want to hit her? The madwoman could not distinguish between rhetoric and reality. Bewildered, she backed away from the cart, and the hem of her cheongsam caught under one of its wheels. The madwoman cried out loudly and freed the hem, craning her neck to examine it for grime. Just then, a bespectacled man was passing by. He jumped off his bicycle and eyed her for a moment, then he grinned, straddled his bike again and rode off.

When the madwoman noticed the man, her eyes kindled and she waved vigorously after his retreating figure: 'Mr Zhang! A real scorcher, isn't it?' It distracted him and he made as if to stop, then decided against it, the hesitation nearly causing him to fall off. He had to put his foot down hurriedly, coming to a stop by the end of the bridge. The madwoman and the Shaoxing woman both looked at the man, or rather at his back. He was clad in khaki trousers and a tunic, with sagging shoulders. The strange, sunken-looking figure hesitated for a long moment on the bridge before glancing back with undisguised interest, but in the end he kept silent and rode hurriedly away.

'Do you know him? And if you don't, why did you call him Mr Zhang?' the Shaoxing woman asked, looking after his receding figure reproachfully. Then she turned back to the madwoman. 'See how you're always accosting people? No wonder they say you act badly. You're indecent, that's what you are.'

The madwoman exclaimed, 'Who's indecent? You're the indecent one. I know him. Mr Zhang – he was the make-up man for the ensemble. He used to do my make-up.'

'Make-up, make-up! Is that all you can talk about?' All the time, the Shaoxing woman was nudging the madwoman towards the end of the bridge, saying, 'You have

18

a nerve, calling a woman *my* age indecent. Still, your mind's gone soft, and I'm not going to quibble with you. You doll yourself up like that and stand on the bridge if you want to. What do you think you look like? A painting? That would be all right – a painting for people to look at – but why is this painting looking back at *them*? Do you have any idea how people think these days? There are so many bad sorts. If they gang up on you, you won't be able to report them, and even if you did, they'd ignore you. Why don't you go home?'

At first the madwoman dodged her, then the Shaoxing woman caught her by her cheongsam and started tugging at it. The madwoman's heart bled for her beloved cheongsam and she began to resist, swatting the Shaoxing woman's hands as if they were flies. But they were strong and persistent, and the madwoman grew flustered. She raised her sandalwood fan and struck out at the Shaoxing woman's arms once, then twice, but when she saw the anger in the Shaoxing woman's eyes she didn't dare continue. Instead she forcibly thrust the old woman away. The Shaoxing woman staggered back, features twisting into a ghastly expression. She stamped her bound feet, gave her clattering milk cart a shove towards the end of the bridge, and said sharply, 'Fine. Don't listen to me then. Hit me with your fan. Just stand there like a peacock flaunting your feathers. No wonder people are cruel to you. You reap what you sow. Even a peacock doesn't spread his tail for just anyone.'

On that autumn afternoon, the madwoman stood on the bridge waiting for her daughter Susu. She would leave school and come home only in the early-evening, at about five o'clock, but the madwoman was standing on the bridge by a little after two. Perhaps she had nowhere else to go; perhaps she had already lost any sense of time passing. Everyone knew that something had gone wrong with her mind last spring. I suppose what happened next was pure coincidence, but it's often the case that if you wait for blossoms to open, you are rewarded with a bee sting. For Susu did not come, Cui Wenqin did.

Cui Wenqin came . . .

Forgive me for interpolating a few explanatory sentences at this point. Wenqin was the youngest doctor in the clinic on Mahogany Road, as well as one of the most famous women on the north side of town. She was extraordinarily beautiful, and she gave injections; it was therefore only natural that some people were given to unwholesome flights of fantasy about her. Apparently there were even a few who, although perfectly healthy, were so obsessed by her that they submitted themselves to injections just so they could be in her company. What they hoped to gain by this you can probably guess without my telling you.

Wenqin had in fact administered injections to the madwoman, but they had turned out to be ineffective for her illness, and were discontinued, so although the madwoman had no recollection of the doctor who had treated her, Wenqin remembered her clearly. The shocking sight of a beautiful woman in a state of mental collapse had touched her, and she kept pointing at her as if she were a painting, gasping in admiration. An intelligent woman openly admiring another woman's appearance is unusual enough, but since the latter's mind had gone, Wenqin's gasps were genuinely heartfelt. Some people wondered if this admiration might simply be a form of pity, though the madwoman provoked no similar feeling in others. Instead, the women who took their children to the clinic for inoculations would try to curry favour with Wenqin by saying, 'Look how pretty auntie is. Look how simple her clothes are. And it doesn't hurt at all when she gives you your injections.'

But Wenqin liked to talk to people about the madwoman's illness, appearance and clothes – especially when it came to her startling, beautiful clothes, Wenqin's praise was unstinting. She would say, 'There's nothing she daren't wear, and she looks good in it all. Have you seen her cheongsam? A white velvet cheongsam! Except for people in movies, I've never seen anyone look as good in a cheongsam as she does.' A colleague, although disapproving, hit the nail on the head when he said, 'You would look good in it, too. Too bad there's nothing wrong with your head! Because even if you did have a cheongsam like that, you'd never dare put it on.'

Wenqin walked past the bridge and spotted the madwoman at a glance – or rather her white velvet cheongsam. You could tell that she approached the madwoman only in order to be closer to that cheongsam. And though she exclaimed, 'Why ma'am, fancy meeting you here!' in her voice, so filled with pleased surprise, there was a quite different greeting, 'Why, white velvet cheongsam, fancy meeting *you* here!' Anyone could see that Wenqin was madly in love with that cheongsam, and that it was a love that ran bone deep, though at the moment it burned white hot as well.

People had only ever seen her in the tailored-to-fit military uniform she always wore; never in a cheongsam. It wasn't that she wouldn't give cheongsams a chance, rather that cheongsams hadn't given her one. She was Wenqin, after all; she wasn't the madwoman, though at that moment who could have said which one of them loved the cheongsam more? Wenqin's eyes betrayed her secret though; the way she gazed at that white velvet cheongsam was like a famished bee discovering a flower garden. She stopped in her tracks and began talking to the madwoman, although really she was talking to the cheongsam.

'What soft material. And tailored so snugly. And aren't the fastenings beautiful. Are these called lute frogs? How are they made, I wonder?' At first, when Wenqin touched the white velvet, she did so reverently, with utmost care, so as not to damage it, but gradually the movement became more rapacious, almost abandoned, her hand stroking in circles about the madwoman's waist. It was as if she were surveying something with a caliper, the result of which always remained unclear and had to be repeated constantly. When her hands slipped down to the madwoman's buttocks, she realized she had gone too far and immediately slid them up to her back. But she was not yet sated and clutched once again at the madwoman's shoulders.

'How unbelievably well it fits!' Wenqin exclaimed. 'I'll bet it was the one you used when you were MC in the performance troupe, wasn't it? You couldn't find another one like it in the whole world now. This kind of velvet – you can't buy material like it any more, even in Shanghai.'

The madwoman gave her a charming smile, and at the same time inspected the cheongsam. Wenqin's fulsome praise gratified her, though she was a little concerned there might be wrinkles where Wenqin had touched it. She arranged her fingers in the orchid position to act like an iron, and flattened out the tiny creases. Wenqin was a little insulted by this and remarked, 'You really take care of this cheongsam, don't you? It won't hurt it just to touch it. Still, no wonder. You only have this one, don't you? I saw you wear it in the summer, too.'

Stung, the madwoman replied, 'Who says I have only one? I have six cheongsams: this white velvet one, then there's the red velvet, two of silk – they're patterned – and two that are cotton but look good anyway. So altogether I

23

have six cheongsams, only my husband cut up the other five so this is the only one left.'

Wenqin was looking at her sideways, listening somewhat doubtfully. Abruptly, she interrupted the madwoman, asking, 'Red velvet? Can you make cheongsams from red velvet?'

The madwoman replied, 'Naturally. They all say my red velvet cheongsam is the one I look best in.'

Wenqin's eyes lit up. 'They *do* sell red velvet in the fabric shop. And I won't even need coupons – the clinic bought some so we could make cloth flowers!'

Wenqin lingered on the bridge a moment longer. She had now stopped staring at the madwoman and her cheongsam, and instead she was looking around herself, deep in calculation. She clapped her hands, reaching a decision, and said, 'I'll go and buy it right now.' With that, she turned round and walked off the bridge.

At first, the madwoman didn't realize what Wenqin had gone to do; she was just waiting for Susu, but instead of her daughter, once again it was Wenqin who appeared. The madwoman watched her as she crossed the bridge with a bolt of red velvet clasped in her arms. As she approached, the madwoman asked, 'What have you bought all that red velvet for?'

Wenqin grasped her by the arm and said, 'Do me a favour. Come with me for a moment to the tailor's. I need you to lend me your cheongsam so Mr Li can make a pattern from it.' Strangely, whenever it was anything to

24

do with clothing or make-up, the madwoman cottoned on right away. She stared at Wenqin, her eyes widening, and protested, 'No, I'm not going. I don't want him to make a pattern from my cheongsam.'

But Wenqin had clearly prepared for this. She caught the madwoman's hand tighter in her grasp. 'Don't be so petty. I'm only borrowing it to make a pattern. It's not as if anything bad will happen to it. Besides, yours is white velvet, mine is red – they're different, don't you see?'

But the madwoman kept trying to free her hand, and said, 'I don't have time to go with you to the tailor's. I have to wait here for Susu; Susu's about to leave school.'

Wenqin looked at her wristwatch, 'Oh, nonsense. It's only three thirty now; much too early to leave school. Don't run away. People will think that I'm dragging you off to do something awful.' Still trying to subdue the madwoman and protect herself from her flailing hands, Wenqin finally managed to catch her tightly by the elbow. In desperation, she grasped at straws and told the madwoman, 'I don't mean to be unfair. If you do me this favour, I'll give you my black scarf with the golden flowers. When you came for your injection, didn't you keep saying how you admired it?'

This one sentence carried more weight than the dozens preceding it. Wenqin felt the madwoman's resistance fade away as soon as she finished speaking. A silk scarf had conquered her. Her eyes glazed over for a moment, as if she were trying to picture the scarf she had just been promised. Then she laughed. 'My cheongsam, with a black silk scarf. A black silk scarf! Wouldn't they look smart together?' She smiled at Wenqin, then said abruptly, 'Fine. I'll hold you to that. And don't tell me you regret it later or I'll think you're a welcher.'

Now that it was already too late to take back her promise, Wenqin was a little discomfited. Frowning, she said, 'Who says you're soft in the head? You earn a silk scarf just for lending me your cheongsam – seems to me you're shrewder than anyone else I know.'

At half past three in the afternoon, the madwoman was seen following Wenqin off the bridge. With one hand she gingerly held the hem of her cheongsam while the other hand was clasped tightly in Wenqin's. They walked towards The East is Red Street. From the back, they could have been two women of equal intellect, their steps imbued with a similar grace. They looked like sisters out for a walk.

Li the tailor had a hunched back. On his head he wore an army cap, and a tape measure hung around his neck. He was drowning in the shop's disorder, the clothes and cloth piled and hanging everywhere. The shop didn't seem to belong to the same era as the spotless street outside, and Li's apologetic expression acknowledged this. Whenever a female customer entered, Li would rise obsequiously from behind his sewing machine, like someone from a grass-roots unit welcoming an important leader for a visit. But it was different when Wenqin came; with her he somehow achieved a surprising role reversal. As soon as she arrived, he began acting like a spoiled woman himself. At first he acted deliberately coy, tilting his head to see who was standing behind her, and when he saw that it was another woman, he heaved a sigh of relief and asked, 'So you've brought along another customer for me today? That's nice.'

Wenqin had brought not only a roll of red velvet, but also a woman in a white velvet cheongsam. She prodded the madwoman towards Li, and told him, somewhat incoherently, 'Make me a cheongsam . . . a cheongsam! I've talked to you about it before – the white velvet cheongsam. I've even brought her along!'

'A person is a person, a cheongsam is a cheongsam. Tell me exactly what you want.' First, though, the tailor took a look at the strange woman: she was in her thirties and pretty at first glance. But she did not bear close examination well: at second glance she looked strained, and yet a third revealed a kind of torpor in her. The tailor's eyes lit up, but she was not looking at him, instead she was fanning herself and having a look about the shop, casually criticizing all the clothes: 'You call this clothing? So ugly!'

The light in the tailor's eyes faded and he stared hard at her cheongsam. 'I'm not dreaming, am I? Is history going backwards now? I didn't think anyone still showed themselves in public looking like that!'

Wenqin, standing behind the madwoman, gestured to her head, which the tailor misinterpreted. 'Hard to deal with, eh? What, you or her? I'm not afraid of difficult customers – that's for other people. You know all about the quality of my work.' Wenqin gave up, and without further explanation threw the bolt of red velvet onto the sewing table. Prodding the madwoman again, she said, 'Take this as the pattern. Make me one like hers.'

'What's got into you? You want to have a cheongsam made now? Well, I won't do it. Even if I did, you'd never dare wear it.' The tailor seemed to want to keep her in suspense. 'Last time I made you bell-bottoms, but I haven't seen you wearing them.'

'How do you know I haven't worn them? I don't wear them for *you*,' she started in a bullying tone, then suddenly switched back to sweetness and light. 'Oh, what does it matter anyway? First, you're not my boss, and second, you're not my husband. You're my tailor, so your place is just to do the job. Besides, where is it written that if I have clothing made I have to wear it outside the house?'

'I make clothes for you, and then you're too scared to wear them? I suppose you want to be named a model worker, afraid of being criticized by your superiors?' the tailor said. 'You mean you'll only wear it at home? Just for your husband? What a waste!'

'You dirty old hunchback! What business is it of yours who I wear it for?' Wenqin picked up a piece of chalk and threw it at him. 'Let me tell you something: a lot of the clothes I've ordered are stored in my chest. Even if I don't wear them, I can still take them out and look at them. They make me feel better.'

'After all the work I put into that clothing, you let it rot away in a chest? When I think how demanding you were when I was making it: if the end of a thread was too coarse you kicked up such a fuss! And then you take it all home to stick in a box?' The tailor looked as if he couldn't quite bring himself to laugh. He stared at Wenqin, and suddenly his face hardened. 'Well, I won't make clothes for you, not any more. The money I earn off you is like a traitor's reward: I end up holding myself in contempt.'

'Oh, yes? Or maybe you don't even know how to make a cheongsam!' Wenqin was clearly irritated. She held it in check for a moment, and then went on baiting him. 'And here was I thinking you were the best tailor in the city! Best tailor my arse, if you can't even make a cheongsam.'

'I never said I was the best in the city, did I? In a profession like this, it doesn't matter who says they're the best; it's the clothing that does the talking in the end.' After clowning about, the tailor grew more serious. Avoiding Wenqin's eyes, he squinted sideways at the madwoman, sizing her up as she stood by the shop window. 'Has the lady comrade come here to stroll around? Why doesn't she take a seat?' Still the madwoman stood by the window, stretching one of her hands into the window display to fondle something.

'Never mind her,' said Wenqin, 'she can't sit still. Just tell me how we should go about taking the measurements.'

'You're a little fuller than she is. Chest, waist and hips will all be different. What choice do we have? Get her to take her cheongsam off and put it on yourself. That's the only way to do it if you want accurate measurements.'

The madwoman raised her head and walked daintily around, pointing at the clothing hanging on the racks with her sandalwood fan. She pointed at a tawny army uniform and said, 'The People's Liberation Army.' Then she pointed at a white shirt and said, 'Red Guards.' Then it was blue trousers: 'Junior Red Guards.' A black skirt: 'Old women.' In the course of pointing at all the clothes she reached a dress with blue polka dots that reminded her of her daughter, Susu. She turned around and asked Wenqin, 'What time is it? Shouldn't Susu be on her way home?'

Wenqin glanced at her wristwatch and said, 'No rush, no rush.' But her body tensed, and with a glare at the tailor she said, 'I'm not in any mood to chatter the day away here. Hurry up and get started. I have a million things to do at home and I must get back.'

The tailor chortled and said, 'You want me to get started? On whom? Shall I help you undress?'

Wenqin raised one finger and tapped herself on the forehead. 'Tricked me again! Every time I come here I'm swept up in your chatter. You flirt away without my even noticing.'

Wenqin lured the madwoman behind a printed curtain, into what passed for the tailor's bedroom. There was a wooden-framed single bed and a portrait of the heroine from *Azalea Mountain*[1] was pasted on the wall over its head; her eyes stared fiercely, while the position of her hands suggested cool calculation. Underneath the bed was a spittoon that hadn't been emptied in several days and emitted a sour, noxious odour. Wenqin had changed in there before and immediately took care to pull the curtain shut behind her before fastening both ends with iron clips. Despite her precautions, the madwoman was far from reassured and cried out in alarm, 'What kind of place is this? I want to go out. I don't want to change here.'

'You're driving me mad,' Wenqin replied. 'You're not the MC for the cultural ensemble any more. There aren't any dressing rooms: the women who come to the tailor's all change here. There's a curtain. What are you afraid of? Do you think Mr Li's some kind of pervert?'

On the other side of the curtain, Mr Li was indeed behaving well. First he went to pour himself some tea and glugged the aromatic liquid down, then he hummed

[1] *Azalea Mountain*, written by Wang Shuyuan, was a popular play about the heroine He Xiang and her revolutionary exploits in the late 1920s. The play was adapted into *pingju* and several Beijing Opera scripts ('revolutionary' and otherwise), as well as a 1974 film version.

something from a revolutionary opera: 'Rosy aurora-a-ha, mirrored in Yangcheng Lake's waters-a-ah-a.'[2] In his bedroom, all was not so harmonious. The madwoman refused to strip and Wenqin was too impatient. After much twisting and turning the struggle died down, and all the tailor heard was the light swishing of cloth against cloth and the sound of rubbing hands. After a moment, Wenqin lifted up the curtain and walked out of the bedroom clad in the white velvet cheongsam. She stretched both hands out to the tailor, then made a half turn. She modelled the clothing in a bashful yet confident manner, as if to ask, 'How does it suit me?'

The tailor called out, 'Ooh-la-la!' and clapping his hands as he advanced on her, he grabbed her by the waist and said, 'It looks great. Even better than it did on her.'

As the tailor took Wenqin's measurements, he forgot the madwoman even existed, and after some overzealous measuring, Wenqin suddenly gave him a resounding slap, saying, 'Nasty hunchback! I'm in a good mood today so I've been letting you get away with it, but you'd better keep your mind on this cheongsam. If you do a bad job, don't think I'll let it go lightly.'

'If I were going to make a mess of it, I wouldn't have

[2]A famous aria from *Shajiabang*, another revolutionary opera, named after a centre of Communist resistance to the Japanese invasion. The town lies on Yangcheng Lake, north of Suzhou in the east of Jiangsu Province.

taken the job,' he assured her. 'Even if I were ten times braver, I wouldn't dare put anything less into it than you deserve.'

The two of them suddenly became aware that the madwoman had begun to pace restlessly behind the curtain. 'What time is it?' she muttered. 'The time? Oh, no – it's totally dark outside already. Susu must have left school a long time ago.' The curtain suddenly bulged – the madwoman had thrust her face against it and was saying, 'It's dark outside. Why don't you let me go home? Give me my cheongsam back and let me go home!'

Wenqin assured her, 'It's all right, all right. There's nothing wrong. What are you screaming about? Are you scared of the dark? There's no light on in there, so it *is* a little dark. If you're afraid, I'll get Mr Li to turn on the light for you.'

For some reason the tailor smirked as he went to turn it on. As soon as he lit it, the silhouette of the madwoman was clearly visible through the curtain. The sudden appearance of the shadow frightened the madwoman and she shouted, 'Oh!' The shadow giving a little jump.

Wenqin saw immediately that the light wasn't helping and rushed to turn it off. Then she turned back to rebuke the tailor. 'I should have known. No sense in trying to stop a dog from eating shit, is there, you wretch?'

'What are you swearing at me for?' demanded the tailor. 'You told me to turn on the light yourself.'

Wenqin was confused for a moment. She went to the

curtain again, intending to lift it back, but then she retracted her hand and said to the tailor, 'Measure my shoulders . . . my shoulders! Hurry up and measure them.'

'I'm trying to but you keep squirming around, you're not making it easy for me.'

Wenqin took a sidelong glance at the curtain and lowered her voice. 'Don't frighten her. Can't you tell she's not right in the head?'

The tailor looked a little ashamed and said, 'I noticed, yes. Too bad.' Still shamefaced, he began to work faster. Then he sighed deeply. He took the tape measure and slid it around her. 'Here, at the waist – I haven't really got it right yet. The waist is the hardest part of a cheongsam so don't blame me if it's wrong . . .'

'If it's not right I'll only pay you half your fee.'

The tailor didn't respond to that but stood sideways on to her and measured every detail of the way Wenqin's body corresponded to the cheongsam's measurements. Identifying a problem, he suddenly took hold of something; it was one of the frog fastenings of the cheongsam.

'I almost forgot – I'm going to have to take off one of these lute frogs. They're really hard to make. If I don't have one for the pattern, I can't make them from scratch.'

This immediately made Wenqin anxious, and she rolled her eyes, warning him to bear in mind that the madwoman was behind the curtain. Then she lowered her voice to confer with him. 'You can draw, can't you? You can draw it now and make it from that.'

'What a great idea!' the tailor responded. 'And then I'll draw an aeroplane and make that too, shall I?'

This retort struck Wenqin dumb momentarily and she twisted her hands and said, 'Then what are we going to do? I couldn't bear to take one off. If she was normal, we could discuss it with her. But her mind's gone and, besides, she's petty; she'd never agree to it. What if you didn't make lute frogs but some other nice ones instead?' Before the tailor could even answer yes or no, Wenqin shook her head. 'No, no. I really love these frogs. If I'm going to go to all this trouble to make a cheongsam, I can't have just any fastenings.'

'Well then, what should we do about telling her? Shoot first, ask questions later? Tell her after we've already gone through with it?'

Wenqin looked at the printed curtain, then at the tailor, gritted her teeth and said, 'Take it off. In any case, we'll sew it back on when we're finished.'

The tailor picked up the razor blade near him and was about to cut the frog off when he hesitated and said quietly, 'I don't know. I'm a bit nervous about this. I mean, not only is her mind gone, this cheongsam is her life. If we take off a frog, don't you think she might make a scene?'

Wenqin put one hand to her mouth. 'My heart's beating like mad,' she said. 'A beautiful thing like that

. . . obviously it's hers, but we'll never get anywhere by asking her.'

The tailor blinked. He thought it over for a moment, then he found a safety pin and gave it to Wenqin, saying, 'I'll take the frog from the collar, it'll be less noticeable. In a second you'll have to fasten it for her with the safety pin. If we just keep talking, maybe we can get away with it.'

Wenqin was staring directly at the lute frog, her expression wavering between fear and resolve. I want this frog. I must have it, she thought, and in the end she said, 'It's not as if it's important. I'm just borrowing it for a few days. Whether she notices or not, we'll have to do it. Take it off.'

As evening approached, Wenqin and the madwoman were seen walking down The East is Red Street. The two women attracted attention in different ways. Naturally people noticed the white velvet cheongsam the madwoman was dressed in, and the sharper-eyed among them soon observed what was different about the madwoman's collar. The safety pin totally ruined the elegant effect and made people burst out laughing. But because they knew all about the state of her mind, the bizarre appearance of a safety pin seemed perfectly reasonable and no one gave too much thought to the question of what had happened to the frog. The impression the madwoman had always given was that she loved to show off her elegant appearance, and now they assumed she had lost even her vanity. But no one really cared; let her wear whatever she felt like. Let her dress in a cheongsam if she wanted, and if she wanted to fasten it with a safety pin, then so be it.

Luckily, the walk passed without incident. When they reached Wenqin's home on Sunflower Alley, she tried her luck. Tentatively she asked the madwoman, 'Now, you can get home by yourself. You know the way, don't you?'

But the madwoman was not fooled, she had a crystal-clear recollection of the promise Wenqin had made. 'The silk scarf. Your black scarf with the golden flowers, you promised to give it to me. You're a welcher if you don't.'

Wenqin rolled her eyes and said, 'Your memory's better than mine. Are you sure there's anything wrong with you? It's just a silk scarf; I'll give it to you like I promised. Wait here, I'll go in and get it.'

'Oh no,' the madwoman said. 'What if you go in and don't come back? I'm coming with you.' Wenqin was growing angry. 'What are you talking about? Just because you're ill, you can't go around behaving like this. Following me around like a little dog, sticking to my heels.' Having raised her voice, Wenqin noticed that people were looking at them, so she adopted a milder tone and said, 'My father-in-law's ill in bed and not in any state to be seen. If you really don't trust me you can come along, but you can't go inside. My mother-in-law is very superstitious, she won't let anyone like you into an invalid's house.'

37

The madwoman stood outside the door of Wenqin's house on Sunflower Alley. There were no sunflowers to be seen, but people had planted white, yellow and purple chrysanthemums on their windowsills and in their gardens, all of them half dead by now. As the madwoman waited for Wenqin's silk scarf, she bowed her head to examine the chrysanthemums in front of the door; then, not satisfied with merely looking, she bent down to pick some. Just at that moment, a loud noise behind her gave her a fright. It was a little girl wearing a red neckerchief, who approached her while twirling a skipping rope. Girls in red neckerchiefs always reminded the madwoman of her daughter.

'You're not Susu. I thought you were my own girl, Susu.' She ran after the skipping girl and asked, 'What time is it? Do you know my daughter Susu? You're out of school now, aren't you?'

The girl stood still and stared at the madwoman in astonishment. First she looked at her face, then nervously she examined her cheongsam. 'Why are you wearing a dress like that? That's the sort of dress women spies wear in the movies!'

The madwoman said, 'This isn't a dress at all; it's a cheongsam. Everybody used to wear them, before.'

The girl seemed only partly to understand this. Finally, her curious gaze rested on the madwoman's collar. She pointed at the safety pin and said, 'You're so lazy! Why don't you sew on a new button if the old one fell off? Why did you use a safety pin?'

The madwoman lifted her hand to her collar and let out the first sharp cry. By the time Wenqin came out with the silk scarf, the little girl who had provoked the disaster had vanished without trace, leaving only the madwoman. Her face was pale as snow, she had thrown the sandalwood fan to the ground, and her left hand gripped her collar tightly. Her right hand was pressed against her chest and she sent forth one sharp scream after another. Wenqin knew that there was no sense in denying the truth; the game was up. She was flustered now, too, and the neighbours were converging on the door to her home. But there was something that frightened Wenqin even more: as well as the missing frog, according to the madwoman's choked cries, a gem-encrusted brooch had also disappeared!

In her desperation, Wenqin forgot the madwoman's precarious state of mind. She poked her in the face with one finger. 'What brooch? What precious stones? That's a malicious lie! I've never seen you wear any brooch.' How could Wenqin be anything but flustered? The frog was a small affair – and it was true she bore responsibility for that, but it was only a frog, it didn't really distress her – the brooch, on the other hand, was a catastrophe that had materialized out of thin air. How could Wenqin fail to be confused? And in her confusion, she began to abuse the victim: 'What butterfly brooch? What precious stones? You loony!

Be mad if you want to, but you needn't try and con me while you're at it.'

The incident that became known as 'the time the madwoman raised Cain' consisted of the events of that early evening. In fact, the madwoman did not raise Cain; she merely gave sharp cries and wept. Everybody there learned from her cries that she had lost two articles: a frog fastening and a brooch. Although exquisite, the frog was only a dress fastening; but the brooch sounded rare and valuable, and its loss accounted for the gravity of the situation. Everyone looked at Wenqin with eyes that demanded an explanation. Then the madwoman seized a part of her dress, as if that would make her produce the missing belongings, and refused to let go; meanwhile, Wenqin refused to explain. She held a black scarf in her hands which she tried to wrap around the madwoman's neck; but the madwoman wouldn't accept it, and the impression given was that she was refusing some kind of bribe. Soon the women were fighting, madly entwined, accompanied by sharp screams from them both.

Wenqin's pretty face flushed red as a pig's liver with fury. 'She's mad! Mad! You all know that!' She tried to shake off the madwoman and raised one hand to make an oath to her neighbours: 'She's sick in the head, but you aren't. I'll tell you what really happened. I borrowed the frog to make a pattern from it. But this brooch or whatever, that's her madness talking. If I've ever seen this brooch of hers, may lightning strike me down!'

At one point, Wenqin's husband Luo came out and tried to part the two women, but to no avail. He took no further steps, apparently thinking of the undignified impression it would make, and instead stood by with a sombre expression on his face and his hands on his hips. That was all he could do as the women flew at one another; for whenever women fight, no man can feasibly intervene, much less if one woman is the Mahogany Street madwoman and the man a cadre in the Ministry of Health. Luo heard the madwoman crying. His wife was crying too, and as she cried she turned around to reproach him, 'Luo, you wimp! Why don't you do something to make this loony go away? Hurry up and make her go away!'

Luo rubbed his hands, took a step forward and grabbed the madwoman with one hand. But then, realizing he couldn't bear the loss of face, he retracted it again. The next moment the neighbours saw him clap himself on the forehead – evidently he had found a solution to the problem. They watched him run down the alley, a few children at his heels. They all ran down to the public phone outside the general store – apparently Luo's solution was going to be found at the end of the phone line – and the children listened as he made the call, instructing someone to dispatch an ambulance right away. Who was the patient? Luo bawled into the receiver, 'What do you mean, is it high blood pressure? Is it heart disease? What do you mean, is it serious? If it weren't serious, would I be calling you? Since you have the nerve to ask, it's a loony, a wild loony on the loose, making a scene in front of my house.'

Eventually a white ambulance drove down Sunflower Alley. By that time the sky was almost pitch black and the ambulance lights worked like searchlights, lighting up Sunflower Alley so it seemed as bright as day. The lights dazzled Wenqin, and on her despairing face arose the dawn of triumph. The light shone on the neighbours gathered for the spectacle and they looked stunned; one by one they blinked and began whispering to one another. When the lights hit the madwoman's face she lifted one hand. It looked like surrender, but at the same time as if she was struggling against the light. It was then that the people in Sunflower Alley heard the madwoman emit the most forlorn of all her cries; it came like a thunderclap from a clear sky. The people couldn't help but cover their ears; cover their ears and watch the madwoman as she tried to escape. She ran a few steps forward – but the ambulance was in front of her; so she ran a few steps back – but the people were behind her. The madwoman, lost to any sense of shame by now, sat down on the ground, covered her face with her hands and cried. She kicked her feet; she even kicked off her T-bar leather shoes, and said, 'I'm not going to cry. You can have my frog, you can have my brooch, just don't come over here. I beg you, don't come over here. Don't come over here.'

But those who had to come over came over. Three

men jumped out of the ambulance; they were wearing white suits and surgical masks, and one of them even had a length of rope in his hands. They seemed prepared for the patient to resist, but now that it was actually happening, the madwoman had lost all her strength. She just curled up into a ball and her whole body shuddered violently. She said, 'I beg you, don't come over here.' She raised one hand, meaning initially to ward them off, but in effect meekly presenting them with it. She said, 'Susu's out of school. I should go home.' With this, she raised another hand, and thereby gave that up, too. In the end, the madwoman ended up cooperating with the ambulancemen. The people on Sunflower Alley watched as two of them lifted her into the ambulance. The third looked to be very strong, but he wasn't going to be needed today. He was the one who took the T-bar shoes from Wenqin's hands and put them inside the ambulance.

Most intelligent people know where an ambulance would carry a madwoman, but some people are born stupid, and they ran after the ambulance asking, 'Hey! Where you going to take her?' And the people in the ambulance answered, 'Where do you think? Sanli Bridge, of course.'

Sanli Bridge was about twenty kilometres from Mahogany Street. To get from here to Sanli means changing buses three times, and in the end you have to take the suburban line from the South Gate. People younger than me all know that Sanli Bridge is ancient and seven-arched. Under the bridge is a white building with a red-tiled roof; that's the activity centre for retired cadres. What they don't know is that under Sanli Bridge there used to be a shady patch of willows, and that there among the willows there used to be a mental hospital. So 'going to Sanli Bridge' didn't mean going to the actual bridge, it meant *under* it. Just a simple rhetorical technique; I expect you know that.

Weeping Willow

Even when he had long since passed the scene of the accident, near the village of Siqian, the driver remained badly shaken.

The highway in the rain was a lonely stretch of road. Outside the lorry's windows the sky was the colour of lead and the rain drummed down without interruption. The wipers swung feebly to and fro and there was a constant but irregular flow of water on the windscreen. In the rear-view mirror the road seemed like a black tide pursuing his lorry, which was buffeted by the wind and rain like a solitary boat. Also reflected in the rear-view mirror was his face, wan and fatigued, with traces of sweat faintly visible on his forehead, and an expression, a look in the eyes, that showed he had not yet recovered from the shock. He had a feeling like carsickness, or more precisely seasickness. He felt as if the road was tossing him up on sky-high waves. In his long career as a driver, this was the first time the highway had provoked such feelings of profound dread.

The rain still hadn't stopped, but once he turned off and drove through a mountain pass the drops became noticeably smaller; the sound of the rain hitting the corn leaves was no longer so pronounced and the swift current of a river could be heard above it. The sky was still dark to the north, but towards the south it had become both bluer and brighter. Now, a few shabby red-brick sheds appeared ahead of him on the left, the sonorous voice of a pop singer drifting faintly from them. It was a song praising the highlands of Qinghai and Tibet. The driver knew he had reached Weeping Willow. He had passed through here a year earlier and the tape player had played that same song all day long: 'Oh, the highlands of Qinghai, and the highlands of Tibet.' Today it was still the same song, but these were neither the highlands of Qinghai, nor those of Tibet. Weeping Willow was a place that survived by serving long-distance drivers and which consisted of three roadside establishments. One was the petrol station, one the general store for cigarettes, alcohol and food, and the last a cross between a restaurant and an inn. The restaurant boldly fronted the road, while the inn was half-hidden behind it. Local people had told him they were all one business, belonging to the same woman.

A girl in a green miniskirt stood beneath an umbrella, trying to stop vehicles and attract customers. She extended one of her arms from under the umbrella in a gesture intended to be seductive, but which looked more like a traffic policeman ordering vehicles to proceed. The girl stood with her legs apart and exposed below her skirt. They were half light, half dark and extremely eye-catching. The driver took a long look at her and realized that it was because she was wearing black silk stockings, onto which were sewn glimmering mock pearls, like a patch of starlit night.

'Hey, big boy. Have a drink and relax for a while.' The girl gestured to him, and after she had finished, she covered her mouth and giggled.

The driver was used to gestures of this kind and didn't respond immediately, letting his eyes wander between the girl's face and the road, undecided. It was his hand that took the lead and chose to stop by pulling the brake. The driver's mind obeyed his hand and his tightly wound body suddenly slumped forward over the steering wheel. 'All right, I'll rest here for a while.' The driver knew his own nature, and was quite astonished by the way the girl's invitation had been able to calm him down so quickly. As he was backing in and parking the lorry, he studied his face again in the rear-view mirror: although it was still pale, his eyes were already more lively, shining with obscure expectations, filled with intense light.

The girl was rather childish, and her graceful smile seemed both ingratiating and shy. She demonstrated great interest in his cargo, standing on tiptoe to look in the back of the lorry. When she saw that it was empty, she was evidently disappointed, and exclaimed, 'Empty! The guest who just left had a lorry jammed with Coke!'

The driver said, 'So what? It's not as if he let you have any.'

The girl didn't yet understand how men's flirtatious small talk worked and concluded mistakenly that he was making fun of her. She closed the umbrella and shook off the water. 'I wouldn't drink it even if they did give it to me. It tastes like cough syrup. Totally gross,' she murmured.

Weeping Willow looked the same as it had a year before. The muddy ground in front of the restaurant was rutted with tyre tracks, which turned into countless puddles of differing sizes as soon as it rained. By the garage wall was a mountainous pile of wet, discarded tyres. A few chickens that belonged to the restaurant wandered among the puddles, looking perhaps for something to eat.

'This way, big boy.' The girl directed the driver with her umbrella towards the restaurant, 'This way, not over there. It's wet over there.'

'You think I can't find the way by myself?' The driver laughed. 'You don't have to be so attentive just yet.'

'The boss tells us to be sure to make a good first impression,' the girl explained earnestly. 'Last month, our boss took a trip to some other restaurants to see how it's done there.'

'What do you mean, "first impression"? I'm a repeat customer. I've been here quite a few times.'

'How come I've never seen you before?'

The driver jumped over a puddle and suddenly recalled the name of the girl from last year. 'There's a girl called Xue. Is she still around?'

'Xue?' The girl's eyes lit up for a moment. 'I'm called Xue. You know me?'

'I don't know *you*, I know the other Xue – the one with the round face and short hair. She's a little bigger than you, and a little darker. Does she still work in the restaurant?'

'I'm the only girl called Xue here. Who knows who all these other Xues are you're talking about,' the girl said. 'What did the other Xue do?'

'Same as you. Stand here, attract customers.'

'No way. I've been here for more than a year and that's *my* name. How could there be another Xue? No way!' The girl looked as if she thought he was having her on. She turned her head to look at the driver's face, and then took another glance at his shoes. 'Oh, man, look at your shoes. They're disgusting,' she cried out. 'I told you to be careful where you stepped and you wouldn't listen. Now look at your feet – covered in mud!'

The driver didn't mind mud on his feet. He frowned, trying to remember something. 'Well, that's strange. You're called Xue, too? I'm sure I remember right. The other Xue had a mole on her cheek, and you don't. Or maybe all you girls here are called Xue.'

'No way! How would that work? Everybody would get mixed up. It'd be impossible to manage things. There's Mei, Hong and Li – they work nights – but during the day there's only me.' She raised her voice and said vehemently, 'I'm not lying. May I drop down dead if I am. My name is Xue.'

The driver was a little bit perplexed and wondered if perhaps he had confused Xue in Weeping Willow with some other roadside girl. But he had always set great store by his memory, and the people he worked with at the transport company agreed that he was good at remembering two things: one of them was his route, and the other the names of the girls he chanced to meet along the way.

The proprietress came rushing out from the back of the restaurant, holding sunflower seeds in her cupped hands. Her bony face was covered in a thick layer of powder and her mouth smeared with lipstick. Her smile revealed jagged, blackening teeth. 'Why, my friend. What a long time it's been.' She squinted as she gave the driver the once-over. Suddenly she extended one finger and poked him in the shoulder. 'You dockside drivers, you've no loyalty at all. We gave you such good service last time and you forgot us all the same.'

Despite this greeting, the driver couldn't be certain whether the proprietress really recognized him or not.

Perhaps she did, perhaps not. He had met a lot of people of this type in roadside inns. The driver just smiled an acknowledgement and sat down on the edge of a table. He said, 'I'll have the same thing as before. Two fried vegetable plates and a bowl of noodles with herbs and shredded meat.'

Not far from the kitchen two men were sitting round a cardboard box, playing poker. They cast sidelong glances at the driver and then bowed their heads again. He had never seen them before, but guessed that they were paid by the proprietress to hang around the restaurant. All the roadside places had men like these, sitting idly while the women moved around them. The counter, painted pink, was right by the entrance, and on top of it stood a black-and-white TV set. The girl who called herself Xue had turned it on as soon as they came in. The TV looked like some kind of relic. It made a droning sound, but the screen remained blank. The girl picked up a slipper and hit the set twice, once on the left and once on the right, and suddenly the image appeared, a TV series from Hong Kong. There was a man and a woman, conducting meaningless small talk in a queer kind of Mandarin. After a moment, it turned out they were talking about love.

The driver said, 'That's really getting on my nerves. No matter where I drive, it's always those two voices. They can't talk normally, they have to drawl like that: *"yala yala yala"*. As soon as I hear them, it gets on my nerves.'

51

Xue stood by the counter. 'No way! It's cool to speak like that now, don't you know that, big boy? If you don't like a programme this good, why would you even want a TV?'

The driver said, 'My TV at home is strictly for decoration. Of the three hundred and sixty five days of the year, I'm not at home for a hundred and eighty. I don't have time to watch. When I do, it's sport. I don't watch anything else; I fall asleep if I do. The series from Hong Kong and Taiwan are OK, so far as the stories go, it's the dubbing that gets me. As soon as I hear two voices like that, I want to fall asleep right away.'

Xue said, 'No way! If I feel sleepy, I just watch TV and then I'm not sleepy any more. I'm watching this show – it's the last two episodes now, so don't interrupt or I can't hear.'

The proprietress came out of the kitchen with his food. She kicked at the cardboard box and shouted, 'Cards! All you do is play cards! It wouldn't occur to you to go into the kitchen and help with the vegetables, I suppose?' As she approached the driver, her expression quickly turned into an easy smile. She remarked to him, 'Just look how hard it is to run a place like this. The staff are all lazy. I'm the busy one while they've got it made: the card players with their cards; the TV-watchers with their TV.'

The driver had wanted to say something, but then yawned. 'I can't stand the sound of that show. I get sleepy as soon as I hear it.'

The proprietress blinked suddenly and scrutinized him. 'You look awful,' she shouted, as if she was genuinely alarmed. 'Your face looks terrible. You really should take a rest. How long have you been driving? You look exhausted.'

The driver shook his head, and leaned back on his chair, giving the proprietress an ambiguous smile.

'Are you all right?' She put out her hand to feel his forehead, saying, 'You don't have a fever. Well, then, as long as you're not ill. Hey, it's not easy the work you do, and it takes the best years of your life, too. Aren't I right? I can tell you're tired. You'll be fine once you've had a rest.'

'It's not that I'm tired. To tell you the truth, I had a bit of a shock. There was an accident out by Siqian.'

'Who caused it?' The proprietress suddenly seemed a little nervous and took a step back from him. She asked tentatively, 'You're all right, though, aren't you?'

'I'd hardly be sitting here if I weren't, would I?' The driver chuckled and moved his legs restlessly under the table. 'I didn't do it,' he said. 'What are you staring at me like that for? I didn't do it, it was the coal truck in front of me!'

'Yeah, those are the worst. Their drivers are all mad. It's as if they're deliberately looking for people to hit.' The proprietress was going along with him now and demonstrating appropriate interest in the accident itself. 'Did you see the person get hit? Who got hit?'

'It was an old man. All I saw was this old man going off like a firecracker. The coal lorry was along with me the whole way. The trucker had just passed me when I saw him hit someone. I heard a big bang – hell, it was just like a firecracker. In all the years I've been driving, I've never seen anyone be hit. Just like a firecracker!'

'Did the other driver get out and help him? There's the rural hospital in Siqian.'

'Help him? He didn't even get out of his truck, he just took off! I was right behind him and didn't know what to do. It was one of those situations where you can't really win. I just gritted my teeth and kept driving. I hadn't counted on the old man still being alive, though, and as I drove past he suddenly popped up, his whole body covered in blood, and tried to flag me down!'

The proprietress gave a frightened shout and said, 'That *is* scary! You mean he wasn't dead? Is he dead now?'

'How do I know? I was scared half to death myself.' The driver had started eating his food. As he chewed he said, 'I'm guessing he didn't survive. He was walking from the fields on to the road. The raindrops were big as soya beans, you couldn't really see for them. He was an old man from a village and his reflexes were slow – you know how they all walk along the road with their heads down, as if the national highways were built for their personal convenience. He was carrying a basket full of chilli peppers. When he was hit, there was a bang, like a firecracker, and the peppers flew all over the place. I'm not kidding, the guy and the peppers both flew up, just like a big firecracker.'

They had been talking very loudly, annoying Xue sitting over by the counter. 'Look, please keep it down. I can't hear a thing. Ms Fang is writing a suicide note. She wants to kill herself!'

The proprietress looked over to where Xue was sitting, and craned her neck a little to see the screen. Obviously she too was preoccupied with the series. 'I thought she was going to die in yesterday's episode – so they dragged the suicide note out until today.' The proprietress said to the driver, seemingly in apology, 'It's a really good show. I watch it every day.' Then she lowered her voice and whispered in his ear, 'In a minute I'll set Xue to work on your back, and then you can get nice and relaxed. Xue's not bad-looking is she?'

The driver hesitated for a second and said, 'She wants to watch the programme. Let her watch. I'll go into the back rooms and have a snooze.'

'Now how could we just let you snooze?' The proprietress gave the driver a knowing nudge. 'Never you mind. When you're as tired as that, you should get some proper relaxation. I'll tell her what to do for you.'

The driver looked at the girl in front of the TV and then glanced out of the window. The rain had stopped briefly, but now it was back. There were no vehicles on the highway and with the rain falling it looked peaceful, like a black river, with little glittering lights. A chicken or duck belonging to the restaurant had ventured on to the highway and was taking a leisurely walk. The driver looked out at the sparsely planted mahogany and pagoda trees lining the road – they were only about half the height of a man – and he reckoned they had just been planted when he last called here about a year ago. He suddenly recalled that the place was called Weeping Willow. How come there wasn't a single weeping willow to be seen?

'Why is this place called Weeping Willow?' he mumbled, but the proprietress didn't hear. She'd already resumed her place in front of the TV and was staring at the flickering screen while spitting out sunflower seed shells. The girl called Xue was now sitting on the counter. Apart from her black silk stockings and the little pearls embroidered on them, the driver could see only the side of her face and her back; her rounded breasts were carefully concealed by her sleeveless top, like corn in its husk. She had put her hands underneath her legs and was sitting on them, and it seemed to him that he had seen this posture before – surely the Xue he remembered had sat like that? Maybe she was the same girl he had met last time after all. Or maybe he was mistaken; after working as a long-distance driver for so many years, the girls he knew from roadside inns were beyond counting. What perplexed him was Xue's attitude towards him; if it was the same girl, she ought to have recognized him. Last year in Weeping Willow the Xue he had met was a tearful country girl; totally clueless, like a lamb being led to the sacrificial slaughter for eighty bucks. He hadn't even done anything to her; her tears and meek acquiescence had moved him to compassion. He had done nothing, but he had still paid, and even given a tip. He remembered how Xue had clumsily kissed him on the face to express her gratitude, saying, 'Mister, I'll never forget you all my life. You're a nice man.' Of course he was a nice man: he hadn't done anything, but had still paid, and he felt satisfied when he thought of that. He had been positive that Xue in Weeping Willow would remember him, and so he felt a double sense of loss now: he couldn't be sure if it was the same girl, but she didn't seem to know him.

The room's furnishings were shabby and rustic: an old-fashioned slatted bed, a washstand and basin; walls covered with posters of stars from Taiwan and Hong Kong. The plastic matting had just been scrubbed and was slippery to walk on. He saw they still had the kind of mosquito net that had long since disappeared from the big cities hanging from the ceiling over the bed. It all felt very familiar, although he didn't remember there being any such net last year, but that might have been because it was autumn then. The driver crawled under the mosquito net and checked everything with his hands; the bedding seemed clean and had been sprayed with perfume. Slowly he lay down and heaved a sigh; he knew what the proprietress was going to fix up for him, what it was he was waiting for, and while he waited, he combed his hair back with his hand. What was different from other times in similar roadside inns was the heaviness of his heart. This time, he was waiting for something without really knowing whether he wanted it.

Xue came into the room carrying a Thermos. It was obvious that she had been hectored inside by the proprietress as she didn't look willing and the smile on her face was stiff. 'Have a wash first,' she said from outside the mosquito net, 'orders from the boss. She says you're to have a wash.'

'What am I going to wash? You mean my feet?'

Xue stood there awkwardly, saying nothing. It was clear from her expression that she was being forced to attend to him.

'What do you want me to wash? Come on, tell me.' The driver pushed his face out of the net. He lowered his eyes when he saw that she had no intention of answering, pulled his head back and said, 'I won't wash. I'm not dirty, so why should I wash?'

Xue said, 'It's not my business if you want to be filthy. In any case, I'll tell you straight out, I'm not on night shift, I don't do that stuff.'

'What stuff is it you don't do?' the driver chuckled inside his net and said, 'I don't think I've ever met a girl like you before. If you don't do anything, why are you here? Get me the boss.'

'No! I didn't mean to offend you.' Outside the net, Xue's voice had suddenly grown milder, more defensive. She put the Thermos on the edge of the bed, and seemed to be pondering something. Then, hesitantly, she said, 'Look, if you don't want to wash, then don't. I'll wash your feet for you, I'll massage your back, I'll even scratch you where it itches if you want, but you have to promise me something, OK?'

'What are you making such a big deal of it for? I just want to relax. I'm hardly going to romance you, am I? What am I supposed to promise you anyway?'

'Fifteen minutes,' Xue said. 'Fifteen minutes, OK? After that I'm going next door to watch TV, and you won't tell the boss.'

'No way.' The driver, having now understood what she was after, could not suppress a smile. Mimicking the girl's voice, he repeated, 'No way!' And then, 'Fifteen minutes, enough to relax me? How about I only pay half, then?'

'Look, I'm begging you, OK? The last two episodes are on today. It'll start again after the ad break's over. Promise me! Promise, OK?'

'No way!' The driver said in a falsetto. 'What do you take me for?' Suddenly he remembered something and asked, 'Why not just ten minutes then? Why fifteen?'

'The first five minutes are for the opening song.' Xue realized that this question was a sign the driver might be willing to accommodate her, and the thought lifted her spirits so she said, 'You know, you're a nice man. I knew all along you were a nice man. I'll remember you all my life.'

'You said the same thing last year.' The driver gave a hollow laugh from inside his net. 'What do girls like you remember anyway? All you remember is the cash.'

'What's that supposed to mean? Why turn nasty all of a sudden?' Xue sounded flabbergasted. For a moment it seemed she didn't know what to do with her hands. She pulled back the one that had been lifting the net. 'Why would you say something like that? Girls like me? What kind of girl am I, then? How do you know what kind of girl I am?' She cocked her head and looked at the posters on the wall. Then she whispered, 'If you treat me like shit I'm hardly going to want to serve you, and I don't care if you *do* tell the boss. Creep.'

'Are you swearing at me?'

'I didn't swear at you. When did I ever swear at you?'

'You called me a creep.'

'That's not swearing. They dock your salary if you swear at a guest. Don't go telling lies about me.'

'How old are you, anyway? And how come you're so clueless? Do you really think you can earn money here without having the first idea about anything?' The driver stared at the girl, and his tone of voice changed. It was halfway between reproachful and teasing. 'Tell me, are you really Xue or not? Do you really not remember me? I came here last year and you kept sobbing like some kind of Lin Daiyu.[3] I didn't even touch you but I paid up, and you said over and over again that you were going to remember me for ever . . . and now, damn it, in less than a year you've forgotten about me altogether! I'm called Lin. It's me, Lin!'

Xue turned her head; the driver's words had caught her attention. She lifted the net an inch. Perhaps she wanted to take a closer look at his face, but in the end she was too embarrassed, so she plopped herself down on the edge of the bed. It looked like she was straining to remember something. She just sat there on the edge of the bed, supporting herself with her hands, swaying back and forth as if the movement were helping to jog her memory. But in the end she shook her head and said, 'No way. If you did something as nice as that, how come I don't remember it at all? You're pulling my leg, right? You drivers all like to joke. I've never met you before, Liu.'

'Not Liu, you illiterate! Lin, L-I-N, your friend Lin!'

'Lin, all right? Don't get so worked up. Look, if you help me out now, I promise you that next time I'll remember.'

'If you don't remember me, then never mind. Damn it, it's not like I was counting on you to remember me.' The driver sat up impatiently under the net, then lay down again. Suddenly he laughed and said, 'Come on then.

[3]Tragic heroine of Cao Xueqin's 18th Century novel, *Dream of the Red Chamber.* Frail and emotional, she is associated with melancholy and tears.

Aren't you worried about missing your TV show? If you want to see that last episode you'll have to hurry up. I'm in a bad mood and I'm tired too. Maybe you won't even need ten minutes.'

Then the driver watched as one of Xue's legs slid under the net; she hesitated over the other, but in the end it came in too. The driver didn't look at her face; he didn't know why, but he didn't want to. He heaved a sigh, swore coarsely under his breath and lifted his eyes to look at the ceiling outside the net. The top of the net was made of white cloth which was yellowing slightly, and through it the driver could dimly make out chilli peppers strung across the room. He asked, 'What's hanging up there? Are those chilli peppers?'

'Yeah, chilli peppers. They use them in the kitchen, but there's no room so they hang them in here.'

The driver's whole body began to tremble, and his gaze was drawn, almost unwillingly, outside the net. Dimly he saw an old man sitting on the ground, his face covered in blood, holding chilli peppers in his cupped hands. The driver's hands trembled until they froze in mid-air. He turned over – the tidal water of desire that had swollen his body abruptly receded and a kind of obscure dread filled his mind. Brusquely he threw off Xue's hands and kicked her off the bed. 'You don't have to pinch me just because you can't do it right,' he shouted loudly. 'Go and watch your TV show.'

This time Xue was frightened; she hadn't been prepared

for his sudden violence and didn't know how to react. At first she stood barefoot outside the net, stunned, then she picked up her green sandals from the ground. 'What was that about? There's something wrong with you,' she said, then finally she started to cry and ran to the door, sandals in hand. 'There's something wrong with all of you, you sick bastards. You're perverts! I'm damned if I'm going to serve you creeps!'

The driver heard her footsteps recede rapidly, together with the storm of weeping. It sounded as if she'd suffered a huge injustice while the driver also felt like the victim of some nameless wrongdoing. An ordinary matter had become so complicated, against all expectation. He didn't know what he was doing, or why he had even come to Weeping Willow in the first place. Before long he heard the proprietress screaming and the hurried footsteps of several people. He crawled out of the bed and quickly locked the door.

When the proprietress knocked, the driver could hear the two card-playing men conferring outside in low voices. He called, 'Don't bother knocking, there's nothing wrong. Watch your TV show, I'm going to sleep. I'll just sleep a while and then I'll be on my way. I'll pay whatever you say.'

'Now come on, what's up with you? If you don't tell me, I can't make it right, can I?' the proprietress cajoled. 'Xue's not very bright, she doesn't always do as she's told. She's no good at this kind of work. I've already sent

63

word to her family for them to come and pick her up. If we've offended you, just be a little understanding with us. It'll be all right when Hong comes in the evening. No matter what kind of service you need, we'll give it to you then.'

'I don't need any service at all, I just want to have a little snooze.' Through the door, the driver could smell the proprietress's strong perfume and suddenly the scent revolted him. He pinched his nose and went over to the room's only window. He opened the curtains and saw a large cornfield outside, a cornfield after the rain, half green, half yellow, the leaves still sparkling with raindrops. The huge fields and the hills in the distance seemed to have been soaked in rainwater and exuded a faint alcoholic smell. The driver saw something flash past the window. Surprised, he poked his head out and saw two white goats, their coats soaked, huddled together. Apparently they had been standing below his window for some time. He stretched out his hand to touch them, stroking one of them on the back; it felt soft and wet, but the beautiful sensation didn't last for long before they ran off.

The driver really did want to sleep, if only for ten minutes; he felt exhausted, close to collapse. Before he crawled under the mosquito net, he went to the basin on the stand and gave his hands a good wash. There he discovered they were filthy, with diesel oil and dirt between his fingers. After he had finished washing his hands, as a matter of habit he took a paper tissue from his pocket. He'd already used them up, though, and all he fished out was the crumpled plastic packaging. He felt something else come out of his pocket along with the packaging and fall softly to the floor. The thing he dreaded most came last: it was a red chilli pepper lying on the inn's plastic matting, shining forth its cool dark red rays.

At night, Weeping Willow was a different world. The business, small and quaint by daylight, emerged in all its thriving, prosperous glory. The day's heavy rain lingered into the evening, stopping for a moment and then starting up again. The lights of Weeping Willow seemed exceptionally bright in the damp air. Perhaps it was because of the bad weather, or maybe because traffic accidents had delayed the drivers, but that night Weeping Willow was very busy. Altogether, there were seventeen drivers spending the night there. The few tables in the restaurant were completely packed and the lights in the inn's rooms were all turned on in readiness. The proprietress was radiant as she commanded her flock of girls in miniskirts, shuttling back and forth between her businesses.

Among the seventeen drivers was a young fellow by the name of Li. He drove a fuel tanker, and he knew Xue. He sat down and started glancing around, looking for Xue among the other girls, but unable to find her. He asked the proprietress where she had gone, and though he repeated his question several times, the frantic proprietress kept telling him to wait. So he waited, and didn't drink, and didn't talk to the other drivers, and after quite a while the proprietress finally came to him, but the news she brought was very unexpected.

'What a shame you should come now. Xue's had a family emergency; it just happened today. Her father was coming to get her, but he was hit by a truck on the highway!'

'Was that the accident by Siqian?' The young man was stunned for a moment, then he suddenly remembered something. 'The site of the accident is still closed off. I heard it was a hit-and-run.'

'That's the one. Xue had only eaten half her dinner when the police came.' The proprietress pointed at a plastic bowl and said, 'Do you see that? She just left her dinner there.'

For a moment Li was at a loss. He opened his mouth, but didn't know what to say. The proprietress clapped him on the shoulder and tittered, saying, 'Don't look so stricken. You're not the one who hit him. Why should you be nervous?'

Li asked offhandedly, 'Who did hit him?' The proprietress winked and seemed to want to tell him some secret, but in the end she rejected the idea. 'How would I know? If I did, I'd arrest the truck-driving creep myself!' Her hands waved ambiguously in the air and then clapped the driver's shoulders again. 'Now don't you pine after Xue, she was nothing special.'

As the proprietress spoke, she bent closer to Li's ear and said in a low voice, 'Give me a second and I'll send Hong to serve you. She's our best worker, and she's beautiful, *and* she went to college. I guarantee you'll be satisfied.'

On Saturdays

The man they called Papa Qi was in fact still quite young. Though Meng and his wife realized that he was younger than they were, they still affectionately called him Papa. It was a habit, and like all habits it arose from particular circumstances. It might be inaccurate, but it seemed wrong to correct it. Calling him anything else would feel unnatural by now, like the time Ningzhu had suddenly asked him, 'Mr Qi, what time is it?' The two men in the room had acted as if a bomb had gone off, and turned abruptly to look at her as she stood by the door. Their gazes expressed shock in different degrees, and their reaction made Ningzhu feel extremely awkward.

'Our wall clock is broken,' she explained haltingly. 'Papa Qi, you have a wristwatch, don't you?'

Papa Qi laughed silently, and glanced at his wrist. 'Nine o'clock. I should be leaving,' he said and stood up. He seemed a bit flustered, and ended up hitting the coffee table with his knee, then almost sweeping a cup to the floor with his arm. After this momentary confusion he gave the cup to Meng, grimaced in embarrassment at the couple, and said, 'I should go. You'll be wanting to get to bed soon.'

'There's no hurry. Why don't you stay a while longer?' An unmistakable look of shame appeared on Ningzhu's face and she blocked the door as she spoke. 'Don't misunderstand me. The wall clock really is broken; it has been for weeks. I told Meng to have it fixed, but he doesn't want to go to the repair shop and keeps putting it off. You know how lazy he is.'

'I should go. It's after nine – I really should go,' Papa Qi said. 'I have a lot to do tomorrow anyway. We've been so busy at the office recently.'

'We just don't have any way to tell the time at home now. I left my own watch at my aunt's,' Ningzhu felt compelled to keep explaining, 'and Meng can never find his. You'd really have to look hard to find someone as forgetful as he is. We've bought so many watches but he just keeps losing them, one after the other!'

Papa Qi had reached the door by now. All of a sudden he turned back and told Meng, 'Go and get your wall clock and give it to me.'

'Sorry?' Meng hadn't caught on right away.

'It's broken, isn't it?' said Papa Qi. 'My brother knows how to repair clocks. That way you won't have to take it to the shop. Besides overcharging you for the repair, they'll probably take out the good parts and put broken ones back. Let me handle it. That way you won't have to pay a penny, and I guarantee it'll run for two years without breaking.'

'You don't have to do that,' Meng glanced up to where the clock hung on the wall. He said, 'We really shouldn't bother you with all our little problems. Maybe it's not broken at all. Maybe I just bought a dud battery.'

'What's the big deal between friends?' Papa Qi answered. 'Go and take it down and give it to me.'

Meng looked at Ningzhu, but she avoided his eyes and sighed ambiguously. He took a chair, walked around her and climbed up to take the clock off the wall.

That was how it came about that Papa Qi left the Mengs' that day carrying their wall clock. Outside it was already completely dark and there were no street lights. The Mengs stood outside the door to see him off, but all they could make out was the dim glow of Papa Qi's white shirt. Apparently, he had placed the clock in his bicycle's wire basket as they could hear it rattling. He straddled his bike and then they heard him say in the darkness, 'Till Saturday then. On Saturday I'll come again. I'll bring the clock.'

On any given day, how many trains are there in the world speeding along the railway tracks? And on every train, how many people become companionable simply because they happen to be sitting next to one another in a crowded carriage? But then again, how many of these chance acquaintances end up as actual friends? Travel acquaintances are quickly made and equally swiftly forgotten; when the train enters the station there may not be time for farewells, and once you've been off the train for an hour you might even have forgotten what your companion looked like. Meng had never imagined that a trip lasting a mere three hours would yield an unforgettable friendship. No, you don't expect some guy making small talk on a train to turn into a real friend.

But that was just the kind of friend Papa Qi was. Meng could no longer remember clearly what topics they had touched on while chatting on the train – the conversation had ranged from UFOs to share prices to AIDS. It had been a congenial chat precisely because it had been so wide-ranging. Both of them had wanted to kill time on the train in the most natural way, and the three hours were easily disposed of. Soon they were standing on the platform and nodding to one another as they went their separate ways.

Later, Meng could not be sure exactly why Papa Qi had checked his rapid steps – more than likely it was because of Meng's luggage. He had three pieces with him: two travel bags and a large cardboard box. He would carry one of the travel bags on his shoulders, and the other bag and the box in his hands. For Meng a little luggage like that presented no difficulty at all. He picked up his travel bags but was beaten to the cardboard box by someone else, who lifted it up. Glancing up, Meng saw that it was his neighbour from the train, an amicable smile on his face.

'Why don't I take this for you?' he said. 'You live in the new housing estate at the station, right? That's only a few steps away. I'll help you take it all home.'

Meng thanked him and declined repeatedly, but finally he reluctantly acquiesced. It was because of Papa Qi's eyes; they seemed so clear and pure somehow, as if charged with some kind of expectation. That was how Meng first hesitantly led Papa Qi to his home. He recalled later that Papa Qi did not come in on this occasion. Meng had invited him in for a sip of tea, but Papa Qi had replied, 'No thanks. I still have to get to the office. We've been very busy recently.'

Meng said, 'Well, look in some time when you're free.' Of course, he just made this offer to be polite but he always remembered Papa Qi's earnest reaction. He had thought seriously about it for a moment, shaking his tired wrists, and then he'd said, 'On Saturday. I'll come on Saturday then.'

And afterwards Saturdays became Papa Qi's visiting day.

The Mengs were not the kind of people who enjoyed a wide circle of friends. On the first day that Papa Qi came to visit, neither of them really knew how to act, although as cultured people, they treated him amiably enough. Ningzhu had not yet met Papa Qi, and assumed he must be a friend of Meng's from university. She sat to one side, lamenting the fickleness of human nature and remarking that Meng's photograph albums were filled with pictures of his former classmates, faces shining with happiness, arms slung around one another's shoulders. How close they seemed to have been, yet now they had scattered to the four winds and Meng was in contact with no one: only Papa Qi had taken the time to visit his old friend.

Meng felt it would be awkward to correct his wife's error, so he just chuckled instead. It was Papa Qi who took the initiative and explained who he was: 'I never actually went to university. I missed the minimum score by a single point. I think I was born unlucky. After that, I didn't bother to retake the exams.'

Ningzhu, reacting quickly to this information, immediately switched the topic of conversation to the worthlessness of university graduates. 'What good are they? Look at Meng – comes out of a prestigious college and can't even install a ceiling light.'

Papa Qi laughed knowingly as she spoke. Then he nodded and remarked, 'You're right. But it's not just him. None of the college graduates I know can. And anyone who *can* put in a ceiling light didn't go to college. It's a social problem.'

'Well, I bet you can do all kinds of electrical work,' said Ningzhu encouragingly. 'Maybe we can give you a shout next time we need something done.'

'No problem. Just give me a call and I'll be there.'

In fact, they never actually asked Papa Qi for help with

anything electrical, nor did they ever intend to ask for help with anything else. But later Papa Qi did do them an enormous favour; something it would have been hard to imagine before it occurred.

For a few years Meng had been wanting to leave the research institute where he worked to find a job in the hi-tech development zone[4], but this hope had remained unfulfilled. One day he mentioned it in passing to Papa Qi. He really had meant nothing by it, he was just adding one more possible topic to their increasingly meagre supply of conversation. Papa Qi merely smiled enigmatically and asked, 'You want to work in the zone, eh? We might be able to work something out. As long as the research institute will let you go, there shouldn't be any problem.'

'I went to the zone once when they were recruiting. They seemed to be really satisfied with me, but nothing came of it in the end,' said Meng gloomily.

'Nothing strange about that, you don't have the connections, that's all. People get high salaries and good treatment in the zone. Everybody's been racking their brains for a way to get in. It all depends on your connections.'

Meng replied, not without scorn, 'I know that, but I can't be bothered to go around making connections. If they don't want me there, then I don't want to be there.'

[4]Many Chinese cities have outlying zones set aside to attract investment, typically offering preferential taxation and financial-support policies. A position in such a zone is, in general, highly desirable.

Papa Qi looked at him closely and after a second was unable to stifle his laughter.

'What are you laughing about?'

'You. That really says it all about you intellectuals.' Meng understood what was meant, but said nothing. Then he heard Papa Qi give his knee a resounding slap and say, 'No problem. I'll take care of this.'

Meng thought his behaviour baffling, but didn't pursue it since he'd only mentioned the matter in passing. It was true he wanted to go to the zone, but it wouldn't kill him to have to stay at the research institute, either – that was how he looked at the matter. So he was almost scoffing at Papa Qi when he asked, 'What? You don't mean to tell me that your father's the general director of the zone?'

No, Papa Qi's father was not a high-placed official in the zone, but he had another relative who was, and Meng was about to find that out. After only three days he was called to an interview in the zone, and what surprised him even more was the comment the official made as he was showing him out: 'We'll make the transfer order out tomorrow.' As Meng sped down in the lift he felt like he was dreaming. He left the building and spotted Papa Qi right away. He was sitting on the flower terrace, waving at him. Meng immediately woke from his trance, feeling now that there had been no particularly dreamlike element to what had just occurred. Of Papa Qi he enquired, 'So what's your connection with Vice Director Wang?'

'What do you want to know that for?'

'No reason. I was just curious.'

At this Papa Qi laughed and said, 'You intellectuals, curious about everything. But can you eat curiosity?' Meng felt a little awkward, but Papa Qi gave him a hearty pat on the back and said, 'He's a relative, I suppose, but that doesn't count for much. We're mostly friends; we gradually got to know each other.'

The Mengs were duly grateful for Papa Qi's help, and the day before Meng reported for duty in the zone, the two of them went to buy gifts for him. Obeying the conventions, they purchased high-quality cigarettes and alcohol. Then Ningzhu, anxious to do right, said, 'Papa Qi's chin is always so stubbly. Why don't we get him an electric razor?'

'If we get one, then it should be top-grade,' Meng replied, so in the end they shelled out a thousand yuan for a Philips razor.

Just as the couple had expected, Papa Qi refused this windfall of gifts, remarking, 'If I'd known you intellectuals believed in bribes like everyone else, I wouldn't have helped you out in the first place.'

Fortunately, Ningzhu knew how to be persuasive: 'We know how things work. You must have spent quite a lot of money running around to get this done for us. If you won't accept even these poor tokens of our gratitude then Meng simply won't report for work in the zone.'

Only when she had put it so boldly did Papa Qi finally agree to take the cigarettes and the alcohol; but when it came to the razor he exhibited his unconventional side, saying, 'I'll accept the razor too, but I won't take it home with me. If I take it home, I'll just end up giving it away to someone else, so it'll be best if you take care of it for me. I come here all the time anyway. This way it'll be mine just the same, right?'

From then on, the buzzing sound of an electric razor was often to be heard in the Meng's home, generally on Saturday afternoons but sometimes also early on a Friday or Sunday evening. And that was how Papa Qi's visits became part of Meng family life. He made them when the working week was done, so naturally those were the days when Ningzhu was particularly busy with her housekeeping. While she was cooking or washing up, she could always hear Papa Qi shaving in the sitting room. Their flat was far too small, and even from the kitchen she could clearly hear the three revolving blades rasping against the bristle of his beard. Not only that: since Papa Qi's beard was very tough, even two rooms away Ningzhu could make out the sound of the stubble rattling around inside the razor. One day, she grew very agitated at the noise and cried out loud, 'That racket is driving me crazy!'

The two men hadn't heard Ningzhu's complaint, but when Papa Qi took his leave that day she didn't see him to the door as usual, but instead vanished into the bathroom. She came out only once he had left, and her expression showed she was annoyed. She said to Meng,

'You two talked together the whole evening. What did you talk about? You talk to him almost every other day. What on earth do you find to talk about? How can there be that much to say?'

Meng, aware of his wife's mood, said, 'I don't really know what we talk about. He wants to sit there and talk, so I just talk back. When there's something to say, we talk, and when there isn't, we sip tea. And while we're sipping, we come up with another topic.'

Ningzhu frowned and said, 'It's very odd. He's always saying he's so busy, but if he is, why is he always sitting around our home all evening or afternoon?'

'Are you annoyed with him?' replied Meng. 'He's not just some run-of-the-mill acquaintance, you know, he did us a huge favour.'

'You're right, I shouldn't be irritated. I don't know what's happening to me, but as soon as I hear that razor it just gets to me. It's like a swarm of mosquitoes buzzing in my ears. If I'd known it would be like this, I'd have made him take it home when we first gave it to him.'

They were greatly in Qi's debt. Except for their parents, their brothers and sisters, was there anyone as interested in their affairs? When the toilet flush broke, it was Papa Qi who fixed it. They felt the deepest gratitude towards him, realizing you could scour the earth and never find another friend like him. On the other hand, they developed an ever-deepening dread of Saturdays. On Friday evenings, when Meng went to bed, he would laugh

79

hollowly and say, 'Tomorrow's Saturday. Papa Qi will be coming again.'

They had once supposed that Papa Qi had an ulterior motive, but the two of them quickly came to realize that to think that way was to do him an injustice. Meng was an automation programmer, Ningzhu an accountant; what use could they possibly be to him? They realized that Papa Qi was someone whose word was his deed; a person utterly devoid of ulterior motives, who paid them visits purely out of friendship. Neither Meng nor Ningzhu was odd or eccentric, and in their opinion making friends was a nice, harmless thing to do, but they didn't understand why Papa Qi had to come *every* Saturday, and why, when he did, he had to stay quite so long.

Ningzhu hatched a variety of schemes to curtail the length of Papa Qi's visits. Once, when Papa Qi and Meng were chatting in the living room, she carried out a pile of accounts books and explained that she was helping a co-worker make a little cash by doing extra bookkeeping, so she had to have them ready for the next morning. Then she sat down right under their noses, thinking it would be seen as an obvious hint. But Papa Qi seemed totally undisturbed, and concentrated on the political joke he was telling. The joke was in fact very funny, but Ningzhu couldn't bring herself to laugh. Instead she enquired of Meng, 'Can't you hear that the water on the stove is boiling? Go and pour it into the Thermos!'

Before he could get up, Papa Qi was already on his feet,

saying, 'I'll do it.' Then he rushed into the kitchen as if he was in his own house while Meng, caught between sitting and standing, said to his wife, 'You're going too far.'

Ningzhu rolled her eyes at him, picked up the things from the table and flounced into the bedroom. Once there, she had a private temper tantrum, throwing Meng's pillow viciously to the floor and stamping wildly all over it. That was the day Papa Qi brought back the repaired wall clock. When he had gone Meng wanted to hang it on the wall, but Ningzhu wouldn't allow it. Meng realized then that she was very angry with Papa Qi.

What could account for his behaviour? Did he really not see how they felt or was he merely pretending not to? Ningzhu sighed, 'I practically ordered him out. How come he didn't react?'

'He's the straightforward sort, that's all. He's not used to people beating about the bush,' Meng replied. 'Besides, it probably hasn't occurred to him that he annoys you. He's helped us with so many things without the slightest hope of getting anything in return. Why would it even cross his mind that he annoys you?'

'Nothing in return?' Ningzhu shouted. 'He takes our time away, he takes our Saturdays away. Other people have seven days in a week, but we only have six. Isn't that compensation enough?'

Meng could think of no immediate response. As a bookkeeper, Ningzhu had a way of presenting facts so clearly that others always saw her point. He chuckled for a moment, and then said to his wife, 'If he's really getting on your nerves, why don't you just go home to your mother's on Saturdays? I'll stay here and keep him company. He'll only be stealing my Saturday that way, so we'll be cutting our losses by fifty per cent, right?'

The next Saturday closed in on them with quick steps. In the morning, Meng was shaken awake very early by Ningzhu and took fright when he saw her haggard face and bloodshot eyes. His first thought was that she must be ill, but Ningzhu said, 'I'm not ill, I just haven't slept. I've been thinking the whole time of what will happen when Papa Qi comes. I try to force myself not to think about it, but as soon as I close my eyes, I hear the sound of that damned razor.' Then she said, 'I can't take it any more, really I can't.'

Meng felt the issue had become a major concern and tried to console his wife, saying, 'It's not as bad as all that. Think of his good points. If you remember all the things he's done for us, you won't feel that way.'

'I *did* think about them. I've thought all I can about his good points, but if he hadn't helped us at all, wouldn't we still have been fine? We could picnic on the mountain, we could go to the movies, or we could not go out at all and stay in reading, just the two of us. Wouldn't that be nice? Why did he have to force himself between us?'

'What do you mean, "force"? He's our friend, after all.'

But Ningzhu was no longer interested in the topic of

friendship, being steeped too far in resentment. 'No,' she said suddenly in a tone that brooked no argument, 'you can't stay at home today. You're coming with me.'

Meng was the kind of man who cherished his wife, and though he was extremely reluctant to agree, in the end he was unable to dissuade her. Before leaving home at noon, he wrote a note informing Papa Qi that they had gone out. Ningzhu was against even this, and said, 'If you say you're busy today, what about tomorrow? He'll come back tomorrow for sure.'

'But won't he notice we're avoiding him on purpose?'

'We *want* him to notice! Didn't you say he was straightforward? This time we won't beat around the bush, we'll let him find out. Maybe he is straightforward, but not to the point of idiocy!'

That night, when they returned home they discovered several cigarette butts outside the door. Meng counted them; there were six altogether. He picked them up one by one and threw them in the rubbish. A strange sensation accompanied the action, as if, bit by bit, he was picking up his friendship with Papa Qi and throwing that in the rubbish too. He felt empty inside, but strangely enough his movements seemed filled with exaggerated glee. Meng himself could not have explained his frame of mind that evening. All he could remember later was the first thing Ningzhu said after they got home: 'Now he gets it! He won't come back next week.' And he also remembered how full of joy and hope her voice was.

Indeed he did not come. Having waited until two in the afternoon, the Mengs felt certain that he would not; they had become familiar with the pattern of Papa Qi's visits. When the clock struck two, they looked at one another and smiled. Ningzhu said, 'Like I said, he won't come today.'

Meng replied, 'He didn't come today; he's given us our Saturdays back.' He'd meant to say it in a humorous tone, but could tell that somehow he'd sounded nervous, serious, anything but humorous.

Papa Qi did not come, and Saturday afternoon seemed very tranquil and empty. For a time, Meng didn't know what to do with himself; it felt as if this interlude had been stolen from Papa Qi. Somehow, he couldn't bear to fritter it away. He wandered around at home, and in the end asked Ningzhu, 'Tell me what I should be doing.'

She said, not without satisfaction, 'Anything you like. Why don't you read? You haven't read in six months.'

So Meng took a specialist book out, read a little and then raised his head, saying, 'What's that sound? I keep hearing something.'

Ningzhu put down her magazine, too, and said, 'You're right. It's some kind of droning. I can hear it. Weird. The noise doesn't seem to be coming from anywhere.'

Both their glances came to rest simultaneously on the shelf underneath the coffee table where the Philips razor lay silent. Since no one had switched it on, it couldn't possibly be making any noise, and both of them knew that this incident could only be attributed to their own hypersensitive nerves.

Meng couldn't remember at what time – perhaps it was three o'clock, perhaps four, in any case later than Papa Qi usually came – they suddenly heard the sound of a bicycle bell outside. Before Papa Qi knocked on the door he always rang his bicycle bell; it was practically a rule. Meng felt stunned for a moment; he watched Ningzhu jump up from the sofa. Panic-stricken, she grabbed his hand, and before he had worked out what was going on, she had pulled him behind her into the bedroom.

'Don't say anything.' Ningzhu covered his mouth and hissed at him, 'You mustn't say anything – you mustn't open the door to him. He'll knock for a little longer and then leave.'

Meng felt like a burglar, his heart beat so fast it threatened to stop altogether. He stared at Ningzhu, wanting to laugh, but couldn't get the sound out. 'Are you sure this is a good idea?' he mumbled as he put out his hand and quietly shut the bedroom door.

Outside Papa Qi knocked on the front door, and as he knocked he called out their names. Initially, the knocking was gentle and patient but gradually it became louder and more urgent, like thunderclaps they could hear all the way from the bedroom. Meng's hand kneaded his chest while Ningzhu covered her ears. They looked at each another and saw the resolve on one another's face. They waited for about five minutes until finally it was silent outside.

Meng sighed first and said to Ningzhu, 'We're going too far. He might realize we're at home.'

She shook her head at him, and walked stealthily to the window. He understood what it was she intended to do as she carefully turned up a corner of the curtain to peer outside. Suddenly he had a premonition, but it was the kind of premonition that comes too late – already he could hear Ningzhu's hysterical screams.

She later described to him the scene as her eyes met Papa Qi's as he rang his bicycle bell about a metre from the window. When he saw her, his expression became vacant and confused, a sight that made Ningzhu feel so ashamed she wanted to sink to the ground. 'I'm so terribly sorry,' she said, choking on her sobs. 'When I think of the way he looked, I regret everything. I went too far . . . oh, I'm so terribly sorry.'

Now that matters had reached this point, Meng had no way of consoling his wife, and when he imagined Papa Qi's expression, he too felt wretched. He said, 'There's no point regretting it now. He gets it. He won't come back to our home again.'

After that Papa Qi didn't return; not on Saturdays, nor Fridays nor Sundays either, not to mention any other day of the week. Meng knew that he had lost his friend for ever. For a very long time after that he would imagine sounds every Saturday: the ringing of bicycle bells in the street always drew his attention, and between two and two-thirty in the afternoon he would dimly hear the buzzing of the razor. One day he took the head off and saw that there was a thick layer of stubble inside, looking just like black dust. He went outside his door, puffed out his cheeks and blew the head clean of stubble. If Papa Qi wasn't going to come round any more, then the razor was Meng's to use. Afterwards, without his even noticing, the imaginary sound disappeared.

How many people meet every day on trains, only to go their separate ways when they reach their destination? In the end, the relationship between Papa Qi and Meng confirmed the conventional wisdom. Of course it was sheer coincidence that they saw one another once more on a train platform; the difference this time was that Meng was getting on a train to go out of town on business while Papa Qi had come to the station to see off some guests. It was a group from the north-east, and Meng guessed that these were Papa Qi's new friends.

Meng was positive that Papa Qi had seen him – his eyes skimmed past Meng several times, but his gaze deliberately blanked him out. Meng was too ashamed to greet him and kept his own head down, observing Papa Qi while he anxiously waited for the train to start. When it did, he saw Papa Qi waving from the platform but Meng knew that he was not waving at him; he was waving to those new north-eastern friends of his.

Thieves

'The thief reminiscing in a box.' An intriguing phrase like that doesn't just come out of nowhere. In fact, it originated from a word game. It was late one Christmas Day and a few Chinese people, in an attempt to be trendy, had consumed a half-cooked turkey and quite a large quantity of red and white wine with surprisingly few ill effects. They chatted until at last there was nothing more to chat about, and finally someone suggested they should play a word game. The rules called for the participants to write down subject, verb and location on separate pieces of paper. The more slips of paper submitted, the greater the number of sentences that could be randomly assembled. They were all old hands at this, adept at choosing peculiar phrases. Consequently, the pieced-together sentences could be quite amusing, and sometimes there were real side-splitters. The participants wracked their brains before writing down the words on separate slips of paper and piling them all on the table. Afterwards one of them, a young man called Yu Yong, picked out the following three slips: 'The thief/reminiscing/in a box.'

The game's purpose had been achieved. The Yuletide merrymakers broke into uproarious laughter. Yu Yong laughed too. When the hilarity had died down, one of his friends teased him, asking, 'Well, Yu Yong, do you have any reminiscences like that you can share?'

He responded, 'What, you mean thieving reminiscences?'

And his friends all said, 'Of course. Thieving reminiscences.' They looked at him as he scratched his cheek, searching his memory, but he didn't seem to be exerting himself unduly, and they were about to start the game again when Yu Yong cried out, 'I've got one – a memory. I really do have a thieving reminiscence – there was something like that, a long time ago . . .'

And to the surprise of everyone present, Yu Yong began a story which no one could have interrupted, even if they'd wanted to.

I'm no thief; of course I'm not. I suppose you all know I'm not from here originally. I was born in Sichuan and grew up there with my mother. She's a secondary school teacher and my father was serving with the Air Force as ground crew at the time, so he was rarely at home. I'm sure you'll agree that a child who grows up in such a home isn't likely to become a thief. The story I want to tell you, though, is about thieves. Keep quiet and I'll pick out some typical anecdotes . . . Actually, I'll just tell one story. I'll tell the story of Tan Feng.

Tan Feng was my one and only friend in that Sichuanese town. He was the same age as me: about eight or nine. Tan Feng's family lived next door to us. His father was a blacksmith and his mother was from the countryside. They had a lot of kids but the others were all girls, so you can imagine how the rest of the family spoiled their only boy. They really adored him, but they didn't know what he got up to, as Tan Feng stole things. He didn't dare steal from my house, but apart from that almost every household in town had lost something to his thieving ways. He would swagger into people's homes, ask whether their kid was in, and that was all it took – while he was there he would swipe a can of peppers or a picture book from the table and slip it under his clothes. Sometimes I would watch him steal and my heart would thump like mad, but Tan Feng was always as cool as could be. He didn't hide these things from me because he thought of me as his most loyal friend, and in fact I used to cover for him.

Once, when Tan Feng had stolen somebody's wristwatch – remember that at the time a wristwatch was something really expensive – he was suspected of being the thief. The whole family came out and shouted for him outside his house, but Tan Feng blocked the door and wouldn't let them in. Then the blacksmith and his wife came out. They didn't believe that their son would

91

have stolen a watch. Tan Feng swore like a sailor, so the blacksmith kept pinching his ears, but he wouldn't be quiet; he just yelled loudly for me to come and testify for him. So I came, and said, 'Tan Feng didn't steal that watch, I can vouch for it.' I remember Tan Feng's pleased smile and his parents' grateful, tear-filled glances at me. To the onlookers they said, 'That's the son of Mrs Yu the teacher. He's taught good manners at home and he never lies.' And because of my intervention the matter remained unresolved. After a few days the victims discovered the watch at home. They even went to Tan Feng's home to tell them they had found it, apologized for having done him wrong and gave him a big bowl of sweet soup dumplings to boot. He carried it over to share with me and the two of us were very proud of ourselves – I was the one who'd told him to go to their house and secretly put the watch back.

My mother disliked Tan Feng and his whole family, but people were very progressive thinking in those days, and she said that being friendly with proletariat children was a kind of education, too. Of course, if she had known what I was getting up to with Tan Feng, she would have gone bananas. 'Pilfer' – my mother liked to use that word – and 'pilfering' was the sort of aberrant behaviour she hated most, but what she didn't know was that this word and I were already inextricably linked.

If it hadn't been for a certain toy train, I don't know how far my alliance with Tan Feng might have gone. Tan

Feng had a hoard of treasure, all of which was stored in the pigsty of old Mr Zhang, who lived on communal welfare. Tan Feng was clever to hide his spoils there as old Mr Zhang was no longer good on his feet and the pigsty had no pigs in it. Tan Feng just burrowed a hole in a pile of firewood, and put all the things he had stolen inside. If anybody saw him, he could say he was bringing Mr Zhang firewood, and in fact he really did bring wood. Half of it was for the old man, and the other half, of course, was to hide his treasure.

Now, let me tell you about this treasure, although the things it contained seem laughable now. There were a number of medicine bottles and capsules which might have been stuff women took as contraceptives; there was an enamel cup, some fly-swatters, bits of copper and iron wire, matches, thimbles, a red neckerchief, a clothes rack, a long-stemmed pipe, an aluminium spoon – in short, a random assortment of tat. When Tan Feng let me in to see his hoard, I couldn't hide my contempt for it. Then, however, he delved into the pile of medicine bottles and brought out a little red train.

'Look,' he said. He carried it with extreme care, at the same time elbowing me away roughly so I couldn't get close to it. 'Look,' he said, but while his mouth repeated the word, his elbow blocked me from getting any closer to the train; it was as if his elbow were saying, 'Just stand there. You can look, but you can't touch.'

Ah, that little red iron-plated train: a locomotive and

four cars. On top of the engine was a stovepipe, and inside it was a miniature conductor. If children today saw a train like that, they wouldn't think it was so amazing, but at the time in a little Sichuanese town, you can imagine what it meant to a boy. It was the most wonderful thing in the world. I remember my hand felt like a piece of iron being drawn to a magnet. Overcome by an irresistible impulse, I kept making grabs for it, but every time Tan Feng fended me off.

'Where did you steal it from?' I almost screamed. 'Whose is it?'

'The Chengdu girl's from the commune hospital.' Tan Feng gestured for me not to speak too loudly, then he stroked the train for a moment and laughed out loud. 'I didn't really steal it. The girl's such a dumb-bell that she just left it by the window. So since she was practically asking me to take it, I took her up on it.'

I knew the Chengdu girl; she was short and fat, and it was true that she was stupid. If you asked her what one plus one made, she would say eleven. I suddenly remembered having seen her crying that day in front of the commune hospital. She had cried herself hoarse, and her father, Dr He, had carried her home over his shoulders like a sack of potatoes. Now I was sure she had been crying for her toy train.

As I imagined the scene of Tan Feng taking the little train through the window my heart filled with a kind of envy, and I swear that this was the first time I'd felt such a thing for him. Strange to say, even though I was only eight or nine, I was able to disguise my emotion. Calmly, I asked him, 'Can you make it go? If you can't make it go, then it's nothing special.'

Tan Feng flashed a little key at me, and I noted that he had taken it out of his pocket. It was the sort of simple key used to wind up a spring mechanism. A sweet, self-satisfied smile appeared on his face as he put the train on the ground and wound it up. Then he watched as it began moving around the pigsty. It could only go in a straight line, it couldn't turn in circles or blow its steam whistle, but for me it was a wonder even so. I didn't want to seem too excited, though, and simply said, 'Well, of course you can make the train go. If you couldn't make it go, then it wouldn't be a train.'

My own terrible plan was hatched at that instant. It took shape vaguely, when I saw Tan Feng cover his treasure back up with firewood. He looked at me with anxious eyes and said, 'You're not going to tell anyone, are you?' By now, my idea was rapidly taking hold and I said nothing. I followed him out of the pigsty. On the way back, he caught a butterfly and seemed to want to give it to me as some sort of bribe. I refused; I wasn't interested in butterflies. It felt as if my idea was gathering momentum, weighing on my mind more heavily until it became hard for me to breathe. But still I didn't have the strength to chase it from my brain.

You can probably guess what I did. I went to the

commune hospital and sought out Dr He, telling him that Tan Feng had stolen his daughter's train. So that he wouldn't recognize my face, I wore a big surgical mask, and after I rushed through what I had to say, I ran off. On my way home, I happened to meet Tan Feng, who was playing football on the school sports grounds with some other children. He called out for me to join in, but I said I had to go home for dinner and vanished like a puff of smoke. You know how the aftermath of tale-telling is the worst thing? That evening I hid at home and pricked up my ears so I could hear what might be going on in Tan Feng's home, and before long Dr He and his daughter paid a call to the Tan family home.

I heard his mother shout Tan Feng's name at the top of her voice; then the hammer in his father's hand ceased its monotonous banging. They couldn't find Tan Feng. All his sisters went around the town calling out his name, but they couldn't find him either. Seething with anger, his father came to our home and asked me where his son had gone. I didn't answer, and then the blacksmith asked another question, 'Did Tan Feng steal Dr He's daughter's toy train?' Even then I stayed silent; I lacked the courage to say yes. That day, Tan the blacksmith's dry, haggard face spluttered with rage like a soldering iron – I thought he might kill someone. As I heard Tan Feng's name resounding through the town in the shrill, crazed voices of his family, I regretted what I had done.

But it was too late for regret; soon my mother returned

from school and stopped for a long while outside Tan Feng's home. When she came in and pulled me out from underneath the mosquito nets, I knew that I had got myself in a fix. The blacksmith and his wife were right behind her and my mother said to me, 'No lying. Now, did Tan Feng take that toy train or not?' I don't have the words to describe the severe and indomitable expression in my mother's eyes then and my last line of defence suddenly collapsed. My mother said, 'If he took it, nod. If he didn't, shake your head.' I nodded. I saw how Tan the blacksmith jumped with rage like a firecracker, and how Tan Feng's mother sank down on our threshold, sobbing and blowing a string of snot from her nose as she cried and tried to communicate something. I didn't pay close attention to what she was saying, but the general idea was that Tan Feng had been led astray by someone and now he had gone and ruined his parents' good name. My mother was livid at this insinuation, but she was too well-bred to quarrel with her. Instead, she took out her anger on me and gave me a smack with her exercise book.

They found Tan Feng in the water. He had wanted to escape to the other side of the little river outside town, but the only stroke he knew was doggy paddle, and once he reached the deep water he just thrashed around wildly. He hadn't even called for help. The blacksmith reached the riverbank, fished his son out and pulled him back on shore, then he dragged Tan Feng, who was soaked to the bone, all the way home. People from the town followed the pair of them as they headed back. Tan Feng was rolled over and over on the ground like a log, but with great effort, he lifted his head to see curious faces on both sides of him. He began spitting and swearing at these people who'd come to see the public spectacle: 'What the f*** are you looking at? What the f*** are you looking at?'

Just as I had expected, Tan Feng refused to confess. He did not deny that he had stolen the little red train, but he refused to reveal where he had hidden it. I heard the blacksmith's oaths and Tan Feng's cries, each louder than the last; the blacksmith had always raised him using a judicious mixture of spoiling and savage beatings. I heard the blacksmith give a last ear-splitting howl, 'Which hand did you steal it with? Left or right?' Before the sound had died away, Tan Feng's mother and sister began to wail in concert. It was an atmosphere of pure terror. I knew something terrible was going to happen, and I didn't want to miss my opportunity to witness it, so while my mother was busy washing vegetables, I rushed out.

I was just in time to see the blacksmith maim his own son by pressing Tan Feng's left hand onto a red-hot soldering iron. I recall that at that same moment, Tan Feng shot me a glance so full of shock and despair that it was like a red-hot iron itself, so searing that my whole body seemed to steam with shame.

I am not exaggerating when I say that a hole was burnt

98

into my heart at that moment. I didn't hear Tan Feng's scream, which resounded high above the town, I just turned around and fled, as if afraid that Tan Feng, who was in the process of losing the fingers of his left hand, might yet chase after me. With dread and guilt in my heart, I ran away, and before I knew it I was at Mr Zhang's pigsty. Despite all that had happened I still hadn't forgotten the little red train, even in this dark hour. I sat for a moment on the stack of firewood and made up my mind to excavate Tan Feng's treasure, taking advantage of the last rays of the setting sun to make my careful search. I was surprised to find, however, that the little red train wasn't there. I took the stack of firewood apart, and still I didn't find it.

So Tan Feng was not as foolish as I had thought; he had moved the train. I reasoned that he had done so after the theft had been exposed. Perhaps while his family had been calling for him he had moved it to an even more secret location. I stood in Mr Zhang's pigsty and realized with a jolt that Tan Feng had taken that precaution against me. Perhaps he had suspected me long ago, thinking that I would tattle one day; perhaps he had another secret hoard. I pondered this and a nameless sense of loss and sorrow welled up in me.

You can imagine the chaos in the Tan household once the deed was done. Tan Feng fainted and the blacksmith wept, hugging his son to him and wandering through the town to find a tractor driver. Then he and his wife got on the tractor and took Tan Feng to the district hospital fifteen kilometres away.

I knew that Tan Feng would spend the next few days in extreme pain, and that time was very hard for me to endure too. There was also the punishment my mother inflicted on me. In her eyes I bore half the guilt for the whole affair, so I was confined to the house. Beside this she required me, like one of her students, to write a piece of self-criticism. Remember that I was only eight or nine at the time. As if I was going to be able to write a substantial piece of self-criticism! I wrote and doodled in an exercise book, and without realizing what I was doing I drew several little trains on the paper; so I threw it out. But afterwards I was still thinking about that little red train. There was nothing I could do – no way I could resist the spell that train had cast over me. I leaned over the desk, and heard in my ears a dim, metallic sound: the sound of the train's wheels rolling over the ground. The four cars, the sixteen wheels, were constantly appearing in my mind's eye; not to mention the stovepipe on top, and the conductor with the neckerchief tied around his miniature neck.

What made me disobey my mother's orders was burning desire: I urgently needed to find that missing train. My mother had locked the door from the outside, but I jumped out through the window and walked down the streets of town positively thirsting for it. I had no destination in mind and just blindly looked for somewhere to go. It was a sweltering day in August, and the town's children were gathered by the riverside, either splashing around in the water or playing stupid cops-and-robbers games on the bank. I didn't want to splash around, and I didn't want to play cops and robbers, all I could think about was that little red train. I walked until the only surfaced road in the town ended and I saw the abandoned brick kiln in the cornfields beyond. This must be what people mean when they talk about a moment of inspiration. I'd suddenly remembered that Tan Feng had once hidden several of old Mr Ye's chicks in that kiln. Could it be his second hiding place for the treasure? The thought made me jittery with nerves. I moved aside the stone blocking the kiln's door and ducked in. There! I saw the freshly piled cornstalks and kicked them apart. Have you guessed? You have. It was that simple. Don't people often say 'Heaven helps those who help themselves'? I heard a clear, melodious ring, and my heart nearly stopped beating. Heaven helps those who help themselves – it's as simple as that. I'd found the Chengdu girl's little red train in the brick kiln.

Did you think I was going to take the toy truck back to the commune clinic and ask for Dr He? No. But if I had, then the rest of this story would probably never have happened. To be frank, it didn't even cross my mind to return the train to its original owner. Instead, I was more concerned with the question of how to take it home without it being discovered by anyone. I finally thought up a plan and removed my T-shirt, broke off some heads of corn, and wrapped both train and corn in my T-shirt to make a bundle. Nervously, I set off for home. Usually I never went shirtless like the other boys in town, mainly because my mother didn't allow it, so as I walked down the narrow street, it felt as if people were looking at me. I was very anxious to begin with, and then someone took note of my unusual appearance. I heard one woman say to another, 'What a blistering day – even Mrs Yu's kid's taken his shirt off!' But what the other woman noticed was my bundle, and she said, 'What's he carrying? Do you think he's stolen something?' This scared me, but fortunately my mother enjoyed a spotless reputation in the town and the gossiping woman was brusquely cut off by her partner who said, 'Hold your silly tongue. As if Mrs Yu's son would steal anything!'

My luck held; my mother wasn't around so I was able to find a hiding place for the train. Besides the box under my bed where I stored things there were two other places for emergencies or temporary deployment: one of them was the padded overcoat my father had left at home, and the other was the pressure cooker in the kitchen, which we weren't using. I hid the toy train there, and from that moment on I couldn't rest. I realized I still had a problem: the key to wind up the spring. No doubt Tan Feng had it hidden about his body, and if I couldn't get the key, I couldn't make the train run. And for me, a train that didn't run had lost the greater part of its value.

The trouble that came later was all because of that key. I hadn't even thought about how to deal with Tan Feng once he got home. Every day I tried to make a key myself, and one day I was at home alone, grinding a padlock key on the whetstone, when the door was kicked open and who but Tan Feng should come in. He walked up to me and glared at me threateningly, then he said, 'You're a traitor, a foreign agent, a spy, a counter-revolutionary and a class enemy!'

His tirade caught me off-balance. I held the padlock key tightly in my fist, and listened to Tan Feng abuse me with all the coarse language he knew. I looked at that left hand of his, wrapped tightly in white cloth, and my guilt submerged any impulse I might have had to retaliate. I remained silent, reflecting that Tan Feng might not yet know that I had been to the kiln. I wondered whether he would be able to guess that it was I who had taken the train.

Tan Feng didn't touch me – perhaps he knew that with only one hand he would come off worse – instead he just swore. But after swearing for a while he grew tired and asked me, 'What are you doing?' Still I said nothing, and he must have thought he had gone too far. He put out his left hand for me to see. 'You have no idea how much gauze they used to wrap it up – a whole roll!' I said nothing, so Tan Feng examined the gauze on his hand and, after looking at it for a while, suddenly he laughed proudly and said, 'I fooled the old man. As if I would use my left hand! It was the right hand, of course.' Then he asked me a question, 'Do you think it pays to have your left hand burnt or your right?'

This time I replied, 'It doesn't pay either way. Far better to have neither burnt.'

He looked stunned for a moment, then waved at me contemptuously. 'Stupid. What do you know? The right hand's way more important than the left. You need your right hand to eat and work and everything, don't you?'

After Tan Feng came home, we didn't play together any more. My mother forbade it, and the blacksmith and his wife wouldn't allow me to play with him, either – they were now both of the opinion that I was the devious kind. I didn't care what they thought of me, but I did listen carefully to the goings-on in their house, since I was anxious to know whether Tan Feng had been to the kiln yet, and whether he suspected me of taking the little red train.

That day finally came. We had already gone back to school when Tan Feng blocked my way in front of the gates. He looked distracted, and the expression in his eyes as he studied me was almost pleading. 'Did you take it or not?'

I had prepared myself mentally for such a challenge; you wouldn't believe how calm and streetwise I sounded. 'Take what?'

Tan Feng answered quietly, 'The train.'

I said, 'What train? The train you stole?'

And Tan Feng replied, 'I can't find it. But I hid it so well, why can't I find it?'

I urged myself to stay calm and not to mention the word kiln. 'Didn't you hide it in Mr Zhang's pigsty?' Tan Fang rolled his eyes at me, and after that he didn't ask me any more questions. He took a few steps back, towards the sports grounds, his eyes fixed on me in confusion. I looked steadily back into his eyes and started walking in the same direction. You would never believe the way I acted that day, that an eight-year-old child could put on such a mature and composed manner. It wasn't in my nature; it was all because of the little red train.

From then on Tan Feng and I went our separate ways. We were neighbours, but after that whenever we ran into each other, we would turn the other way. On my part, it was because of my guilty secret; on his the result of a deep wound. Because I believe Tan Feng's heart was hurt as badly as his hand, and I have to take responsibility for both. I remember very clearly how, a few months later, he was brushing his teeth outside his home. I heard him call out my name and I ran out. Though he was still calling to me, he didn't even glance my way. Instead he seemed to be talking to himself, saying, 'Yu Yong, Yu Yong, I know what you are.' I turned a deep red. He had obviously fathomed my secret. What puzzled me about it though was that ever since Tan Feng had returned from hospital, I had kept the toy train hidden away in the pressure cooker. Even my mother had failed to discover it, so how could Tan Feng know? Had he perhaps also relied on inspiration to guide him?

It sounds ridiculous, but after I got my hands on that train I rarely had a chance to play with it, let alone experience the joy of making it go. Only occasionally, when I was sure it was completely safe, did I take the lid off the pressure cooker and sneak a little look at it – only a look. What are you laughing at? At a thief's guilty conscience? I did have a guilty conscience – actually it was more painful and complicated than that – I even saw the train a few times in my dreams, and in the dream it was always blowing its steam whistle. Then Tan Feng and the kids from town would come running to hear it and I would wake up quickly from fright. I knew that the steam whistle in my dream actually came from the Baocheng railway two kilometres away, but still I woke up in a cold sweat. You ask why I didn't give the train back to Tan Feng, but that would have made no sense. Reason dictated I should give it back to the Chengdu girl, the real owner. The idea had occurred to me, and one day I even went up to the commune clinic's door. I saw the girl in the courtyard playing Chinese skipping, happy as anything. She had forgotten all about the train a long time ago. Well, I thought, if she's forgotten about it, what's the point of doing a good deed and giving it back to her? And in an epithet I had learnt from Tan Feng, I swore at her, 'Porkhead.'

Was I very bad? Yes, when I was a child, I was pretty bad: I went so far as to misappropriate stolen goods. But, in fact, that's not the right question to ask. The real question is, with a secret like that – put yourself in my shoes – how could I surrender the train? And then, very soon, it was the winter holidays, and in the winter of that year my father was released from military service and we moved to Wuhan – our whole family moving here from our little town in Sichuan. This news made me extremely excited, not only because Wuhan is a big city but because it gave me the opportunity to put all the trouble with the train behind me. I looked forward more each day to our move; I looked forward to leaving Tan Feng and the town behind.

On the day we left, cold, heavy rain was falling. I was waiting with my family at the long-distance bus station when I saw somebody's head appear and disappear outside the waiting-room window, then, after a moment, it appeared again. It was Tan Feng. I recognized him but decided to ignore him. It was my mother who had to tell me to go and say goodbye. 'Tan Feng wants to say goodbye to you. You used to be good friends, how can you ignore him?' And so I had to walk outside and go over to him. His clothes were soaked from the rain and he used his maimed hand to wipe away the water dripping from his hair; his eyes too were wet. He seemed to want to say something, but he didn't open his mouth to speak. I grew impatient and turned away. He gripped one of my hands and I felt him slip something into it. Then he ran off, so fast he was almost flying.

As you will all have guessed, it was the key. The key to wind up the little red train! I remember that it was very wet, though whether from sweat or the rain I couldn't say. I was very surprised; I hadn't expected things to end like that. Even now I feel surprised by the way it ended. I wonder what Tan Feng meant by it?

None of the man's friends seemed willing to answer the question. They were silent for a moment, and then someone asked Yu Yong, 'Do you still have the train?'

He said, 'No, not for a long time now. On the third day after we got to Wuhan, my parents packed it up in a box and sent it back to Dr He.'

Someone said awkwardly, 'That's really too bad.'

Yu Yong laughed and replied, 'Yes, I suppose. But you have to consider it from my parents' point of view. How could they have agreed to conceal stolen goods? How could they have let me become a thief?'

How the Ceremony Ends

It was last winter that the folklorist paid his visit to the village of Eight Pines. Carrying his rucksack by the straps, he jumped off the public bus from the city and started walking north-east. The road was covered in a thin layer of fine snow which, from afar, assumed a light-blue tint; shadows from the winding lines of high-voltage wires and telephone poles chequered the surface evenly. Occasionally, flocks of birds passed over the man's head: sudden, but orderly nonetheless. The folklorist walked towards Eight Pines. By now, he too has become part of the landscape of my memory.

By the entrance to the village, an old man sat on the ground mending a large ceramic urn, his kit bag lying to one side. A tiny, dark red flame licked at a piece of melting tin; the smell of it crept through the air, which otherwise held only the crispness that comes after snowfall. The old man grasped a tin clamp with his tongs and squatted to examine the urn for cracks, but hearing the crunch of footsteps in the snow, he interrupted his work and glanced behind him. He saw a stranger walking towards Eight Pines, then turning back to the task in hand, he took no further notice of him. Spitting on a crack in the urn, he exerted all his strength to force the clamp inside; it held for only a moment before falling into the fire. The old man frowned, and as he did so he discovered the stranger was now standing behind him, gazing intently at the urn.

'I held it in too long, now it's gone too soft,' the old man explained.

'What period is it from?' asked the folklorist.

'What?' said the old man.

'The urn.' The folklorist flicked the side of it with his index finger and a clear ringing resounded from it. Then he observed, 'Dragon-and-phoenix pattern. *Longfeng. Qing Dynasty.*'

The old man picked up another clamp with his tongs, and this time it fitted easily into the crack, filling it. He grinned at the folklorist and said, 'There! That's the way to do it! I've been mending pottery for fifty years now all around these parts. Where are you from?'

'The city. Is this Eight Pines?'

'More or less. What brings you here?'

'I collect folk stories.' The academic had hesitated before answering, thinking that an old man from the countryside might not understand what he meant by that.

'Then you'll need to find a storyteller. Who do you have in mind?'

'I don't know. I don't know anyone here yet.'

'You should look for Wulin.' The old man grinned again. Then he bent over to blow out the fire and repeated, 'Go and look for Wulin. He has stories coming out of his ears.'

The folklorist rested one hand on the urn and gazed around at the village in winter. The sun shone dimly on the paddies which were turning dry and white. The trees, scattered among the graves and ditches, had all let their leaves fall, and there was nothing to be seen of the pines he had envisaged. The most striking thing about the scene was a solitary scarecrow among the paddies, blackening with age, wearing a straw hat, in whose brim an intrepid bird had pecked holes.

Apparently the folklorist stayed in a classroom at the primary school. There are no hostels of any kind in Eight Pines, so that's where outsiders are generally housed. You can sleep on the desks free of charge, but you have to be out by the time the morning bell rings. So in the mornings, the folklorist put on his rucksack and set out from the primary school. He demonstrated a particular interest in the village's recessed doorways, walking in and out, examining them. His face was very pale and his upper lip clean-shaven; this, along with his beige anorak and the rucksack, made a deep impression on all the locals.

Before long, some of the older villagers of Eight Pines were relating what they knew of the area's remaining customs while the folklorist took notes. They would sit in front of the village tavern's stove, eating meat and drinking rice wine. By paying for everything, the folklorist was able to reap a new harvest every day. Once, remembering what the old man on the edge of the village had told him about Wulin, he asked the old people, 'Which one of you is Wulin?' The strange thing was that none of them could recall any such person, but then one of the old men, looking startled, called out, 'I remember! Wulin . . . Wulin the ghost! But he's been dead almost sixty years. He's the one who drew the ghost, back when they used to cast lots for them.'

That was how the folklorist discovered that Eight Pines had once had a custom of casting ingot-shaped lots to designate a 'man-ghost'. Immediately he sensed that this was likely to be the most valuable find of his research. He told the old people to take their time and give him a complete account of the practice, but they were all over eighty and expressed themselves so vaguely that he was only able to note down these brief impressions:

Notes

The custom of ghost-casting in Eight Pines was passed down from ancient times until the thirteenth year of the Republic[5]. The ceremony, held once every three years,

[5]The Republic of China was established in 1912 (Year 1), after the fall of the Qing Dynasty. The thirteenth year of the Republic would therefore be 1924.

consisted of choosing a human sacrifice from among the living in deference to the dead ancestors of the clan. All the people of the village gathered for the ceremony at the clan hall. Small ingots made of tinfoil were placed on the altar and unwrapped, one by one, by an elder. A single ingot was marked with the outline of a ghost, and the villager who drew this became the man-ghost. The man-ghost was then wrapped in white cloth, thrown into the large *longfeng* urn and beaten to death with sticks.

The folklorist was not particularly satisfied with these sketchy notes. Never in his entire career had he encountered such an appalling custom. In the heat of the tavern stove, his thoughts began to race feverishly, and finally it occurred to him that the ideal way of recording this custom for posterity would be to recreate it. Turning to a white-haired old man, he asked, 'Do you recall how the ceremony used to be performed?'

The old man replied, 'I remember it very clearly. No way of forgetting.'

'Well then, why don't we cast lots for a ghost, just so I can get a sense of it?' said the folklorist.

The old man laughed merrily. 'You can't cast lots for ghosts any more.'

But the folklorist bought more bottles of rice wine and meat dishes and placed them in front of the old people, saying, 'Don't worry about it. We'll do it just for fun. But I need you to help me a little, all right?'

From what I hear they were quick to consent, setting the winter solstice as the date and the elementary school as the location for the ceremony's re-enactment. The arrangements were made in accordance with their recollections: they said that ghost-casting had always been conducted on the winter solstice, and that the school had been constructed on the grounds of what had once been the clan temple.

The weather preceding the solstice was chill but humid, and as the thin layer of snow melted into the black mud, the village recovered its former austere appearance. With the snow gone, barefoot farmers began to venture out into the paddies. They gathered the dried rice straw that had fallen throughout the autumn, and hurried home with it. Only the scarecrow stood still, watching over the frozen endless lands.

At the edge of the village, the folklorist saw the urn once again. It was listing slightly and an inch of water had accumulated in the base – melted snow, he presumed. He bent over to feel the moulded *longfeng* pattern of dragons and phoenixes, and then, giving it a few raps, said to himself, 'This must have been the urn.' The cracks had now all been filled by teeth-like tin clamps sunk solidly into the fissures. He nearly burnt his fingers on them, they were still scalding hot. He looked around and glimpsed the old pottery-mender with his kit bag, passing behind a grave mound and gradually disappearing from view.

'Wulin,' murmured the folklorist, remembering the ghost of sixty years ago. Then he couldn't stop himself from laughing out loud. He walked around the urn once more; it was like walking into an older era in village life. It seemed as if the urn, which had once held corpses, was revolving on its base behind him. The fantastic customs of this village were provoking his imagination to greater and greater heights.

'Wulin.' Now he stretched his hand into the urn and felt the imaginary outline of Wulin's wrecked skull. It was a mixture of blood and flesh, like jellyfish floating on the surface of the water. Removing his hand from the urn, he shook it to rid himself of the sensation, but nothing came off. Of course there was nothing in the urn but an inch of melted snow, and beneath that grey-brown moss. Nothing else. He hadn't even really believed the illusion. Nevertheless, he couldn't help but wonder about the old man who had given him that useless, even malicious piece of advice to look for Wulin, a dead man, and ask him to tell stories.

The folklorist examined the fingers he had put in the urn, but there was nothing unusual about them except for their bloodless pallor; the result of the weather and his own anaemia.

At the winter solstice, the ghost-casting ceremony was re-enacted at Eight Pines. Some of the participants were old people who had come spontaneously, and through the help of the village council, the folklorist had managed to assemble even more of the local people. The folklorist wanted the ceremony to be as realistic as possible, saying that for him the best thing would have been to go back in time sixty years.

The altar was formed by pushing together school desks in a long line on the dirt floor. The villagers lit several candles and set these on the altar, along with offerings of meat, fish and dried fruits. More troublesome was the question of the foil ingots. Since there were approximately three hundred villagers, it was necessary to make that many ingots to put on the altar. The folklorist helped the old people as they rolled the foil into shape. Finally, on the paper lining of one of the sheets of foil, he sketched the outline of a ghost in red ink. This he gave to the venerable white-haired old man who rolled the foil into an ordinary-looking ingot and threw it on the pile. Next, four people standing with their backs to the table mixed up the shimmering pile of ingots. Numbering over three hundred by now, these were arranged in a single long line, which wound from one end of the altar to the other, ceremonially confronting the villagers.

The villagers waiting to draw ingots stood solemnly in a similar winding line and filed gradually towards the altar. One after another, each of the villagers took an ingot and gave it to the old man. He unfolded each in turn, spreading it out on his palm. It was a long and solemn procedure and the villagers kept their eyes fixed on the old man, waiting for him to raise one of the pieces of foil above his head and say, 'The ghost. This one's the ghost.'

The folklorist's place was towards the end of the line, and while he proceeded towards the altar he paid close attention to the events unfolding ahead. The villagers were passing one by one through the old man's hands; the ghost was proving slow to appear. A thought occurred to the folklorist, but he dismissed it as too improbable. Shaking his head, he continued shuffling slowly towards the altar. Reaching it, he took one of the ingots, just like all the villagers had: there weren't many left, but he had to choose one of them. As he walked up to the old man, he saw that there were thin white streaks of light, like snow, shining in his long beard, and as the old man held out his hand to take the ingot, it too was streaked with grey-white rays of light. The eerie sight made the folklorist shudder. Giving the old man the ingot he had selected, he thought, That's not possible. It would be too theatrical. But he saw that the same light was now shining from the old man's eyes too. He opened the ingot and raised it slowly above his head. Then the folklorist clearly heard the old man's voice, brimming with emotion.

'The ghost. This one's the ghost.'

The folklorist laughed. He felt light-headed, although he knew there was no good reason to be. He turned around to face the now restless crowd. Laughing, he said, 'Isn't that funny? I'm the ghost.' At this point, four men rushed out from behind the old man, dragging a

117

large sheet behind them. They wrapped the folklorist in it from head to foot and, lifting the bundle, ran outside. Initially the folklorist retained his composure at this turn of events, but when he heard their wild, ear-splitting cries, he began to feel afraid. Summoning all his strength, he cried out, 'Where are we going? Where are you taking me?'

The ghost-bearers answered, 'To the *longfeng* urn! How could you forget? It was your idea!' At this the folklorist calmed down again. Through the white sheet he could dimly see a dense crowd of villagers running along like madmen. Some of them were shouting, 'The ghost! The ghost!' He was being carried above Eight Pines now, soaring, flying over the village. Suddenly he remembered the old man at the urn who had mentioned Wulin's name. The memory made his heart skip a beat. The ghost-bearers gradually picked up speed. They were heading to the urn so quickly that their feet barely touched the ground. The folklorist could dimly see the great urn, with its cracks and clamps, its inch of melted snow and moss. He suddenly called out sharply, 'No! Put me down! Put me down right now!'

Finally, the ghost-bearers and the crowd stood still and set the folklorist down. They unwound him from the enfolding sheet, and when his face emerged it was deathly pale. He kicked himself free from the sheet, brushed down his clothes and hair and told the village elder, 'This is purely a re-enactment. It's not real. I research folk customs. I am not a ghost.'

'Of course it's not real,' said the old man. 'If it were real it wouldn't be like this at all. It wouldn't be finished yet.'

'I'm a little out of breath. I almost suffocated in there.'

'It's not finished,' repeated the old man. 'We have to put you in the urn, and then everyone has to hit you once, until you die.'

'This far is fine. It's been quite realistic enough.'

The folklorist heaved a sigh of relief, sat down on the urn's edge and stared around him at the stupefied-looking villagers. The crowd drifted away reluctantly. Feeling strangely weak, he remained there until the moon rose over the distant chimney of the brickmaker's kiln.

Gradually the people dispersed until finally only the scarecrow by the paddies was visible, rustling in the sobbing wind. His straw hat was gone; someone must have knocked it off during the confusion.

How could this have happened? The folklorist patted his throat, which felt constricted after the ordeal; it was still hard for him to breathe. He struck the lip of the urn a few times with the flat of his hand, then stood up. Though he had been unlucky to be named as the ghost, the incident once written up would make for his most outstanding piece of research yet.

I heard that it happened on the day he left Eight Pines.

As he walked through the lanes with his rucksack,

several villagers bade him farewell from their dark, humid homes. He couldn't hear what they said exactly, but he knew that they were words of parting. Lost in his own melancholy thoughts, he walked along the unsurfaced roads towards the main highway. The road was slippery with melted snow which had now refrozen. The wind was blowing very hard that day, and he had to zip up the collar of his anorak and walk sideways. As he reached the edge of the village, he took a last look at the *longfeng* urn. Over the course of one night, the water inside had frozen into blue-tinged ice. It was then that he scented the acrid smell of melting tin in the air, a curdled odour streaming from the urn, tainting his face and luggage. He lifted his head and looked around him. The old man who had recently mended the urn was already quite far away.

The pottery-mender was walking along the road ahead. Flame flickered from his kit bag, floating above the road like a firefly. The reappearance of the old man made the folklorist aware of a mysterious circle of events. All of a sudden he wanted to catch up with him, wanted to grasp the substance of that circle. Quickening his pace, he took the same gravelled road. He judged the old man to be about 300 metres away, from the length and speed of his stride, so the folklorist ought to be able to catch him up in five minutes or less.

He broke into a jog, but soon realized that the gap between him and the old man wasn't decreasing in the slightest. It remained at about 300 metres and this bewildered him. He kept running, but his forehead became beaded with sweat and his legs felt limp. Assailed by doubts and suspicions, he was staggered along like a worn-out old mare. Then, faintly, he heard a call resounding down the road, from somewhere out of sight, indistinct and echoing:

'Wulin . . . Wulin . . . Wulin . . .'

The folklorist stood in the middle of the road and looked around in every direction, but except for the old man's flame ahead of him, there was nothing to be seen. The village behind him seemed deserted. On the brink of desperation, the folklorist turned on his heel and sent a loud cry echoing up to the skies: 'Wulin!' He listened to his cry reverberate across the desolate fields and at virtually the same time, a powerful current of air pressed in on him from behind, closely followed by a blunt object. It sent him flying a little distance before he sprawled to the ground.

The lorry driver was a young man. He recalled sounding his horn from a long distance away, but the pedestrian stood blankly in the road without making the slightest movement. The driver had taken him for a hitchhiker, but he didn't want to give him a lift. He had driven on believing that, like other hitchhikers, this one would move out of harm's way in the end. But there was something wrong with this man: even when the front of the lorry hit him and he was sent soaring, he'd looked astounded, like an unwieldy bird frightened into flight. The terrified driver shifted into a higher gear instead of stopping and fled the scene of the accident as quickly as he could. But when he had driven all the way to the noisy, flourishing city, his own feelings of guilt began to oppress him. After parking his lorry in front of the county public security bureau, he jumped out and entered the building.

The officers sent to examine the scene of the accident walked along the road, the young driver at their head. They all moved with their heads down, looking for traces of blood. Dusk was falling on the road and its gravelled surface was flooded with clean, white light. Neither blood nor body was evident.

The driver told the policemen, 'This is really odd. I'm sure I hit him around here. I don't understand why we can't find anything.'

Someone suggested, 'Maybe the villagers carried him back? We should have a look there.'

They turned onto a narrow unsurfaced road and walked towards Eight Pines. As they reached the edge of the village, the driver cried out suddenly, 'His rucksack! That's his rucksack over there!'

They saw a dark brown bag lying by a large urn. As they ran towards it, they began to make out the two legs protruding from the urn, while the rest of the body was curled up inside.

The dead man's eyes were open. From his clothing and appearance it was easy to identify him as an academic. His face was pale and cold as ice, and frozen on his brow was an expression of astonishment.

'In the urn?' murmured the driver. 'How did he get into the urn?'

The police officers, all experienced men, opened the dead man's rucksack. Besides his clothing, towel, tooth-brush, toothpaste and Thermos, they found a notebook with a plastic cover, the pages of which were covered in dense writing. The most notable circumstance was that a piece of foil fell out from between its pages. Though it was torn and damaged, a drawing of a ghoul could be discerned on the paper backing, along with the word 'ghost' written in large red letters beneath.

'"Ghost!"' said the driver. 'He was a ghost!'

I knew the folklorist in question. His death was certainly shrouded in mystery. But at his memorial service, I heard another folklorist murmur to himself, 'It's how the ceremony ends, that's all.'

The Private Banquet

The last long-distance bus reached the town of Maqiao at dusk, and it was at that point that the passengers' fears were realized: the bus broke down. Fortunately, it broke down at Memorial Arch, only fifty or sixty metres from its destination, and the driver decided to park the bus where it had failed. It turned out, however, that there was also a problem with the switch that opened the bus doors. The driver began by patiently, cool-headedly, pressing one button after another, but his movements became gradually more erratic, until he hit out at the controls with abandon. The bus passengers began to get up and look towards the driver's seat and those at the back asked those further up front, 'Why doesn't he want to open the doors?' And those up front answered, 'It's not that he doesn't want to. It's because the doors won't open.'

Inside the bus, a variety of sounds emanated and subsided: agitated murmuring, indignant calling. Somebody shrewd suggested loudly, 'We should report a bus like this, and make the company give us half our money back!' Other passengers excitedly echoed this sentiment, but then a more resigned voice spoke up mildly, 'This is Maqiao, not Beijing or Guangzhou, you know. If you report something like this, they'll think you're mental.'

Then someone in the know about certain particulars of the long-distance bus company's ownership said, 'If you want to report it, then you should go straight to Fatcat: that's Huang Jian. Didn't you know that he's the contractor on this line?'

Amidst the general uproar, the bus doors began to clatter. They carried on clattering for quite a while, then suddenly they threw themselves half open. Somebody nearly tumbled down, but it was a young man with good reflexes and he managed to catch the railing, though his luggage got jammed in the crack. The young man had a quick temper and he began to swear. 'Motherf***er! Why the hell did you only open the door halfway? My bag's stuck now; hurry up and open it!' But the driver was in a foul mood himself and retorted, 'Grandmotherf***er! You think it was easy to get the door open this far? This old dinosaur should have been sold for scrap ages ago. It's no use swearing at me. If you're such a bigshot, why don't you give Fatcat's old mum a screw?' The passengers were all anxious to get off the bus, and those at the back didn't have time to join in the recriminations or bother to help the young man out. They lifted their legs one by one to step over the obstructive duffel bag, pushing violently at one another to squeeze through the narrow space offered by the half-open door.

The station's PA system operator had wandered off, so the loudspeakers didn't announce the arrival of the bus. Instead, the gay melody of *March Of The Athletes* poured out of it. The eagle-eyed members of the crowd waiting for the bus's arrival spotted the commotion and said to each other, 'I bet that's the bus, but how come it's stopped by Memorial Arch?' They became restless, and some of them strode quickly towards the bus.

'You're late!' they said, and those disembarking said, 'Well, yeah, and no wonder. The bus is no good, the roads are no good and they couldn't even get the door open! It would have been a miracle if we *weren't* late!'

It was already the evening of the Little New Year,[6] and everyone who was coming home for the holidays had done so already. Since Bao Qing refused to join in the rush for the exit, he was the last one off the bus. He carried his suitcase to the bus doors, and outside he glimpsed his primary school classmate Li Renzheng in wellingtons, gripping a long brush in his left hand and hauling a rubber hose with his right. Bao Qing quickly turned his face away and, swivelling his body sideways to fit through the door, stepped off the bus.

Bao Qing was a classic example of what people in Maqiao meant when they spat out the word 'intellectual'.

[6] A festival on the twenty-third of the final lunar month, a week before the New Year's Festival.

Intellectuals lacked warmth. Rather than exchanging conventional greetings, they often made the cowardly choice of pretending not to have seen you. This is precisely what Bao Qing did now. Like a thief, he crept around the bus and started walking west. Immediately, Renzheng's voice called after him, 'Bao Qing! Bao Qing! You're back?' Bao Qing couldn't very well continue to feign deafness and so, much against his will, he turned around to face Renzheng.

Uncharacteristically, Renzheng was sporting a red baseball cap, and above the brim was an eye-catching line of white letters: 'Singapore–Malaysia–Thailand. Eight-Day Tour'. Bao Qing chuckled, and asked, 'What are you wearing that cap for? I didn't even recognize you. Have you been travelling abroad?'

Renzheng stretched his hand up to touch his hat, and said, 'I should be so lucky. No, someone gave it to me. My hair is, well, I'll tell you later.'

Bao Qing did not try to leave, as he could tell from Renzheng's expression that there was something more he wanted to say. He had assumed it was going to be an explanation about his hair, but this turned out to be quite wrong. Instead, raising his voice, Renzheng suddenly said, 'Fatcat is inviting you to have a drink with him. He's told me many times to let him know if you came back, because he wants to treat you to a drink.'

Bao Qing, said, 'Who? Fatcat? You mean Huang Jian?' Renzheng was now spraying water from the hose onto

128

the glass of the bus's rear windows, and said, 'Of course, Fatcat. Don't you remember Fatcat?'

Bao Qing was speechless for a while, and in the end he murmured, 'How could I forget him? A drink, then. I suppose.'

So it was that Bao Qing returned from his distant Beijing home to celebrate the New Year. Going home was just as much trouble as not going home. For Bao Qing, the tradition of returning home for the New Year had become a ceremonial burden. A few years ago, when his mother had still been hale and hearty, she had come to the station to wait for him. It seemed a cruel ordeal to put her through, so he had withheld the exact date of his return from her. Even so, she had waited at the station for two days before Little New Year, a puny, emaciated form, standing in the wind underneath the archway. It made Bao Qing sick at heart to think about it, but he couldn't refuse to come home, and so his visits became pilgrimages of filial piety. Only the thought of his mother made him return to Maqiao; and since his wife was sure he had no ulterior motives, she had no objections. Thus every New Year, he and his wife set off in different directions. His mother, too, understood the situation, so she hadn't complained about the absence of her daughter-in-law in recent years. She spoke candidly on the phone: 'I won't live much longer. You have a few more years of filial responsibility before you, and after that you can go with your wife to spend New Year in

129

Guangdong. It's lively there at New Year, and the weather is warm. Just one sweater is warm enough.'

As he walked over the New People's Bridge, Bao Qing saw his brother-in-law coming towards him from the direction of the meat-processing factory, pushing his bike. He was running and Bao Qing's elder sister trailed behind him. Evidently, they were late and were now hurrying to make up for it. He could see that his sister was telling her husband off. She was still wearing her white uniform. Bao Qing disliked it when his family made a big fuss over him, so he knitted his eyebrows and stood motionless on the bridge. Just then, a woman in a purple leather overcoat was leading her dog up onto the bridge. At first, Bao Qing didn't notice her, but then the short, curly-haired dog began sniffing at his shoes and the bottoms of his trousers. Simultaneously, he picked up the same perfume which in summer suffused Beijing's big department stores, and when he turned his head, Bao Qing found himself looking at Cheng Shaohong. She had assumed a flirtatious pose and gave him a sidelong look. Though he recognized her straight away, he couldn't recall her name. The boys in town had all known her as Morning Glory. Shaohong took the initiative and pulled the dog towards her and then up onto its hind legs, commanding the curly-haired pooch, 'Jubilee, bow to the professor.'

Even after all these many years, Bao Qing was flustered to see Shaohong. As a matter of habit, he extended his hand, but seeing that she was not going to take it, he took it back and stared at a button on her overcoat. He said, 'It's been many years since we last saw one another. Are you still at the fruit company?'

Shaohong responded, 'As if there would still be a fruit company! That broke up a long time ago. I work in a private enterprise now. I have to live how I can; I'm not a clever clogs like you going around doing important things.'

Bao Qing responded, 'Oh, I don't do anything that important, either.'

Shaohong punched Bao Qing on the arm, and said, 'No need to be modest. In a small place like Maqiao everybody knows who's a lightweight and who's got clout. Fatcat says he saw you on TV.'

Bao Qing waved this off and said, 'That's not being "on TV". I was just reading a paper at a conference and somebody took a shot of it.'

Shaohong responded, 'And yet you're modest about it. Not too shabby: still as modest now as when you were a kid.' Some memory had occurred to Shaohong as she spoke, and now, covering her mouth, she made a tittering noise. Bao Qing was embarrassed, for he inferred that she was laughing about his past, although he couldn't know which particular incident she was remembering. He turned away and watched as his sister and her husband walked up the bridge, apology written all over their faces. Bao Qing said, 'I have to go now, my family's here to fetch me.'

He felt Shaohong give him another light slap, this time on the back. Then he heard her say, 'Fatcat says he wants to invite you for a drink, but you've been all hoity-toity with us lately. The last two times he let you decline, but there's no running away this time.'

It rained on the second day of the new year. An unbroken cloud cover hung over the town, and the roads, where underground optical cables were being installed, became an expanse of mud. Underneath his umbrella, Bao Qing rushed between his relatives' houses, bearing gifts and New Year greetings. At his uncle's he heard once again that Fatcat wished to invite him for a drink, and his uncle even encouraged him: 'If Fatcat asks you to dinner, see if he won't give your cousin a job at the eiderdown plant or as a ticket-taker on the long-distance buses. You have a lot of prestige, maybe he'll do you a favour.'

The subject annoyed Bao Qing as soon as it was brought up, but he couldn't very well lose his temper. Instead, he told his uncle, 'I don't have time to eat with him; I've even declined the mayor's dinner, and I'm leaving tomorrow. Besides, I still have to go to the banquet the Education Committee Director Liu's giving.'

By the time Bao Qing left his uncle's home, the rain had become very heavy, so he took a short cut through the little alleys. As he passed Maqiao's second Primary School, which he had attended long ago, he automatically glanced through the school gates. What he saw, however, was not the familiar sight of the school, but rather Fatcat's eiderdown plant. Four red lanterns hung from the factory gates, making up the words, 'Happy New Year Wishes!' On both sides, the walls of the factory grounds were pasted with the conspicuous slogan 'Demand Quality From Management, Reap Profit From Quality'. Bao Qing stood beneath his umbrella and listened to the sound of the raindrops as they struck the red-brick building's gutters and the plastic awning over the propaganda board. The sound was so desolate that Bao Qing shuddered, and then he felt a strange sensation of resentment. 'So he bought the school and made it into a factory. That's new money for you! New money!'

Fatcat's invitation hung like a shadow over Bao Qing as he paid his various family visits. Using the weather as an excuse, he had resolved to decline Fatcat's invitation to dine at Prosperity Restaurant. His mother did not encourage him to go, for she could still remember the humiliating price her son had once paid for the privilege of Fatcat's friendship. As Bao Qing was making excuses on the telephone, he heard his mother denouncing Fatcat: 'Now he treats you like a human being, but back then he treated you like you were his servant; actually worse than any master would ever treat a servant. He used to ride on your shoulders and shit.' Bao Qing did not want to hear his mother prattle on about the matter, so he motioned for her not to hover by the phone while he spoke. She moved a few paces away and sat down, remarking, 'He's rich. So what? There'll be great food. So what? Leave it for the folks who like that sort of thing.' His mother's attitude reminded Bao Qing that he could safely shift all blame onto his mother. Into the receiver, he said, 'Of course I don't wish to offend, but I'm off to Beijing tomorrow and my mother says she simply won't let me eat my last meal anywhere but home.'

Bao Qing presumed that, with this, he had successfully declined the invitation, but that evening, just as the whole family was sitting down to dinner, they heard the sharp squeal of motorcycle brakes outside, followed by the sound of knocking on the door. Bao Qing's sister went to open it and came back to inform him that it was Renzheng. She reported furthermore that he refused to come in and was insisting that Bao Qing go out to speak to him. As soon as Bao Qing went outside, he saw Renzheng standing stiff and perfectly upright in the rain. He had removed his helmet and Bao Qing saw that he was now half bald. There were only a few tufts of hair closely pressed to his brow, dripping from the rain. He stood there in the rain with a mixed expression of terror and disquiet, seasoned with a pinch of mystery. 'Well, Mr Professor, don't you think your high horse is a little too high? Your old classmate is just asking you to have a drink with him, not to pass through fire and brimstone. So how come it's so hard to get you to agree?'

Renzheng had been sent to pick Bao Qing up for Fatcat. Apparently, he had no delusions as to Bao Qing's feelings about the matter, and so had prepared some ploys to make him to submit. 'Bao Qing, if you don't give in, I'll just stand here and wait.' Renzheng lifted his head and looked at the sky. 'I don't mind if I get wet. In any case, I've never heard of someone being rained to death.'

Bao Qing's mother was the first to falter; pitying Renzheng, she sent Bao Qing's sister out with an umbrella, saying, 'When a man is that devoted, you'd be wrong not to go. People will talk. They'll say my Bao Qing goes round with his nose in the air now that he's made good – it'll make a terrible impression when it gets round.' Then, just as he was on the point of leaving, his mother picked up a piece of smoked fish with her chopsticks and stuck it in Bao Qing's mouth. So it was that he left the house chewing fish.

Bao Qing held the umbrella with one hand and hugged Renzheng's waist with the other as they passed through the streets of Maqiao in the freezing wind and bitter cold. It was the holidays, but night in this small town exuded an unseasonal gloom. Bao Qing could feel the little patch of warmth that was Renzheng's waist: even through the poor-quality, rain-soaked leather he wore, Bao Qing could feel his body heat. The situation seemed both strange and familiar. Suddenly, the memory of a New Year's night many years ago came back to him with great clarity: he, Fatcat and Renzheng had ridden two bicycles into the county capital to see the concert of some famous singer. On the way back, Renzheng's bicycle tire had burst. Fatcat had then compelled him to change bikes with Renzheng, and they had left him behind like un-loaded cargo. Bao Qing remembered that he had pushed the useless bike 15 kilometres alone.

Bao Qing had not realized that Shaohong would also be among Fatcat's guests, but there she was, gorgeously decked out and the first thing he saw as they entered Prosperity Restaurant. She stood fixing her make-up in a mirror on the second floor, in the hallway leading to the private dining rooms. There was an excessive grav-ity about the way she made herself up, as if she were a folk singer preparing for the stage. Seeing Bao Qing, she tossed her lipstick hurriedly into her bag, and said loudly and sharply, 'What, so you agreed to come? Even without a cortege of eighteen sedan chairs?'

Bao Qing could say nothing and instead forced a smile. Then he complimented Shaohong: 'You look very nice tonight.'

She responded, 'Like hell I do. I know what you're thinking: you think I'm made up like an escort girl, don't you? Well, that's exactly what Fatcat intended: I'm to keep you company through dinner, drinks and then right on through the night. He told me it's an honour for me to bask in the companionship of the great professor!'

The hostess, dressed in a red cheongsam and wearing a golden 'Welcome' sash over her shoulder, greeted them and led them to a private dining room called the Paris

Hall. Bao Qing entered and then watched as an obese man in a suit rose slowly from his chair. This, apparently, was Fatcat, although it didn't look like him. Only when Bao Qing noted the wine-coloured birthmark on his forehead was he certain it was him. At first, Fatcat made to embrace Bao Qing, but since the latter shrunk away reflexively, the movement became a handshake. Fatcat's lukewarm hands held Bao Qing's in a tight grip and wouldn't relax their hold.

'Bao Qing, just feel my heart, feel how strongly it's beating,' he said, tugging Bao Qing's hand and pressing it onto his suit over his chest. 'Bao Qing,' he said. 'I was less nervous about meeting the provincial governor, and that's the truth.'

Bao Qing laughed, and extricated his hand. Then he remarked, 'If I had run into you on the street, I certainly wouldn't have recognized you.'

Fatcat answered, 'You might not have recognized me, but I sure would have recognized you. You just flashed on TV for a second and I knew it was you.'

A mixed group of guests was present and they immediately chimed in, 'That's right. When the boss saw you on television, he recognized you straight away.'

Fatcat pulled Bao Qing down to sit by his side. Except for Renzheng and Shaohong, the others at the table were all his employees. There was a bespectacled girl in a pink sweater who kept looking at Bao Qing evasively but glowingly. Bao Qing was too embarrassed to ask her

137

name, but Fatcat had the foresight to introduce her. She was the daughter of Mr Zhong, a teacher at Maqiao Middle School, and she was now employed as an accountant at Fatcat's factory. 'And how is . . . ?'

Bao Qing hadn't finished his sentence, because he gathered what had come to pass from the general change of expression as Ms Zhong bowed her head. Fatcat kicked him under the table, and said softly, 'He passed away two years ago. Cancer.'

Bao Qing was silent, remembering how Mr Zhong, the physics teacher, had been the only one of his teachers to take to him, on account of his aptitude for the subject. Bao Qing was at a loss what to say when Ms Zhong stood and raised her glass to him. 'Mr Bao, when I was a child my father often told me how he had trained a future professor. Now that I'm finally getting to meet you, I want to offer you this toast.'

That was how Bao Qing happened to drink the first cup of wine. On the way over, Bao Qing had prepared his excuses: he had a bad stomach, he was allergic to alcohol, he would be travelling tomorrow – anything so that he might be allowed to abstain from the drinking. But Ms Zhong's peculiar identity, not to mention her peculiar glances, robbed him of the courage to decline, and now that he had made a start it was difficult to retract. He was able to fend off Fatcat's employees, but Renzheng's obstreperous exhortations were harder to decline. Shaohong's toasts were coercive to a degree, and also contained a barrage of tactless sexual innuendoes, which deeply embarrassed Bao Qing, who didn't know how to forestall them. Presently, she suggested they all drink with interlocked arms and her audacity shocked him. His face flushed scarlet and he said, 'We can't lock arms for no reason.' Shaohong replied, 'Of course there's a reason. It's a forfeit to punish me for having no judgement back then – I underestimated you, I didn't realize your potential. Now I regret it, because I could have been Mrs Bao, the professor's wife, couldn't I?'

Bao Qing didn't know how to respond, so he joined in her laughter. But then he leaned back on his chair and refused her encircling arm. At this point, the others started jeering, which embarrassed her and cooled her ardour. Suddenly she could take it no longer, and she spilled the cup out on the floor, saying, 'Well, it's not gonna kill me if you won't drink with me now you're a bigshot, but I'd like to know who stole my bra once upon a time. Hm?'

Suddenly the room became quiet. Bao Qing had not expected her to play this card and he began to get angry. 'Are you insane? I can't believe you would even think to bring up childhood pranks now!' He raised his voice, 'Fatcat stole your bra and hid it in my bag. Fatcat's here, right beside me, and he can testify to my innocence.'

Beside him, Fatcat chuckled and gave Bao Qing a shove. 'Holy-moley, Bao Qing. There's no need to take things so seriously. It was a joke. Who can remember the

139

things they did when they were kids? I don't remember anything about a stolen bra.'

But Bao Qing did not use this opportunity to back down, 'Perhaps you've forgotten, but I haven't,' he said sternly. 'You hid it in my bag when her mother came after you. If you don't admit it now, then it is I who must live with the blot on my reputation.'

Fatcat looked momentarily uncomfortable, but soon regained his good humour. Laughing, he said, 'All right then. I remember now. I stuffed it in your bag; we used to let you take the flak. I admit it, OK?'

Bao Qing saw Fatcat make a signal to Renzheng with his eyes and he recalled how many years ago they had also communicated with these signals. Each time he had seen them, he felt a nameless fear grip him. Now he no longer feared the exchange, it just disquieted him. He set his glass down, bottom up, on the table and said, 'I've finished with drinking. I've never been able to drink very much and now I've had more than enough.'

As he set down his glass, Bao Qing could feel everyone staring at him, their eyes variously revealing displeasure or nervousness. Deliberately ignoring them, he informed Ms Zhong, 'I have ulcers and hyperglaecemia.'

Ms Zhong nodded and said, 'Drinking is bad for your health – all the magazines say so.' Besides passing on this nugget of magazine wisdom, it seemed that the girl wanted to say more, but didn't dare. She held back for a moment, but then she could curb herself no longer and rashly came out with the following question, 'Mr Bao, I've always wondered about something. You were a good student in those days, so why would you have been friends with Manager Huang and Mr Li?' The question stunned Bao Qing, and his chopsticks froze over a vegetable platter. Fatcat's employees half-seriously criticized Ms Zhong for having said something untoward, but in the end it was Fatcat who, in a generous and self-deprecating tone, said, 'So you're saying I was a bad student? Well, maybe I was – I can't pull the wool over her eyes. It's not my fault she's so smart; she's Mr Zhong's daughter, after all!'

But the girl had hit on a sore point with Bao Qing. She had posed the same reproachful question that his mother and sister had been in the habit of asking, and that he had never been able to answer. The truth was he did not have the courage to analyse his motivations for sticking with Fatcat and Renzheng. He had no way of facing up to his disgraceful choice, nor enough wit to evade the question. His cheeks suddenly blushed a full, deep red, and all he could produce were a few paltry lines: 'I don't know either. You know how children are. No reason, really, to speak of.'

Shaohong, who had been sulking, suddenly let off a burst of cold laughter. She said, 'I know why. It's like this: have you ever heard the story about the chick who ingratiates himself with the weasel? And why does he do it? He wants the weasel to eat the other little chickies and spare his own life.' Ms Zhong must have thought that

Shaohong had uttered a bon mot, because she clucked with laughter. Then, when she saw no one else was laughing, she realized her error and covered her mouth.

Fatcat looked at Bao Qing's expression and turned to glare at Shaohong. He was agitated and angry. 'Motherf***! You always complain that other people don't know how to talk properly, but look at the kind of s*** that comes out of your mouth!' What surprised Bao Qing was that Fatcat's exceptionally crude way of reprimanding Shaohong provoked no reaction from her whatsoever. Fatcat's language was both foul and rough: 'You festering c***! You think you're the only one around smart enough to open your mouth. Would it kill you to shut up sometimes?'

Shaohong said, 'Fine, then I won't say anything. Naturally, I'm unworthy to speak to the professor and anything I say is crap.'

Fatcat said, 'Of course it's crap. You're here so that everyone can have some fun. And look what happens, just because you can't talk like a normal person and keep talking crap.'

Shaohong rose slightly. 'Fine, then I won't say anything else. I've made everybody unhappy; I'm off.'

Fatcat gave an angry shout, and said, 'You think it's that easy, huh? Off? You can go to hell, but you can f***ing bet you're not leaving this room. Renzheng! Pour her more wine! The big cup! She has to drink a forfeit – three big cups!'

Bao Qing would never in his wildest dreams have thought that Fatcat could treat Shaohong in this way. His common sense told him that their relationship was in all likelihood no ordinary one. His relatives had kept him posted about the extraordinarily self-indulgent private life Fatcat had begun to lead following his sudden rise to wealth, but Bao Qing had never imagined Shaohong could act so submissively towards him. He was also taken aback by Renzheng's attitude – he had presumed that he would try to calm Fatcat, but he said nothing, just picked up the rice wine bottle to bring it over to Shaohong. Bao Qing rose and almost instinctively rushed at Renzheng to wrest the bottle from him. Renzheng smiled evasively and said, 'Don't worry about it. You don't know how much she can drink.'

Bao Qing replied, 'She's a lady. There can be no question of forcing her to drink.' They were grappling with one another when Shaohong suddenly grabbed the bottle herself and banged it down heavily on the table. She said, 'If we're going to drink, then let's get on with it, and if I die from it, then that's not a problem. People's value depreciates, like everything else. If I go and sell myself for a f*** I wouldn't even get enough money for the alcohol. So if the drink doesn't kill me, I'll be making a profit!'

At this point, a waiter opened the door to the room and, taking fright, poked his head in to have a look. Fatcat screamed at the door, 'Screw off! If you come in again I'll have your boss sauté you!' In case this threat alone was unconvincing, Fatcat grabbed a porcelain spoon and threw it at the waiter, making everyone near by jump. They heard a bang as the spoon shattered against the wall like a miniature bomb and covered the floor with its shards.

Dead silence prevailed in the room and three words popped into Bao Qing's mind: The Hongmen Banquet[7]. On the one hand he realized that he was being over-anxious, but he was also sensitive enough to be certain that the atmosphere of the banquet was growing increasingly destructive. Unable to stay seated, he told Fatcat, 'Since I have to leave tomorrow, I'll need to be getting home a little early.'

But Fatcat shook his head and said, 'You can't go.' Bao Qing felt one of Fatcat's hands restrain his arm like a handcuff. 'We're not finished drinking. No one can go until we've finished drinking.'

Bao Qing said, 'I *am* finished drinking. I can't take any more.'

Fatcat said, 'It's up to you if you drink or not, but Shaohong offended you, so she has to drink the forfeit. And as I haven't shown you a good time, I have to drink a forfeit, too. Renzheng and Ms Zhong were invited to

[7]The Hongmen banquet was an incident during the Chu-Han contention (206–202 BC), a civil war which followed the end of the Qin Dynasty. The warrior Xiang Yu tried to eliminate his rival Liu Bang during a feast held in his honour. In modern Chinese, it suggests a trap during festivities.

make pleasant company, and for failing to do a good job of it, they have to drink forfeits too!' Then Bao Qing heard Fatcat roar to those outside, 'Where the hell have you gone? Hurry up and bring more drinks! And don't bring them by the bottle – bring a crate in!'

Bao Qing felt like he was sitting on a bed of needles and deeply regretting giving in to his pity for Renzheng and foolishly getting on the motorcycle. When a waiter arrived carrying the crate of liquor, Bao Qing felt a twinge of dread. He asked Fatcat, 'What's that for? One bottle will be quite enough, make them take the crate back.'

But Fatcat patted Bao Qing on the shoulder, 'We won't necessarily drink the whole crate, but it's my habit to do this for my guests. Don't get flustered; you're an intellectual, so my policy allows an exemption. If you've had enough, then fine – don't drink if you don't want to.'

Bao Qing said forthrightly, 'I *have* had enough to drink. I'm setting off tomorrow. I'll have to change buses and connect to a train, so I need to go home early tonight and get some rest.'

Fatcat said, 'What's that supposed to mean? Are you worried you won't get back to Beijing? If you miss your bus because you've been drinking with me, I'll have them take you there direct, in an Audi.'

Bao Qing smiled but shook his head, gritted his teeth, stood up and said, 'I'm afraid I can't stay. I'll have to bid you farewell.' He watched as Fatcat's expression turned sombre. This time, Fatcat didn't try to stop him, but the others at the table looked at Bao Qing with expressions that were almost fearful.

Renzheng looked at Fatcat, then suddenly took a big stride towards the door to block it. He spoke quietly, 'Bao Qing, don't make us lose face. You can't go now.' Bao Qing saw that Renzheng's expression was one of desperate entreaty, and at such close quarters he noticed the crow's feet at the corners of his bloodshot eyes; his half-bald pate, too, seemed to tell a tale full of misery. The two men confronted each other at the doorway.

Shaohong staggered over to them, hooked her arms around Bao Qing's neck and pulled him towards the chair. She said, 'I have to say, the great professor is really fastidious. I said the wrong thing. OK, so I had to drink three big cups to make up for it, and you're still not satisfied. Maybe you want me to do a striptease?'

Before Bao Qing could refuse, Fatcat chuckled and clapped his hands, 'Good idea! Her forfeit will be a striptease.'

The liquor had obviously made Shaohong speak lightly, but now that she was expected to perform, she sobered up and became mulish. 'You know Ms Zhong is still an unsullied maiden. How could I possibly dance in front of her?'

'Don't make excuses. We'll have Ms Zhong go outside for a moment,' Fatcat said. Ms Zhong turned bright red, stood up and made to leave, but Shaohong held her back, 'You're really going to pretend an old woman like me is

146

an innocent girl? Pah! You think I'll let you see a free strip? What about money? Where's the money?'

Fatcat turned in his chair, grabbed a briefcase from a small table and said, 'The money's right here. What's your price for tickets plus tip?'

Bao Qing saw the joke was reaching the point of no return, so he took Fatcat by the hand and said, 'That's enough nonsense. It's all my fault; I've made everybody unhappy. Why don't I drink a forfeit, too?'

Bao Qing sensed that he needed to make a sacrifice, so he took a drink. As soon as he did, the atmosphere at the table warmed up substantially. Bao Qing had intended to go as soon as the atmosphere returned to normal, but Fatcat made his driver fetch a damask box, declaring that he wanted to show Bao Qing something. He opened the box and Bao Qing saw a coloured porcelain vase lying inside. Fatcat said, 'You're the expert. Make an estimate. How much is this vase worth?'

Bao Qing said, 'I'm in geology, not art appraisal,' but Fatcat responded, 'Don't be so modest. In any case, you know more about it than any of us.'

Renzheng came over and carefully removed the vase for Bao Qing to have a look at. Bao Qing glimpsed an inscription in the floral design which said Tang Yin,[8] but his expression was suspicious. 'This was painted by Tang Bohu?'

[8]Tang Yin (1470–1523), also known as Tang Bohu, a leading Ming Dynasty painter.

A little nervously, Fatcat answered his question with another, 'Why, aren't Tang Bohu vases valuable?'

Bao Qing said, 'That's not what I meant. I think there might be a problem with the vase.' Bao Qing took the vase and looked it carefully up and down; finally he could not suppress his laughter. 'You've been cheated. I'm not an art expert, but they've written Jiaqing reign[9] on this vase. By that time, Tang Bohu had been dust for years; so how come he was still painting vases?'

Fatcat blanched, 'Take another look, carefully.'

Bao Qing, 'No need. You've definitely bought a fake. It might even be that the vase itself is counterfeit as well as the attribution. How much did you pay for it?' Bao Qing didn't hear what Fatcat said in response. He raised his head and saw that everyone was staring at him with wide-open eyes, as if they were waiting for him to retract his comments. Fatcat's expression was exceedingly strange: part of it was embarrassment, but a greater portion was rage.

He gave an oblique, squinting look at Renzheng, whose face had already paled, 'I'll go to Shanghai tomorrow and find Sanzi. He's the one who vouched for it – he guaranteed it was real.'

Fatcat snorted and said, 'How much was your kickback?'

Renzheng, panicking, shouted, 'If I got one single

[9]A Qing Dynasty reign name, lasting from 1796 to 1820, more than 250 years after Tang Yin's life.

penny, may lightning strike me dead; may the first passing car run me down.'

Fatcat sat down, staring sternly at Renzheng, who had dropped his head while looking up with an expression of pure innocence. Fatcat dropped the matter for the moment and rocked back on his chair, looking around the gathering, 'Oh, stop all looking like your daddy just died. I'm the one who's lost money – what the hell is it to you?' He waved his hands dismissively and said, 'Never mind. It's only two hundred thousand yuan. I've been in business for long enough; it's not like it's the first time I've been cheated. I get cheated out of two hundred thousand, fine; but I'll earn back two million.'

Everyone sat in silence; only the dishes on the table still sent off their warm fragrances. Bao Qing realized that he was at the root of all the unpleasantness and it filled him with regret. Bao Qing stood up and offered Renzheng a toast. He had been wearing a frozen, funereal expression, but now he bounded up as if there had been some pleasant surprise.

'I'll drink a forfeit! A forfeit!' Bao Qing felt that, indirectly, he had also harmed Shaohong, and so he offered her a toast as well.

Shaohong, said 'Now this's more like it. You're not even red in the face; you can keep drinking.' Bao Qing noticed that Ms Zhong's gaze seemed to linger on him. It wouldn't be right to ignore Ms Zhong, so he offered her a toast, once again with reference to her father, his teacher, saying that he had always remembered his kindness, but that when he went home it was always so busy with his family that he had never got around to visiting him.

Ms Zhong said nothing, so Shaohong put in her tuppence worth, 'You can still go and see him now. Go and check out his grave.' He knew Shaohong was taunting him, but still he explained earnestly to Ms Zhong, 'I won't have time this visit. I'll go next time.'

Bao Qing returned to his seat, labouring under a misconception that he had now done his best to carry out his obligations. He took up his soup spoon, intending to take a sip of chicken soup, but a liquor glass was suddenly extended to him from the side, bumping against his soup bowl.

It was Fatcat. 'Bao Qing, we haven't drunk yet. Why don't you have soup and I'll have wine? We'll have a little drink, OK?'

Bao Qing put his bowl down and picked up his wine-glass, saying, 'If I have any more I'll fall down.'

Fatcat said, 'And if you fall over I'll get a car to send you home. You're drinking in Maqiao and you still worry about getting home?'

The liquor was stronger than Bao Qing. In his forty years, it was the first time he had drunk so wildly and he began to throw up. He remembered Renzheng taking him to the bathroom where he threw up out of the bathroom window and saw that the rain outside had stopped. The night was bluish, and you could vaguely hear the sound of firecrackers coming from the town. Bao Qing remembered he was about to go home: 'I want to go home. My mum must be worried out of her mind.'

Renzheng said, 'You'll go when Fatcat lets you go. Have another drink with him and ask him to let you go.' He was half pushing and half carrying Bao Qing. Renzheng remembered an autumn day when they had pushed him in the river. He hadn't been able to climb the bank by himself, and in the end it was Renzheng who had felt sorry for him and hauled him out of the water and onto the bridge.

Suddenly, Bao Qing said to Renzheng, 'Renzheng, I know you're a good guy.' But this displeased Renzheng and he spat out curses fuelled by alcohol, 'What f***ing use is it being a good guy? If you don't have money, a good guy turns into a bad guy soon enough.'

When he returned from the bathroom, Bao Qing kept Renzheng's advice in mind: have one more drink with Fatcat and go. Taking the initiative, he proposed a toast, but Fatcat said, 'Farewell toasts have to be three cups.' Bao Qing vaguely knew that he was being toyed with, but he didn't know whether it was because Fatcat had had too much to drink or because he was annoyed with him. But clearly he was being toyed with. 'Never mind', he thought. 'I'm not afraid of you now. I don't depend on you for my livelihood. I'll put up with it for a while and then go.' But things did not turn out as he'd anticipated. His body was acting unreasonably and impatiently. It was soft and intractable. The gravity of the earth was exerting an extraordinary force on him, and Bao Qing suddenly slipped off his chair and fell to the floor. He sat by Fatcat's feet and drank the last cup of wine. What Bao Qing saw were Fatcat's black leather shoes and piercingly white cotton socks. The shoes had a little streak of mud on them that made Bao Qing feel uncomfortable. Sometimes, the so-called corridor of memory can be bridged in a single step. The past had stealthily crept up on him and now Bao Qing heard a crude, familiar voice. The voice carried violence and threats in its commands. 'Wipe the mud off! Wipe it off! Wipe it off!' It was Fatcat's voice when he was young: 'Faster! Wipe the mud off!' Bao Qing obediently took a napkin, just as he had been forced to do many years ago, spat lightly on the shoes and said, 'I'm wiping. I'm wiping.'

Bao Qing heard the ebb and flow of their laughter, but he had no time to look up, for he was too absorbed in the task of shining Fatcat's shoes. He saw that they had become glistening and new, and were now emitting a luxurious sheen. Then he heard a crisp bang and felt a slap on his face; Fatcat had struck him. The abruptness and unexpectedness of the blow ensured the slap was powerfully felt. Bao Qing had to put his hand out not to keel over. At the same time, he heard Fatcat snarl irritably, 'Why have you only shined the left shoe? What about the right shoe? Hurry up! Shine the right shoe!'

Professor Bao Qing returned to Beijing on the third

day of the new year. Everyone in Maqiao knew that his New Year's visits were brief and hurried. Once again, it was his sister and her husband who accompanied him to the station, and once again they encountered Renzheng there. Bao Qing turned his back to him and blatantly ignored him, but Renzheng ran over and squeezed a big paper bag into his hands saying, 'It's wine, a present from Fatcat. The Wuliangye brand.'

Bao Qing was determined to fight off Renzheng's hands and said, 'I don't drink. Take it back to him. He already made enough a fool of me last night.' Renzheng held the wine up, carefully selecting his words.

'He had a drop too much last night, but he asks you not to take it to heart. This is high-quality wine, a token of goodwill for you to take back to Beijing.'

Spitefully, Bao Qing responded, 'I don't drink. If I take it back to Beijing, I won't drink it. Why can't you guys get that through your thick skulls no matter how often I tell you?'

Renzheng winked and said, 'That's true. You intellectuals don't drink all that much.' He took a look at Bao's sister and smoothly slipped the wine into her hands. He said, 'Well then we'll just let your brother-in-law take it home. In any case, I can't take it back to Fatcat. He'd have my head.'

Frostily, ignoring Renzheng, Bao Qing took out his cell phone and phoned his wife from the station waiting room. Renzheng took the hint, but just as he was about to leave, Bao Qing's hand restrained him, pulling him all the way down the steps. 'Renzheng, you're a good guy. When I was making such a fool of myself yesterday, why did you just stand by and watch? Tell me the truth: did I shine Fatcat's shoes? Did he actually slap me?'

Renzheng's eyes were sparkling, but what he said was, 'No, no. Nothing like that.'

Bao Qing watched Renzheng's expression nervously, 'Don't play dumb with me. Why didn't you stop me when I was shining his shoes? He used the drink as an excuse to go crazy and you just watched as he slapped me!'

Renzheng waved his hand and said, 'Hey, nothing like that happened. You shined his shoes, you say? You think he slapped you? We're all grown-ups now – Fatcat would never have made you shine his shoes, let alone slap you. Besides, he would never dare to bully you any more.'

Bao Qing instinctively rubbed his cheek, thinking, Well, it doesn't hurt, but I wasn't in a very clear state of mind at the time. He looked at Renzheng suspiciously, 'It seems drunken people all make fools of themselves, and there isn't any stopping them. Or am I perhaps remembering things wrongly? Did you shine his shoes? Were you the one he hit?'

Bao Qing watched Renzheng lift up his head, and on his face was a remarkable expression; a mixture of wiliness and pride that was hard to describe. 'No, I didn't shine them, sure as I'm my mother's son. Ever since we were kids, I haven't shined his shoes for him, not even once.

And he's never slapped me, either.' Suddenly he laughed and poked Bao Qing in the stomach. 'Don't let it stick in your throat. You can't make a fuss over what people do when they get drunk. Forgive him this once. A great spirit forgives the trespasses of his inferiors.' Without knowing why, Bao Qing suddenly covered his face with his hands. Then he heard Renzheng sigh: 'You can never tell what changes time may bring. You've both made good. Out of all of our friends and classmates, you're the only one who can stand up to him. If he hadn't been drunk, he would never have dared to slap you.'

As they were speaking, the long-distance bus emerged from the depot. A crashing noise gave Bao Qing a fright, until he realized it was the sound of the doors opening automatically. The holiday was over and everyone glowed with health. Even the bus had celebrated the New Year, for it seemed that the doors had been fixed.

Goddess Peak

The steamship pier was far dirtier and more crowded than a village market; people loitered around, some squatting, some standing, some lying with their limbs splayed wherever space would allow, their mouths wide open, breathing in the filthy air and snoring indulgently. The piercing whistle of the steamboat didn't bother them; it was quite obvious they weren't passengers.

Miaoyue and Li Yong were almost the last two passengers aboard. Li Yong was pulling Miaoyue along firmly by one hand. With the other hand, she held up her long black skirt as she was dragged like a puppet towards the ticket-taker. She seemed to know what sort of a figure she cut, judging by the mortified expression frozen on her face. Reaching the ticket examiner she bumped into someone who looked like a farmer, and instead of apologizing to the man, her reaction was to shrug off Li Yong's hand. 'What's the bloody rush? The boat hasn't even left. There's no need to hurry.'

Li Yong turned back to cast a fleeting glance at his

girlfriend; he was carrying a travel bag slung over each arm and shoulder and Miaoyue's purse hung around his neck. Li Yong realized she was angry, but he remained calm. He stood on his tiptoes to look up to the deck of the steamboat and called out loudly, 'My bro! There's my bro!' He waved to a man on the deck, at the same time pulling Miaoyue towards him in an embrace. 'Do you see my bro? He's waving at us right now.'

Miaoyue could see a man wearing a collared blue-and-white striped shirt. A cigarette was dangling from his lips and he was leaning on the railing, one hand raised high in a salute. It was a quick, casual wave, much like that of a VIP. Miaoyue's automatic reaction was to look behind her, but of course there was no one there; in fact, she had realized immediately that he was waving at her, but she deliberately looked away. Actually, even without Li Yong pointing him out, she would have known that he was Mr Cui.

As they boarded the ship, she continued to look steadily in front of her; but then she said, 'Your bro? Hmph! Is *that* your bro?'

Miaoyue was quick to make remarks, often resulting in comments she didn't even know the meaning of herself. She was a girl who liked to take men down a peg. With regard to Mr Cui, the truth of the matter was that when she had seen him on the deck she had found him taller and better built than she'd imagined, and also a little younger and a little more handsome than she had expected.

The three of them had reserved a second-class cabin. The room was not particularly big, but quite clean. It was Miaoyue's first time on a boat and her face lit up with pleasure despite herself; her eyes strayed over the room, then she felt the bedclothes with her fingers, 'Pretty comfy, huh?' As soon as she spoke she regretted it, for she saw the look Cui cast towards her. It was only a brief glance, but it made her desperately want to take her words back.

Smiling, Cui said, 'Is it your first time on a boat?'

'Maybe. So what if it is?' Miaoyue said. 'Is it such a big deal to take a little steamboat? It's not like we're on an aircraft carrier or something.'

For a moment Cui was taken aback, then he looked at Li Yong and remarked, 'Pretty tough.'

'She talks tough,' Li Yong said, 'but she has a good heart.'

'Who says I have a good heart?' Miaoyue said. 'You don't even know me.'

Li Yong laughed awkwardly and changed the subject. 'Fuck, man. It's just the three of us, nobody else. This is gonna be nice. That was really smart, bro, to book the cabin.'

'Oh, he's got the money. When you've got it, flaunt it.' Miaoyue had retrieved a cosmetic case from her bag and was delicately retouching her make-up. Addressing herself to the little mirror, she said, 'Well, at least I know *I* wish there was someone else here; someone a little more fun, otherwise I'll probably die of boredom.'

When neither man had anything to say in reply, she felt she had finally worked off her anger. Still, she was free to consider them as clumsy conversationalists, and at this thought she smiled secretly. She sneaked a glance at the two men in the back of her mirror; they were smiling with similar expressions of tolerance. Li Yong approached her and spoke quietly into her ear, 'You could be a little politer to my bro. Have you forgotten how he got you your job?'

Miaoyue curled her lip, but swallowed what she'd meant to say. She was prepared to regard her revenge as complete, but she hadn't expected Li Yong to commit yet another blunder straightaway. He was taking three pairs of slippers from underneath the bed. He gave the first pair to Cui, the second to Miaoyue, and slipped the third pair on himself. Miaoyue looked with great displeasure at the order with which he had distributed the slippers, but it was Cui who began to speak. 'Now that wasn't right, Li Yong. You should have given the first pair to your girlfriend.' But before he'd finished his sentence, Miaoyue had already kicked the slippers away.

'Useless!' Miaoyue shrieked at Li Yong, 'Are you even a man at all? Just because he's got money, you're happy to be his slave?'

'What's that supposed to mean? He's my big bro.' Li Yong's face flushed scarlet, and he said awkwardly,

160

'They're just slippers. Does it matter who gets them first?'

Cui, sitting to one side, shook with belly laughter, a kind of laughter simultaneously merry and suspect. And while he was laughing he slapped Li Yong on the back, then leaned over and whispered something in his ear. Miaoyue glared at them; she wished she could make out what they were saying. She saw only that Cui had his eye on her, and that the look he gave her was a little peculiar. It seemed to be approbation, but then again somehow it was not. It struck her as a secretive kind of look.

Without knowing why, Miaoyue didn't dare to look Cui straight in the eye, so she turned her face away and gazed out of the window instead. Outside, the scene on the pier was beginning to move and the turbid river-water was slowly retreating: the boat had finally left the harbour. The trip had begun, and with that, little by little, Miaoyue's mood slowly improved. Place names flashed rapidly through her mind – Nanjing, Wuhan, Wanxian, Chongqing – the names of cities she knew they would pass along the way on this Three Gorges trip. Miaoyue's mood slowly improved as she imagined the beautiful, magnificent scenery of the Yangtze Three Gorges. It seemed to her that she could already dimly perceive a strangely shaped, precipitous mountain peak: the famed Goddess Peak. Miaoyue had found out about it from a Yangtze tourist map, and the shape of Goddess Peak really did resemble a woman holding vigil over

161

the river, though Miaoyue couldn't be sure why it was Goddess Peak alone that had inflamed her boundless imagination.

She found the crumpled tourist map in the small bag and let her fingers move along the scenic spots of the river, then suddenly her finger paused on the red dot that indicated Goddess Peak: 'Goddess Peak,' Miaoyue smiled and sighed. 'This boat is so slow. When are we going to get to Goddess Peak?'

Li Yong had already taken off his shirt, and had picked up a towel to rub under his armpits. 'What's your hurry?' Li Yong said, 'The boat has only just left. Whatchamacallit Peak's on the Three Gorges and the Three Gorges come after Wuhan, so you can see it once we're in the Three Gorges.'

'Thanks for the newsflash.' Miaoyue shot him a contemptuous glance and realized that her question had been directed at Cui, but for whatever reason, as soon as her glance met Cui's she felt discomfited and looked away. Miaoyue stared down again at the map and said, as if she were talking to herself, 'Goddess Peak will probably be on the third day. Or maybe on the fourth?'

'I don't know what day it's on, either,' Cui, who was sitting on the other berth, put away his newspaper, 'All I know is that we get to Wuhan on the second day, and that's where I get off.'

'What's so great about Wuhan?' Miaoyue asked, still bent over the map, 'My aunt lives in Wuhan, and my mum's been there. She said it's boiling in summer, freezing in winter, and boring all year round.'

'I realize the Three Gorges are stunning and Wuhan is Dullsville, but I don't have time to keep going upriver with you – it's just a question of time. If I were as free as you guys, then it'd be fine, but the businessman's life is hectic, and I can't afford to keep you company all the way up.'

'Bro has to get off at Wuhan,' Li Yong sat down next to Miaoyue, 'I told you, remember? Bro has a lot of business in Wuhan.'

'I'm sorry, was anybody talking to you?' Miaoyue pushed Li Yong away with her elbow and frowned. 'You know, I really don't think I've ever met anyone quite so annoying. When you open your trap all you do is jabber. Aren't you worried you might exhaust the human word supply?'

It seemed Li Yong would never lose his temper with his girlfriend, for he switched from her side to Cui's with a wink and said, 'What do you think? Tough cookie, eh?'

Cui just gave his belly laugh, 'Don't be angry, little bro,' he said, slapping Li Yong several times on the back, 'a man is lucky when he has a girlfriend with a sense of humour. If you can't take a woman's fury, then you aren't a real man!'

Miaoyue sniggered, or to be more precise, a knowing snigger was emitted somewhere between Cui and Miaoyue. This subtle event had come about very suddenly. Miaoyue's heart gave a little thump and she suddenly turned her face, having felt a faint pang of discomfort. She didn't even know how this had happened – suddenly it seemed like she and Cui had reached a secret understanding, an alliance to tease or bully Li Yong.

The boat growled slightly as it moved over the water. Looking out the window they could see the sky growing dark, and the rural scenes along the riverside became shrouded in the thin mist of evening; a monotonous, hazy aspect. Miaoyue wanted to open the window, but it was nailed shut. Li Yong walked over to her and tried with all his strength to pull the window up. This time Miaoyue didn't censure him, she simply pointed at the nails and informed him with a look at the ceiling what an idiot he was. Then she popped a preserved plum in her mouth and picked up a fashion magazine.

Even before night had fallen the two men began to drink. Miaoyue couldn't understand the pleasure of drinking, but they plunged into it with gusto, especially Li Yong. With his fair skin and delicate features, the flush of drink quickly began to show, and at the same time his speech became more animated and coarse. He talked the whole time about a colleague who had embezzled five million bucks of public money before absconding abroad. 'Bro, you wouldn't believe it. Monkeyman really had the balls to do it.' Li Yong said. 'Fuck, man. I thought I knew the guy, but I didn't know what was going on in his head. Monkeyman was totally yellow, but then he really had the balls to do it. Fuck, man, people today are crazy for money.'

'You've said that a hundred times,' Miaoyue said in disgust. 'It looks to me like you'll be crazy for money soon, too.'

But Cui was very patient with Li Yong's talk and remarked, 'If we were all crazy, it'd be fine. If we were crazy then we wouldn't want any money.'

Miaoyue sniggered a little, or to be more exact it was again the snigger of understanding between her Cui. She was a little embarrassed and turned away, looking at the small bottle in Li Yong's hand. Of the two roasted chickens that had been on the table there was now only half a chicken left. Li Yong was still trying to tear off a wing and Miaoyue was poking at him with her magazine.

Li Yong turned to her, 'What's the matter? It's not as if the news about Monkeyman is a national secret. It's been all over the papers; why shouldn't I talk about it?'

'I don't care about your stupid Monkeyman or Elephantman or whatever,' Miaoyue said. 'I was trying to tell you not to be such a glutton. You didn't buy the chicken, but you've eaten it all up.'

'Hey, what are you talking about?' Li Yong said, 'Me and bro, we don't split hairs. Me eating it is the same thing as him eating it. Isn't that right, bro?'

That secretive smile once again appeared for a moment

on Cui's face and he nodded at Li Yong to indicate his approval. But then, to her surprise, Cui extended his liquor glass towards Miaoyue. 'Boat trips are boring,' he said, 'How about it? Have a sip?'

'I don't drink!' Miaoyue almost screamed. The movement with which she pushed away the liquor glass seemed too shocking, her voice too piercing, as if Cui had offered her a glass filled with poison. She realized she had been rude. Her face flushed with shame and she walked to the cabin door, glancing first at Li Yong, then at Cui, then suddenly she opened it and ran out.

Underneath the lamps the deck was half-lit. Deeply perturbed, Miaoyue stood in the darkness. The river was murky in the night and not many people were looking out into it from the deck. The sound of their talking fell into the oblivion under the thunderous slapping of water against the hull. According to the original plan, Li Yong ought to have been out there with her, watching the night scene. But the trip had taken a somewhat peculiar turn; now she was standing alone, and what she saw in front of her was a liquor glass, the liquor glass Cui had held in his hand. Miaoyue reflected that perhaps she had been too sensitive – maybe the liquor glass had no particular significance. He and Li Yong were so close; what significance could it have?

The curtain of darkness was hanging heavily over the river's surface, the nightscape being admired by the passengers on deck was in fact just a boundless navy blue, with a crescent moon, pinpricks of stars and scattered lights near and far. The breeze from the river was both strong and fierce, and after standing in it for a long time she felt a little chilled. An odd thought suddenly crossed her mind: if Li Yong came now and draped a piece of clothing over her shoulders, perhaps there might still be some hope for their love, but she knew it was only her romantic imagination.

Miaoyue went back to their cabin to fetch some clothes, but when she had reached the door she decided to eavesdrop on the men's drunken banter. She put her ear to the door, but all she heard was the sound of someone throwing up. Then she heard Li Yong's voice, 'What's a girlfriend, after all? A bro is like an arm or a leg, but a woman's like clothing: you can throw her off whenever you feel like it.' Miaoyue could hardly suppress her anger, but just as she was about to storm in, the door opened and Cui dragged Li Yong out, totally soused. Cui wasn't at all surprised to see Miaoyue. 'He's drunk,' Cui said casually. 'I'm taking him to the bathroom. He'll be fine when he's finished puking.'

Miaoyue walked a few paces with them and saw that Li Yong had a slipper on one foot, but that the other foot was bare. They had only taken a few steps before Li Yong threw up. A foul liquid spouted from his mouth and splattered onto the floor of the corridor. Miaoyue stopped instinctively, turned her head away and screamed, 'Yuck!'

The cabin reeked of liquor. Miaoyue waved her hands around in a vain attempt to dispel it, but after a moment gave up. Then she removed a jacket from her travel bag and hurriedly took to her heels. As she passed the bathroom she caught a glimpse of the two men crouched inside; one puking, the other with his head raised high, throwing a look at Miaoyue that was bright but penetrating. She lowered her head and walked on quickly, then she heard Li Yong call out her name, 'Miaoyue! Miaoyue! Where are you? Why are you ignoring me?'

She laughed coldly and carried on walking, 'You've got your bro. Puke away! Puke away and get right back to your drinking!'

Miaoyue had nowhere to go, and her steps led her back onto the deck. A crew member was working on something by the railing, but kept on looking up to stare at her. She blew up at him. 'What are you looking at? I'm not going to jump!' She rolled her eyes, then leaned on the railing to sulk. She was angry with Li Yong and she was angry with Cui. She didn't know why she was angry with Cui, maybe it had something to do with that glass of liquor.

A few people came on deck and a few left. A couple snuggled up to one another under the cover of darkness – the girl's hair had been blown loose by the wind and the boy was holding it in both hands. Miaoyue began observing them covertly but it made her feel dejected and heavy-hearted. All at once she remembered a night not long ago, when she and Li Yong had kissed in the city gardens. It had been just as ardent, just as romantic, but now it had become impossible to call to mind the flavour of those hot kisses. It had all become false and distant, and Miaoyue didn't know whether it was a problem with Li Yong or herself.

The steamboat passed another port, and the lights in the houses slowly dimmed one by one in the distance. The faint sound of a TV emerged from somewhere on the banks; the evening news had just pronounced its earnest farewells. More people went below, and now only she and the couple remained. Miaoyue was still reflecting on her relationship with Li Yong; but since those are the kinds of questions that actually get more confusing the more you think about them, she ordered herself to stop. Instead, she spread her fingers, and counted them one by one. She didn't know how many times she had counted them when she realized a shadow had crept up softly behind her. It wasn't a stranger, though, it was none other than Cui.

'Don't bother counting.' He laughed, 'No matter how you count, there will always only be ten.'

Miaoyue glanced at Cui and said nothing. After a moment she enquired, 'How is he?'

'Asleep. He threw up all over the bathroom,' Cui said, 'Don't worry. Getting drunk is nothing to worry about, he's fine now that he's finished puking.'

'And why did you stop drinking? You're not drunk,' she said.

'I don't get drunk so easily,' Cui said, 'Don't you know what they say? Good guys are easy drunks. Li Yong's an easy drunk; ergo, he must be a good guy.'

'I know he's a good guy. You're not, though.'

'For a bad guy, I'm a good guy. Li Yong's a good guy straight up.'

'Why are you telling me this? That's a weird thing to say.' Suddenly she laughed and turned her head towards the river. 'What's all this good guy, bad guy stuff? Is this a morality court?'

'A morality court is wherever you conduct one.'

'Is this a trial? What right do you have to judge me?' She lifted her head to look straight at Cui, her expression one of defiance.

'I don't have the authority to judge you; I just suspect you.'

'Suspect me of what? Of being an American spy?'

'Oh no, a simple girl like you wouldn't make a good spy.' Cui muttered to himself and one of his hands kept hitting the railing. Then he said, 'Li Yong's a pretty simple guy. He doesn't really have women figured out, but I saw right away that you don't love him.'

Miaoyue's heart gave another thump and she turned her head to look at the faraway riverbank. In order to cover up her bewilderment, she wiggled her shoulders with a forced display of nonchalance. 'Maybe I do, maybe I don't,' she said. 'And what does it have to do with you?'

'It has a little to do with me.' The equivocal smile still played on his features. He brought out his cigarette pack, shook one out and stuck it in his mouth. 'Li Yong's a very nice guy. As you know, he depends a lot on me.'

'I know he does,' Miaoyue said, 'You men like to say that when a friend's in need, sharpen your knife. Are you going to stab me now?'

The smile on Cui's face appeared even more mysterious; and his eyes were luminous in the night. After a spell of silence, Cui said in an exceptionally tender voice, 'No. I'd stab anyone who told me to first.'

The darkness of night obstructed Miaoyue's face, which suddenly flushed. She had lost the courage to look straight at Cui. 'You don't have to go on,' she said, almost faltering. 'I get it now.'

Whenever Miaoyue found herself in a bewildering situation, she would slowly count her fingers. But on that night, when Cui's eyes were so bright, Miaoyue couldn't even see her own fingers; all she could see was his hand, a large hand which stretched leisurely out to her, and gathered up all her fingers. Miaoyue did not resist him, and the only thing that made her uncomfortable was that it all happened too fast.

Miaoyue let him hold her fingers. She could not speak.

'We get to Wuhan tomorrow,' Cui said. 'There's no Goddess Peak in Wuhan, but there is a Crane Tower. It's not as exciting as Beijing or Shanghai, but it can be a pretty fun city. Why don't you come along for the ride?'

Miaoyue could not speak and gazed fixedly at Cui's hand. After rather a long time, she said, 'My aunt's in Wuhan. She keeps writing for me to visit.'

When Miaoyue had finished this sentence, she saw the moon swaying in the sky. Then it seemed to go behind a thick cloud, for the deck seemed vaster and darker and all the banners on the mast were flapping in the breeze, making clear, splintering noises.

It was near evening of the second day that the boat reached Wuhan. Many passengers got off the boat there, taking a great deal of luggage with them, so the pier was unusually chaotic. It took quite some time for the boat and the docks to quieten down. The crew on the pier closed up the exit's iron door, took down the plank that had been used as a gangway and the steamboat pilot pulled the departure whistle. Just at that point, we saw a strange young man running madly from the second-class cabins, his clothes dishevelled and looking like he'd just woken up with a hangover. We watched him bumping around in the corridor, and as he ran he shouted a girl's name, 'Miaoyue! Miaoyue! Where are you? Miaoyue! Miaoyue! Where have you got to?'

Anyone could see that the young man was mad with worry, which was only natural; if someone else's girl-friend had disappeared, he too would have been driven to distraction. But the spectator is always more clear-headed than the person affected. Someone said, 'If you were in the second-class cabins, why don't you go and ask the steward there?'

The young man was in a dream-like state and asked, stupefied, 'Where is the steward?'

A large group of people led him towards the steward. Luckily, he was extremely competent and thoroughly familiar with the particulars regarding every traveller in the second-class cabins. 'You mean the girl who was dressed like a crow? She got off in Wuhan, didn't she? She left with her boyfriend.' At this point, he realized something and scrutinized Li Yong with questioning eyes. He said, 'That's what I wanted to ask you. There were three of you in the cabin, right? Two guys and a girl. Now, the girl, just whose girlfriend is she exactly?'

We all interrogated him with fervent eyes. His face was ghostly pale and he gave off a series of snorts, then he slowly squatted down and clutched his head in both hands. He turned first to the right, then to the left, and refused to answer any questions. His behaviour confused everybody. We vaguely remembered the young man travelling with him, dressed in a brand-name tie with a brand-name collar. Somebody had seen him with the girl on the deck the night before. Who would have thought that a simple matter could become so strange? And whose girlfriend was the girl called Miaoyue exactly?

After the boat left Wuhan, the trip towards the

Three Gorges began. That was the destination of most remaining passengers. We all remember that Li Yong was in low spirits for the rest of the trip, but when the boat passed the famous Goddess Peak, an unusual, peculiar smile appeared on his face. He fixed his stare on Goddess Peak for some time and said, 'Fuck, man. Is that thing Goddess Peak[10]?'

[10]There is such a place on the Three Gorges. The word being used for *goddess* in this story can, however, also be a (rather archaic) euphemism for a prostitute. The Chinese reader is likely to make this association by the end of this story.

The Diary for August

The inspector looked at the suspect who had been brought in for the incident at the city wall. He was an adolescent of fourteen or fifteen, poking his head out and peering at them, with his hand clutching the door frame. He had been picked up at a swimming pool and brought to the station immediately, so his hair wasn't yet entirely dry. Some tufts of it had congealed into two spikes that resembled a pair of scissors poking up from his forehead. His swimsuit, which was dripping water on the floor, consisted of two Young Pioneers' red neckerchiefs knotted together. The inspector saw that his eyes were full of fear and that his long thin arms and both his legs were trembling. It looked like he knew he had caused a disaster.

'What's your name?'

'Snot.'

'I didn't ask for your nickname. Don't you even know your own name?'

'Li Dasheng, but no one calls me that. They all call me Snot. Even my mum and dad call me Snot.'

'Where do you go to school?'

'Red Flag Middle School. But we're on holiday, no one's at school.'

'I know you're on holiday. Don't get smart with me, just answer the questions, OK?'

'Yeah, OK. I won't get smart.'

'Good. Then, scoot forward a little. Not on your ass – move the chair. Are you really that stupid? You little thugs, every last one stupid as a pig.'

'Little thug,' the teenager mumbled. 'I'm not a little thug.'

'If you're not a thug, I don't know who is. What are you, then? A model student, I suppose?'

'No.' The teenager squirmed in his seat, his eyes avoiding the mocking gaze of the inspector.

He looked at a water stain on the floor, cleared his throat and said quietly, 'I almost made model student last year, but I thought they'd laugh at me, so then I did badly in my exams on purpose. Wang Lianju even had a talk with me because of it. That's the truth, cross my heart and hope to die.'

'Who's Wang Lianju?'

'The class teacher. But that's just a nickname, too. You know, Wang Lianju, the traitor from *The Red Lantern*. All the teachers at our school have nicknames.'

'All right, that's enough of your wittering. Let me ask you this instead: were you the one who threw that stone from the city wall?'

The teenager stole a glance at the inspector, then hung his head and said nothing. With his finger, he traced some words on his knee.

'So you're not going to admit it now, huh? Just goes to show you little thugs are all cowards at heart. You have the guts to do this kind of crap, but you don't have the guts to own up to it.'

'I was just tossing it. I didn't think it would hit anybody.'

'And why did you toss it?'

'I dunno. Cat Head and the others dared me to. They cheated, you know; they made me throw it and then they chickened out and didn't throw any themselves.'

'Are you totally brainless? They dared you to throw it so you threw it? Don't you know you can crush someone if you throw a stone from that height?'

'I didn't think about anything like that. They were below the wall and I was thinking, We can see them, but they can't see us. I didn't think it could kill anyone. If I had thought it could kill someone, I wouldn't have thrown it.'

'Did you know either of them?'

'The couple? No, I didn't know them. But we saw them a whole bunch of times when we went to the wall to hang out. They always went there to meet up and hide in the bushes, and we just, we just—'

'You just what?'

'Well, we were on the wall . . . and we watched.'

The teenager became a little embarrassed and tried to suppress a smile tugging at the corner of his mouth. 'They were . . . they . . . Cat Head said he knew the girl; he said it was the girl from Fresh Wind Hairdresser's. She shaved his head once, he said.'

'How often did you watch them?'

'I don't remember. In any case, if we were there at five in the afternoon, eight or nine times out of ten they were there too. Below the wall is the People's Park, you know, and they used to buy their tickets and go in through the back door.'

'Did you go to see them on purpose?'

'It wasn't exactly on purpose.' The adolescent's face suddenly glowed crimson and he twisted his head uneasily this way and that. His voice faltered as he said, 'In any case they didn't . . . they didn't do much . . . of that stuff. Really, they were mostly just hiding there to talk.'

'And you were eavesdropping.'

'We couldn't hear them, or at least it wasn't really clear what they were saying. Once the girl started crying, and she cried for a while, and then the guy started to cry too. When he started crying we all laughed. We thought they would hear us and that they wouldn't come back next time. We didn't think they were such morons, but then they were back in the same place the next day. They were really dumb; they must have thought with all the trees and bushes and stuff that no one could see them. I bet they never imagined we were watching them from the wall.'

'Oh, so you were watching them? Then why would you throw a stone at them?'

'I dunno.' The teenager hung his head again. He pulled on his fingers and cracked the joints. Suddenly he asked, 'Are they dead? Did it hit the guy or the girl?'

'Which were you trying to hit?'

'I didn't think it would hit them. I just wanted to scare them a bit.'

'You're still trying to wiggle your way out of it. If you just wanted to scare them, you could have thrown a pebble, couldn't you? Why did you have to pick such a big rock?'

'I just took the stone Cat Head gave me. He said I couldn't take the real shit.'

'Excuse me?'

'He said I was chicken. He always says I'm chicken.'

'He said you were chicken and so you have to kill people if he says so, is that it? Just to prove him wrong?'

'They're all right, aren't they? They're not dead, are they?' The teenager was watching the expression on the inspector's face, then he gave a light sigh of relief, unable to conceal a self-satisfied grin. 'I can tell they're fine from how you're talking. You were just trying to scare me.'

'I can't believe you just smiled. If you smile one more time, there'll be no more Mr Nice Guy, understand?'

'I wasn't smiling.' The boy covered his face with his

palm and mumbled under his breath, 'It's not like smiling proves anything, anyway.'

The inspector was silent for a moment and ran over the notes he had on his pad with the tip of his ballpoint pen. He hadn't written much, so he added in the punctuation he'd omitted.

'Where did you go after you did it?'

'I took off. When I heard them screaming I took off right away. I thought maybe I'd killed them, you know. I ran home, but it was boiling there so I stood in front of the electric fan forever, but I was still hot, so I ran to the swimming pool to go for a swim, and I swam five hundred metres, no, actually more like a thousand, and then I saw you guys standing there. I knew I could run away if I wanted to, but I didn't see the point. Like they say, you can run but you can't hide.'

'You were swimming the whole time? You didn't go anywhere else?'

'No, I didn't go anywhere.' The boy looked at the inspector in confusion. 'I just couldn't stand the heat, so I went swimming.'

'That's a lie. Why don't you tell me the truth? Where did you go after you came down from the wall?'

'It's not a lie; I swear it isn't, cross my heart and hope to die. I was scared stupid and I went home to cool down by the fan but it was no good, so I went to the swimming pool. You can see I'm still wearing my swimsuit, can't you?'

'Well then what happened to the couple?'

'Can't you find them?' The boy's eyes grew large, but then he quickly regained his composure. He scratched his head and said, 'If they're not in the park, that just proves they're fine. I bet the rock just hit them on the foot. I guess it must have hit the girl's foot, because she screamed louder than the guy.'

'I would advise you to shut up now, because we already know all the details, and let me tell you, it's shaping up to be pretty serious. There are bloodspots all over the path in the People's Park, and the guard hasn't seen either one of them.'

'What does that prove?' the boy asked, blinking.

'That's for you to say. Why don't you tell me, now, honestly? Was it you who moved the bodies? Where to?'

'That's a load of crap!' The teenager, alarmed, had forgotten where he was. Even before he had finished his sentence, he realized he had spoken impudently. He bit his finger, as if by doing so he could take the sentence back. Then his dark features began to twitch, and finally he began to cry. He said, 'You just want to scare me. I know they're fine, they're not dead. If they were dead they couldn't have gone anywhere. There can't be blood-spots on the path.'

'Go ahead, now that it's too late you can cry. After you've already killed someone you start to get weepy. You little thugs are all the same, every one a coward. You're all tears as soon as someone mentions a coffin.'

The teenager covered his head and cried, 'I know they're not dead. Why do you all keep talking about corpses and bodies? As long as they're not dead, you have no right to talk about bodies.'

Apparently the teenager wasn't a bad student. The inspector gave him an hour to write his account of the case, but he finished in thirty minutes. Furthermore, his handwriting was clear and the composition logically structured. When the inspector read up to the part where he threw the stone, he couldn't help but smile. The teenager had included an elaborate, rather overdone half-page explanation of his conflicting emotions: to throw or not to throw, and whether to throw a big stone or a little one. It was very much in the style habitually used by middle-school students for essays assigned to record their good deeds. The inspector didn't know whether to laugh or cry, so ended up saying, not without irony, 'Well, it's quite a good composition.'

The teenager knew that the inspector was mocking him. Nevertheless he took advantage of the opportunity to expand on the topic of his writing talent. 'I'm best at compositions. Wang Lianju often gives me full marks for them. I know he just wants to encourage me, but I do write pretty well all the same.'

'Well I'd have to say I'd give you full marks for crime too; you're even better at that. You kill someone and remember to dispose of the bodies.'

The teenager didn't say anything, but turned his face

to look out of the window. It was already pitch-dark. He gazed around the room a few times, finally resting on the inspector's wristwatch, and asked timidly, 'What time is it?'

'What does it matter to you what time it is? You still think you're going to go home tonight?'

'Is it eight thirty yet? If I were at home I would be writing my diary.'

'What do you write in it? How many crimes you commit every day?'

'Wang Lianju assigned it as our homework for the holidays, one page a day. We have to hand it in when school starts. Actually, keeping a diary's pretty fun, and it kills time.'

'I don't think you'll be handing in your holiday homework. When other people start school isn't going to matter too much to you any more.'

'I only have three pages left to write, because in three days the holidays will be over.' The teenager sat in front of the desk and stared at the ballpoint pen and paper in front of him. He hesitated a moment before making a peculiar request. 'Let me write my diary. You're not questioning me any more anyhow. Can't I just write the entry for today?'

If the inspector assented in the end, it was mostly out of a curiosity about what this juvenile delinquent would write.

183

An Entry from the Diary of Li Dasheng,
Middle School Student
28 August 1974, sunny

The wind blows strong, the red flag flutters, splendid are the
hills and rivers of our motherland.

Today I went to the People's Park. Walking past a
construction site, I suddenly heard cries of distress. It
seemed that a large stone had fallen from the scaffolding
and hit a passer-by on the head. At the crucial moment
of this catastrophy, disregarding my own safety, I rushed
over immediately to help the victim. I helped the hurt old
man into a sitting position. The blood from his wound
spurted onto me like a fountain, dyeing my new white silk
shirt red. I was concerned about getting myself dirty, but
as I relaxed my support of his body, the glorious images
of Lei Feng, Wang Jie, Qiu Shaoyun and other heroes[11],
flashed through my mind. I realized that when the lives or
the property of the people are at stake, heroes do not shy
away from anything, even death. Was I going to let myself
be frightened by a little bit of blood? Having remembered
this, my heart was filled with revolutionary pride. Moving

[11]A short canon of Chinese Communist heroes. Lei Feng (1940–62)
was the archetype of the 'nameless hero', selfless and revolutionary.
Having died in an accident, he became the model for an official
'Learn from Lei Feng' movement. Wang Jie (1942–65) sacrificed
his own life and saved those of twelve other men in an accidental
dynamite blast. Qiu Shaoyan (1931–52) was a Korean War hero who
burned to death rather than move and reveal his unit's position.

as fast as I could, I carried the old man to the hospital on my back, the blood from his wound and the sweat from my body dripping along the path. The whole time I kept thinking of how important it was for him to get medical attention quickly, entirely forgetting about being tired or worried about stains. We finally reached the hospital and the old man was saved. The doctor asked me my name, but I said, 'When you do a good deed, you shouldn't leave your name. I only did what I should.'

It was really a very interesting day!

When the inspector had finished reading the teenager's diary entry, he didn't speak for a long time and his face turned very grave. He folded the diary entry up length-wise, and put it in the drawer. The teenager said, 'It's our summer homework. We have to write a diary. Everybody writes their diaries that way.' He was trying to offer him some kind of explanation and the inspector knew it, but he didn't need an explanation, he just said, 'Today you hand your homework in to me.'

Even after that, the matter of the incident at the city wall remained unsettled. Colleagues of the inspector managed to find the two people concerned. The girl was a pretty little thing with narrow, foldless eyes, who did in fact work at Fresh Wind Hairdressing. Her long, raven-black braids were coiled into a bun on her head and no trace of a wound was apparent. In the inspector's experience, if there had been any injury to the head, the doctors would have shaved all her beautiful hair off at the hospital. The hairdresser didn't admit to being a victim, and furthermore claimed that she never went to the People's Park and that if she did it was only to walk with her parents. How could she possibly have been in among the bushes and weeds beneath the city wall? Then, after a few days, the officers located the other victim, a man who had just returned home from a business trip. As the inspector recalled, he was a mid-level cadre in a large enterprise, one of those people you can see at first glance have unlimited prospects. On his face there had been a suspicious scar. But when the young cadre touched on how the scar had come about, he said that he had been at a cheap hotel in another city and had slipped on the stairs returning to his room at night. That was all there was to it, the young cadre said, and he categorically denied his status as a victim. He said, 'I'm a very busy man. When would I find time to go to the park?'

In fact, the investigators of the city wall incident actively sought to drop the case, realizing that neither of the victims would cooperate with their proceedings, and the investigator later told his colleagues, 'Screw this. Who the hell is going to take on this rubbish case? It doesn't really matter. What bothers me is that the little hoodlum got away with it.'

The 'little hoodlum' was of course Li Dasheng, who was then entering his third year at Red Flag Middle School. The inspector kept the peculiar diary entry in his drawer, expecting that the adolescent would sooner or later fall back into his hands, but that was the strange thing: the inspector never saw him again. Perhaps when he said that he wasn't a little thug it had been true after all.

Twenty years passed and in preparation for retirement from his beloved post, the inspector was cleaning out his desk drawers when he found the diary entry, folded lengthwise. It reminded him of the incident, and he gave an involuntary chuckle at the yellowing paper. His curiosity piqued, a young colleague took it from his hand and began reading. He got halfway through it before he stopped, remarking 'What's so funny about that? I wrote a diary like that back then, too; a whole bunch of diaries like that.'

Of course, the young colleague had never heard of the incident at the city wall twenty years ago, and the inspector didn't feel like going to the trouble of explaining it to him. He slowly tore up the paper, and said, 'Yeah, there used to be lots of diaries like that. Nothing strange about it.'

Dance of Heartbreak

Men, too, have hopes; soft, malleable things, like aquatic plants. In general, they are hidden deep inside, but the pain they conceal can easily well up again, if some little fish takes a nibble at the sore spot. This sensation is known as recurrence, or wish recurrence.

My thickset frame means I'm destined for a life without dance, but the story I wish to relate took place in my childhood. People are all identical when they're small, and I was as lively and clever as the rest of you. And I was a good dancer. It's true. As a kid, I was a very good dancer.

It happened when I was in Grade 4, at Red Flag Elementary School; but even today the whole affair remains fresh in my mind. On one enchanting spring afternoon, Ms Duan Hong called me over from the rope-skipping crowd. She held my hand as we crossed the playground while all the other children cast envious glances my way. Ms Duan was a lady in her fifties who wore white running shoes and had started teaching dance and choir when my father was still at school. I should tell you that if Ms Duan took you by the hand it meant you were in luck. Perhaps you were going to be chosen for the cultural propaganda team.

When I came into the office with Ms Duan, I immediately spotted Li Xiaoguo standing by the window, drawing chalk airplanes and artillery on the glass. Ms Duan said, 'Xiaoguo, behave. Take a seat and don't fidget.' He came running over with a titter and sat down on the one and only stool. His face had been brightly painted with rouge, and he cocked his head, looking contemptuously at me with the whites of his eyes. I knew what he meant by this. He meant, 'What are *you* doing here?'

Ms Duan made me stand up straight and then, her hand tightly clasped on the cosmetic case, she started to do my make-up. Her fingers worked tenderly and ably over my features. Finally, she clapped her hands, subjecting me to close scrutiny and proclaimed, 'Yes! Now you look like a Red Child.' At this point Xiaoguo almost knocked over his stool. Pointing at me, he shouted, 'Ms Duan, he's not pretty! He hides crickets in his desk. He disturbs class discipline.' She just laughed and patted Xiaoguo on the head. 'You're pretty and he's pretty too. You're both Red Children.'

At that moment, Xiaoguo had made me so angry I could've dragged him out and shot him dead – so what if his dad was some stupid chairman? But I knew I couldn't thrash him in the office, because all the teachers watched out for him. In any case, Ms Duan soon had me doing a movement where I hopped up and down while pretending to wipe windows. I had to repeat this movement ad infinitum, but in the end she called for me to stop and said, 'Excellent hopping; just like a Red Child.' She fished out a handkerchief and wiped the sweat off my face. 'Tomorrow you and Xiaoguo will come and practice together, OK?'

I suddenly realized that the movement I had been doing was straight out of *The Red Children*. This was a dance for twelve, six boys and six girls, holding brooms, mops and rags, and making cleaning movements. It was always the finale of our school's performance, but now the window-cleaning boy had changed schools, so Xiaoguo and I were being called in to substitute. Ms Duan said, 'Now you two make certain you practise, and whoever dances better will be selected for the performance.'

Only many years later did I realize that what she had meant was for us to compete. I didn't catch on at the time; back then all I knew was how much I hated Xiaoguo. I was just itching to ask Cat Head, Jia Lin and some of the others in the big kids' gang to break his legs. No doubt Xiaoguo's thoughts were equally truculent. 'The east wind blows, the war drums boom, now we'll see who's scared of whom.' There was a song that went like that.[12]

[12] The song is 'The People of the World will Be Victorious', written 'collectively' by the national philharmonic in reaction to Mao Zedong's statement in May 1970 for the 'people of the world to unite, and defeat the American aggressors and their running dogs'.

I was in fact only provisionally a member of the cultural propaganda team; not really so very glorious a position. The thirteen children of the cultural propaganda team gathered in the big classroom on Wednesdays and at weekends, and, at the sound of the music, began dancing around Ms Duan like chicks around an old hen. I mingled among them, filled with the kind of joy you don't ever forget.

What I will relate next concerns the dancing of another child. She was an extraordinarily beautiful little girl and her name was Zhao Wenyan, which means swallow. Later, when I read about the art theorist Cai Yi's 'typical image',[13] I felt that he must have had someone like her in mind; no doubt this association was inspired by impressions of her back then. For me, she was an archetype.

And she was the Red Child who held the mop.

Wenyan's mother had been a dancer, but afterwards, why I never knew, she kept trying to hang herself. This happened over and over again, but she never actually succeeded in taking her life. From what I heard, it was always Wenyan who found her and, screaming and wailing, would slide a chair under her mother's feet. Her mother then had no choice but to resign herself once more to soldier on. I had seen her mother on the street before;

[13]Cai Yi (1906–92), Marxist thinker whose work *New Aesthetics* contained an influential discussion of the 'image'.

she looked almost identical to Wenyan, except she was a little taller and a little older. She had two maroon stripes on her neck, groove-like scars, left from the noose.

Once Wenyan had her make-up on, she had the power of an angel to induce love and pity, but as soon as she came on stage she began to get nervous. And as soon as she was nervous, she squatted down and peed onstage. This is called urinary incontinence, and I've heard that many beautiful girls are afflicted with this peculiar illness in their childhood. That the propaganda team had not dropped Wenyan was in the first instance because of her extraordinary beauty and in the second because Ms Duan couldn't bear to part with her. Ms Duan said, 'She's had so many frights, poor child.'

I've never met another girl like her; she was a little child of glass. Yes, exactly, a little child of glass, beautiful in her sorrow, glowing cautiously with some emerald light. She wore a little patterned dress, and when she ran to centre stage, radiating her innate beauty, she held her mop with such natural elegance that it might have been a bouquet of fresh flowers. But as soon as you saw her squat down, you knew that before long the cotton dress would be wet. Even someone who was only a little boy at the time could never have forgotten this archetypal image of her, and that's all there was to it.

Then, on another enchanting spring afternoon, I fought with Xiaoguo. I made his little garlic-bulb nose bleed, while he kept trying to pull down my trousers and rip them. I had to cover up the seat of my pants with my school bag all the way home that day.

Analysis today would conclude that I lost. Xiaoguo was a wily old fox.

The east wind blows, the war drums boom. Spring passed very quickly.

Only seven or eight days before the performance, Ms Duan called me aside and whispered secretly into my ear, 'Dance nicely and I'll let you go on.' That was precisely the whispering-in-your-ear kind of woman Ms Duan was, a rare kind of woman for this world. Her waist was more supple than an eight-year-old's, her dance steps more graceful than the bending of a willow in the wind. She had danced that way since her youth and forgotten to get married or have children, so that she was an old maid.

That whisper was the last time she ever spoke to me. During the rehearsal that followed, something terrible happened. On that day Ms Duan's cheeks were flushed; as always, she was leading the team in our dance like an old hen with her chicks: 'Arms a little higher.' And then, 'Why do you always forget to smile? You must smile. Smile beautifully like little red flowers.' I remember Ms Duan gripping Xiaoguo's arm to prevent it stiffening, but Xiaoguo was a born nincompoop, and his arms kept flailing randomly in the air like wooden rods. Ms Duan leapt in and out of our dancing ring, hopping about and mimicking window-cleaning movements. I saw her as she suddenly stopped moving, and her two lovely arms

194

hung in the air freeze-framed. During the space of that moment, the light in her eyes slackened, then I watched as her plumpish body fell backwards.

Wenyan was the first one to burst into tears; before the rest of us reacted, she cried out, 'Ms Duan's dead!' and ran down to the office to fetch a teacher. After a spell of confusion, we thirteen children went along to see Ms Duan at the hospital.

It was called cerebral thrombosis: a sudden attack brought on by high blood pressure. Given how much we understood of the workings of the world, we children were unable to comprehend the connection between haemorrhage and death. I had always assumed that school teachers were immortal; that if Ms Duan had passed on for a moment, she would return to life a second later. But the next day, as soon as I arrived at school, I heard that Ms Duan had died. Wenyan was bent over her desk, bawling her heart out. Her school bag was flung out on the desk, and inside was a pair of white running shoes – they had dropped off Ms Duan's feet on the way to the hospital.

The concept of a connection between death and dancing was even harder to grasp. It was as if Ms Duan was leading us as we danced, but how was it that she suddenly had one foot in the Kingdom of the Dead?

People die all the time. Sometimes it comes heavy as a mountain, sometimes as light as a goose feather.

After Ms Duan's death, I assumed the propaganda

team had been disbanded because no one called me to practices. Those were enchanting spring afternoons – in simple stories, it is best to use phrases like 'enchanting spring afternoon' quite frequently in order to avoid complicating a simple matter. The redbud tree blossomed. Wenyan started to wear skirts. And that's all there was to it.

One day, as I walked past the window of the big class-room, I discovered to my amazement that Wenyan, Xiaoguo and the others were rehearsing; the principal and a strange woman were conducting them. There were twelve children – six boys, six girls – but not me.

What about me? Hadn't they said I would go on and Xiaoguo would go to hell? I leaned on the windowsill and peered in at them; I wanted to go in, but didn't dare. I couldn't understand how they could have dropped me and picked Xiaoguo, that champion nincompoop. It was the first time in my life that I felt a sense of loss. I was twelve at the time. A sense of loss at that age! And dance being to blame. First they say they'll let you perform, then they suddenly don't even want you at rehearsal; how could you not feel hurt?

On yet another enchanting spring afternoon, I fought Xiaoguo again. This time I held him down in the sand-box so he couldn't rip my trousers. With superhuman strength, I began to fill Xiaoguo's mouth with sand, then suddenly I remembered what Ms Duan had said, 'Dance nicely and I'll let you go on.' So I let Xiaoguo go and instead broke into tears myself. I was facing a broken-down wall, and vaguely through my tears I saw that outside the wall was a rapeseed field filled with grieving golden flowers. This time I had won the fight, and yet incomprehensibly I was the one who had ended up in tears. It was the most embarrassing incident in all the historical records of my brilliant youth.

The east wind blows, the war drums boom. Spring passed very quickly.

The day I feared most finally arrived: the day of the performance. The venue was the school's large assembly hall. On the day our school had a kind of orioles-singing-swallows-darting-one-hundred-flowers-contending-bunting-flattering-firecracker-popping atmosphere. The children, ignorant of worldly affairs, were scampering and scurrying all over the place, making so much merry noise that the heavens threatened to fall. I was the only heavy-hearted one, sitting straight-backed like an old man in the last row of the classroom, playing with a box of matches. I piled the matchsticks on top of one another and then took out a little mirror to reflect the light onto them. Slowly, the pile of matchsticks spluttered and caught fire. The smell of burning saltpetre surrounded me and drifted through the deserted classroom.

Would you have played such heartbroken games when you were twelve years old?

Carrying my stool, I fell into the back of the line of my

team as we trooped into the assembly hall. Enchanting spring. No one wanted to know what was troubling me. Who ever wants to know what's troubling you? Suddenly our group began to make a great hullabaloo as the six boys and girls – the twelve red children with their make-up on – processed past with their props. Xiaoguo, that nincompoop, was of course among them. His face was made up redder than any of them. I turned round in order to avoid looking at them, and then I heard the principal jog up to Wenyan and say, 'Don't be nervous, and whatever happens, you must hold it.' I knew what the principal meant, but I reflected that if I were Wenyan I certainly would not hold it, I'd definitely pee, since they were blind enough to choose Xiaoguo and not me.

As you know, in the early seventies, the great masters of dance were, by default, children, and anyway, watching kids bounce around was better than watching nothing at all. So for the performance that day, all the old men and women in the street had brought along their stools and chairs and sat glowing happily at the back. I saw Xiaoguo's grandma and Wenyan's grandpa, both looking as joyous as if they were on the stage themselves. I felt like there was something pernicious about the merriness of the world that day.

Then it was the turn of the red children to begin their piece. The six boys and six girls danced in two rows, holding brooms, mops and rags, and started to clean. I saw how Wenyan's eyebrows were knitted like an old woman's; she made only a few dance moves and then squatted down. The principal, standing offstage, immediately covered his head and rolled his eyes at the sky.

Wenyan couldn't hold it after all. She had peed again.

I bolted up, clapped and laughed out loud. The sound of my laugh was keen and resounding. The class teacher rushed at me from the front row and pushed me down onto my stool, but still I couldn't stop myself, and I opened my mouth wide and carried on laughing. Then the class teacher slapped me in the face.

Would you have laughed like that when you were twelve?

And I guess that was the story I wanted to tell you about dancing.

I'll need to tell you about what happened to the other two kids to round off the story. Before Wenyan even got to high school, she was selected for a dance school in Shanghai. From what I heard the selection committee took one look at her face and those two long legs and refused to part with her. She really was a born dance genius. Later, I was lucky enough to see her do the lotus dance, and let me tell you, it was a far cry from *The Red Children*. She moved you to tears with her beauty when she danced.

Once I was watching TV with a friend and I said, 'She used to pee as soon as she got on stage.' My friend laughed; he thought I was just talking rubbish.

'I'm not kidding. I danced with her once. Why would I lie to you?' And that's all there was to it. In the first year that Wenyan danced in Shanghai, her mother hanged herself; now that Wenyan wasn't at home, her suicide attempt had finally succeeded. I don't know what it was she died for. In the end, it was as if Wenyan's mum had a furrow in her neck. It was the mark left by a noose.

That leaves the nincompoop Xiaoguo. If I tell you what happened to Xiaoguo, you'll really think I'm making things up. Xiaoguo's the handicapped guy on our street who goes around in a wheelchair. One day, while he was working on a construction site putting up scaffolding, he fell ten metres through the air and broke both legs.

I think that's called a tragic fate. A tragic fate is when you've only danced once in your life but you break your legs. And that's all there was to it.

I often discuss dance with my wife. As it happens, my wife was one of the twelve red children back then. Remember? She was the one dancing with the broom. Now she hates it when I talk about dance with her. She says, 'Men who like dancing disgust me.' And when I think about it, she's right. It's not quite normal for men to like dancing.

Can you tell me what dance is all about? My wife asked me once, 'When did you first fall in love with me?'

and I said, 'When you were a kid in that Tibetan dance – you used to throw your sleeves back and forth; it was incredibly beautiful.'

'Really?' she said. 'Did I do a Tibetan dance?'

I watched her expression carefully. It was totally blank and not at all like she was pretending. I could only conclude that she really had forgotten about her own dance.

And that's all there was to it.

Can you tell me what dance is really all about?

The Water Demon

The river flows east. The boat, filled with oil drums, floated wearily on the water's surface. The rhythmic sweeping of the oars seemed hesitant, even shy. The oil boat passed under the arch of the bridge and emerged, leaving behind an oil trail of irregular width, its colour changing depending on the reflected light. The oil boat moved along on the open expanse of the river's main current, and the girl on the bridge could see the seven colours of the rainbow glistening in its wake.

The girl stood on the bridge, and gradually saw off the oil boat with her gaze. She could just make out another bridge, and a bend in the river where the boat disappeared. By the bridge was a factory, which stood out because of its chimney stacks and a cylindrical tower. The girl didn't know what the tower was for. Though it was far away, its discharge culvert was clearly visible where it met the water, and the girl used her glass prism to shine light on it. Just as she had expected, it was too far away and she failed to make a glare, so the tower was completely unaffected. The clouds in the western sky, floating across the water surface, began to redden, and the sky around the tower began to dim.

Yes, the sky began to dim. The girl saw her aunt walk past the bridgehead and quickly turned away, but she had already been spotted.

'Look at you! Why don't you stay at home instead of running around on a scorcher like this? What are you doing here, anyway?'

The girl said, 'Nothing. My mum said I could go out.'

Her aunt said nothing more and turned to leave, but when she had walked off the bridge she turned back and yelled, 'Don't be home too late. If you're going to stand there like a lemon, they're bound to come and bully you again.'

The girl stood on the bridge. She didn't want to go home yet. A boy with mumps wearing a striped sailor shirt ran up; he lived above the general store at the base of the bridge and the girl knew him. He covered his cheeks, which were coated with medicinal herbs. 'What's that in your hand? Show it to me,' he said. The girl knew he meant the glass prism, but she clutched both hands behind her back and fixed him with a bold stare.

'I won't,' she said, but suddenly held the glass prism up in one hand. 'Don't touch it. It's for shining on the water demon.'

The boy, who had intended to plunder some treasure,

drew his hand back. 'Liar,' he said. 'What water demon? Where is it then?'

The girl pointed at the river beneath. 'He's in the water now.' She indicated the trail of oil, which had not yet dissipated. 'You can't see it, but I can.'

'You're lying. Tell me where he's gone.'

A mysterious smile appeared on the girl's face. She tucked the prism away. 'I've found out where the water demon lives, but I would never tell you where.' She began to walk down the bridge, then suddenly turned back to say, 'You all think he lives in the water, but that's not true. You're all wrong.'

As she left the bridge, she could still see the boy standing there, covering his cheeks and staring vacantly. He didn't know a thing. And even though he could see the distant tower, he would still never guess its secret.

A young man slid into the water with frog-like hops while another young man followed behind, using a kind of doggy-paddle. Maybe it was because they couldn't go any further, or maybe they had got to where they wanted to be, but suddenly they stopped beneath the bridge and hauled themselves out of the water to sit on the rocks beneath the arch.

The girl opened her nylon parasol and, standing on the bridge, watched for them to come out from under the bridge. She'd assumed they would keep on swimming, but now that they had stopped under the bridge, she couldn't see them. They were talking loudly.

'That water's disgusting. Shit, man, did you see the dead cat? I nearly threw up.' The other boy caught his breath, and said, 'Yeah, I saw it. Sort of tawny. It probably ate rat poison.'

The girl attempted to bend over the railing so she could see the faces of the two young men. Instead, she could see only a leg with a very dark tan. There was a dense mass of hair on his calf and it looked like he had recently cut the back of his foot; there were obvious traces of antiseptic left on the skin.

'A dead cat! That's nothing!' said the girl, breaking into the conversation from above. 'A few days ago I saw a dead boy! He looked just like a rabbit.'

'Who's talking up there?' one of them asked.

'It's got to be that stupid Deng girl,' the other one answered. 'She's got a screw loose. Ignore her.'

She drew back her head, then stuck it back out over the railing to spit, 'You're the stupid one!'

After delivering this furious retort she went back to playing with her glass prism, making shapes on the water. The only target she could find was the dark, hairy leg. Then she heard someone below say, 'Don't pay any attention to her.'

The girl said, 'No one's paying any attention to you, anyway.' She heard her own voice amplified by the arch.

It sounded clear and sweet. She began to twirl the nylon umbrella one way and then the other.

'Cross my heart and hope to die, a dead boy floated past a couple days ago. He was swimming too, like you, but then the water demon grabbed his foot and dragged him down to the riverbed!'

The two youths under the bridge chuckled, then one of them flopped into the water and started yelling, 'Oh no! Help! The demon! The water demon! He's got me!' While the other youth laughed even harder.

The girl watched them toss up riverweed from the water with their horseplay. 'Don't be so noisy,' she said. 'The water demon's away right now, but if you make him angry he'll swim through the water and grab you.'

'He's here!' The youth somersaulted in the water and cried out, 'My leg! The water demon's got my leg! Somebody! Help! Help!'

The girl knew they were just playing around and ignoring her warnings. It made her a little angry, so she picked up a shard of glass lying on the bridge and threw it into the river. 'Fine. Go on playing your stupid games; carry on swimming if you can. Why don't you swim all the way to the tower, because that's where the water demon lives.'

Her mother did not allow her to go out by herself. One day her mother dyed her nails with jewel-weed, saying, 'We agreed, didn't we? If I dye your nails, then you won't go and do those foolish things. Today you're going to stay at home and do your schoolwork.' Her mother saw that the girl was sitting by the door, carefully examining her ten peach-red nails. 'The sun's fierce today. If you go fooling around outside again, everyone will think you're a dimwit.' The girl held her ten fingers up for the sun to shine on them. She saw that they had become like ten jewel-weed petals, sparkling and transparent.

'I'm telling you, the sun's really fierce today,' her mother said. 'If you go outside today, the sun will definitely scorch you. If you sneak out again the sun's sure to burn you to death!'

Outside, the sun seemed to be boiling. Barely visible white smoke was rising from the concrete road. A woman was hawking cold water somewhere in the distance. The schoolteacher from across the road, Ms Song, hurried off with a jug and a nylon parasol in hand to go and buy some.

'Other people are going outside,' the girl mumbled. 'Who says no one's going outside? As long as you have a parasol it's fine.'

She looked back and forth, searching for something. Her mother knew what it was already and said, 'Don't bother looking. I've put your parasol away. You don't take good enough care of your things. With such a fierce sun, you'll ruin it if you take it out.'

Her mother sat in the bamboo chair and seemed to doze off. She could vaguely feel her empty hand where the palm-leaf fan had been, but she didn't open her eyes; it had probably fallen on the floor.

The girl had sneaked off again with her mother's palm-leaf fan. The girl was standing on the bridge using the fan to keep off the afternoon sun. Nobody noticed her newly-dyed fingernails or, for that matter, the girl herself.

Just as she was walking onto the bridge, a man walked off in her direction with a plank on his shoulder. He almost swept her off as he passed, and she called out, 'Watch out!' The flustered man turned around. He was a stranger, a farmer or something like that. The girl saw that his wife-beater and trousers were wet and dripping as he walked past. The girl laughed and asked, 'What are you doing?'

For a moment, he seemed not to understand her question, but then he asked back, 'What do you mean, what am I doing?'

'Why are you so wet? Are you the water demon?'

The man shifted the plank from the left to right shoulder. 'The water demon? What water demon?'

He looked at the girl in puzzlement, but after a moment seemed to understand and chortled. He pointed to an embankment not far from the bridge and said, 'No, I'm not the water demon. See? We're working in the water.'

The girl's eyes followed the direction of his finger. Labourers were assembled on the embankment by the factory. They were all bare-chested, some standing on the embankment and some of them in the water making a terrible noise. The girl hung on the railing and said, 'I want to see.' She turned back towards him and repeated, 'I want to see.'

The labourer squinted at the girl, then laughed, revealing his yellow teeth. The girl watched as he walked off the bridge with his plank. She noticed the sturdy, protruding veins on his legs, like so many worms. His shins and ankles were stained all over with yellow mud.

That summer a gang of labourers constructed a small pier for the chemical factory. The girl stood on the bridge and patiently observed the entire process: how they drove in the piles, built the retaining walls and pumped out the water. At the beginning, no one noticed the girl on the bridge. She just stood there, holding a palm-leaf fan to keep off the afternoon sun. No one knew what she was doing or what had provoked her interest; she just stood and watched. Sometimes she adjusted the fan's position in her hand, so that it was still covering half of her face, then she carried on watching. Once she called out, 'Here comes the water demon!' At first she called out tentatively, feeling a little bad about frightening them, but later it seemed as though she wanted to provoke their enmity, as she called out loudly, 'The water demon! He's here! Quick! Get out of the water or the demon will get you by the feet!' Often the labourers would stop what they were doing and stare angrily at the girl on the bridge. Each time the girl would run away, tearing down the bridge with only a few strides. Then in the blink of an eye, she was gone.

The labourers started talking about the girl on the bridge; they all thought there must be something wrong with her. Fortunately the girl had made no impact on the progress of their work. They had planned eight days to build the pier, but it was complete after only seven. The day they finished work, they kept looking up at the bridge, but they saw no trace of the girl. They didn't know why she wasn't there that day, just as they had no idea why she had been there on every other day previously. Without the girl, the bridge seemed very empty.

The labourers did not know she was away, visiting her aunt.

On the seventh day, the girl had crossed the city to visit her aunt. She returned home only at dusk, and cried out in surprise when they crossed the bridge. Her mother had been dragging her along by the hand, but now she dropped it. 'What did you do that for?' her mother asked, 'You scared me half to death. There's nothing the matter. Why did you scream like that?' The girl stood on the bridge, looking at the new pier not far away. She wanted to stay there, standing on the bridge, but her mother dragged her away roughly with her powerful grip 'You shouldn't be standing there like a halfwit. Do you know that's what everyone thinks you are? Standing all day on the bridge in the heat. If you're not a little dim-witted, I don't know what you are.'

As the girl was being dragged off the bridge, she said, 'Don't pull so hard. You're going to pull my hand off!'

But her mother replied furiously, 'If I don't drag you home, you'll just stand on the bridge for everyone to laugh at.'

The girl struggled to free herself, 'Don't drag me! You're as bad as the water demon!' She looked at her mother pleadingly and suddenly the girl screamed, 'I can see the water demon! *You're* the water demon!'

Her mother raised her hand and slapped the girl in the face. 'It's just non-stop nonsense with you, isn't it? One day I really will tell the water demon to drag you down to where the Dragon King lives!'

On the night of the seventh day, the girl sneaked out of the house, right under her mother's nose. She had never gone out at night before, so when her mother spotted her walking around the bamboo chair and going out with something like a flashlight in her hand, it didn't occur to her that it might actually *be* a flashlight. And that was how the girl sneaked out, right under her mother's nose.

On both sides of the concrete road there were people who had come out to cool down in the night air. A few of them looked over at the girl and called her name: 'Where are you going so late?' they asked.

The girl said, 'I'm going down to the bridge to cool down.'

'Smart girl. It's windy on the bridge; good place to cool down.'

The girl walked towards the bridge, where a few young men there leaned on the railing with their cigarettes. When they saw the girl, they stopped talking and turned to look at her. Someone started chortling, saying, 'It's her again! The Deng family dumbo, standing all day on the bridge.'

She swept over them with disdainful eyes and said, 'You're the dumbos. You're the ones standing on the bridge all day.'

She leaned on the railing on the other side, wearing an expression that said as far as she was concerned they should just stay out of each other's business. She shone the flashlight on the riverbank below the bridge, then turned it off again. What she had wanted to see was the new pier; the new pier that been raised above from the waters. The newly poured cement diffused an indistinct white light under the moonbeams. The girl stood there and felt strangely hurt, yearning as she did to go down to the pier. She had kept watch for six days, seeing every detail of the labourers' work, missing only the process of raising the structure out of the water. She wanted to have a thorough look at it, but the horrid young men behind her were talking, laughing in a peculiar way that made her feel uncomfortable.

Suddenly she decided to leave the bridge. She began walking away and headed in the direction of the riverbank. The young men on the bridge yelled after her, 'Hey, dumbo, where are you going?' but she ignored them.

To herself, she said, 'If they want to monopolize the bridge, then let them, it's not like I can't go whenever I want to.' She turned the flashlight on and began to walk towards the new pier. She saw the river water rushing underneath the bridge, and in the darkness the water looked thicker and darker than the night itself.

A large block of cement ground lay bare in the moonlight, emitting its naturally fishy smell, welcoming her. She carefully stretched out one of her feet to test the firmness of the cement. It wasn't yet completely set, and in the flashlight's beam, the girl could see her sandalprints in it, clearly marked.

The building shed had not been taken down. It was very dark inside and there was no movement. She shone inside it with her flashlight. The beam hit a straw mat and next to it was an enamel washbasin and a mess tin. This told the girl that there was still someone guarding the pier, but though she shone all around with her flashlight, she saw nothing and no one besides the large wooden cases and discarded machinery the chemical factory left there all year. A little further away, in a spot where the river was suddenly hidden from sight, the tower was bathed in moonlight, giving off a somewhat reddish glow. The discharge culvert wasn't visible at all. The girl listened carefully to the sounds of the flowing river, her ears filling with the sound of the river talking to itself. Suddenly, coming from the tower she heard the unfamiliar sound of something smacking the surface of the water, getting closer and closer. With her eyes almost popping out of her skull, she stared at the surface of the water but saw nothing. There was no one swimming. But there was the sound of something striking the water, becoming ever clearer, and ever closer. She began to feel quite frightened and looked towards the bridge in the distance. The young men were still there.

'The water demon! The water demon's coming,' she shouted.

Although the shadows on the bridge swayed a little, no one responded. The girl began to be really afraid and started to bolt back along the bank. The flashlight in her hand swung wildly back and forth, and as she ran she saw the river running silently beneath her feet. The water in the darkness was darker and deeper than the night as she carried on running across the newly built pier. She could hear the sound of her rapid breathing, but she could hear the breathing of the water demon, too. It was there! Her sandals were suddenly held down by something. She screamed and looked down at her feet, but it was only the drying cement; her sandals had got stuck. At the same time she heard a burst of jumbled noises from the water and caught sight of a shape emerging from the dark water, dripping with glistening algae. The girl gave another piercing scream as she saw the labourer with the plank who she had seen on the bridge.

'The demon! The water demon! The water demon!' she screamed.

The man was holding something in his hands.

'The demon! The water demon! The demon!'

If the young men on the bridge had believed in the legend of the water demon, they might have testified to the Deng girl's story, but they did not. That was what made the account, which was at first only a few sentences from the girl, into a real story.

On that night, at about nine o'clock, they had dimly heard sounds coming from the new pier. One of them had wanted to go and see what was happening, but was prevented from doing so by one of his friends, who had said, 'What water demon? Don't pay any attention to that stupid girl. She's just screaming for the sake of it.'

So they stayed on the bridge smoking and shooting the breeze. Later, at about ten o'clock, they saw the girl coming towards them. They didn't know what had happened, but they did notice that she was totally wet and that she held something cupped in her hands. None of them had wanted to acknowledge her, but she seemed to be crying. The youths on the bridge ran over to her. She looked as though she'd only just got out of the water. She was crying as she approached them on the bridge, and in her hands was a lotus flower. A very large, red lotus flower. At first they were all quite baffled by the flower. The young men surrounded her to look at it. It was a real lotus flower, not plastic, and there were still drops of water on its petals. All talking at the same time, they asked her where she had got it. The girl was still crying, crying as if she were in some kind of dream. She cupped the flower tightly with her hand, and between her pale fingers, drops of water fell, glistening. One of the young men said, 'Let's not get overexcited about something like this. It must have floated to the bank from the lotus pond in the park.'

The others looked questioningly at the girl, 'Is that right? Did it float there?'

The girl said nothing, but clung to the flower and walked towards the road. The youths walked behind her and someone else said, 'You stupid girl! Did you really jump into the river to dredge out lotus flowers? Aren't you afraid of drowning?'

That was when the girl turned suddenly around, her voice hoarse and unsettling. 'The water demon gave me the lotus flower,' she said. 'I met the water demon.'

This story circulated all summer. If she were to relate it herself it would be incomprehensible, so it's better if I summarize it. In fact, it was a very simple story: the Deng girl had met the water demon. Not only that, he had even given her a red lotus flower.

A very large red lotus flower.

Atmospheric Pressure

The train was late. Under the dim lamplight, the platform was cast in half shadow. As Meng left the train, a snowflake floated down and landed on his neck. The wind was blowing open his coat at the bottom. It produced a whistling sound which reminded him that the weather here in Tiancheng was colder than he'd expected. Bag in hand, he walked with the throng towards the station exit, and though he kept looking around him, he couldn't spot the brick Song Dynasty tower that he remembered. Beside the darkness and the lamplight, he saw nothing but the ungainly contours of the high-rises, which looked the same here as everywhere else. No doubt the buildings had blocked his view of the tower.

The station square, covered in snow and mud, was almost empty, since the people, cars, pedicabs and bikes were all crowded chaotically up against the railings by the station exit. The people all seemed so familiar to Meng, though every last one of them was a stranger. He set down his bag, a little surprised that he couldn't find his cousin waiting for him outside the railings. He glanced again at his watch; he was two hours late, and it occurred to him that his cousin and the others might have gone somewhere to kill time.

Suddenly someone tugged at his arm through the railings: 'Comrade, do you need a place to stay?' It was a middle-aged woman with an accent that marked her as a non-local; there were also several others, similar women holding signs, soliciting for this guesthouse or that hostel.

'I don't need any accommodation. I'm a local, myself.'

But then he began to laugh, because even he could hear how stiff his dialect had sounded. After more than ten years away, he could no longer speak it.

Meng smoked two cigarettes. The people who had come to the station to meet arrivals had all departed, and still Meng hadn't caught sight of his cousin nor, for that matter, any of his other relatives. He had no idea what could have happened. Meanwhile, the wind, sweeping in off the square, had a bone-chilling edge to it, and Meng was growing a little anxious. So when he saw a battered old Chinese-made van drive up and stop by the entrance to a public bathroom, it raised his hopes. As soon as the man got out of the van, however, his spirits sank again. He watched as the man walked towards the station exit, the sign in his hand growing clearer and clearer as he approached. It said, 'No. 2 Education Hostel. Excellent service. First-class facilities. Low price. Discount for teachers.'

Meng looked around and heard several of the guesthouse women urgently expounding something to him. He paid no attention to them; he didn't need to. Even if he didn't have anywhere to go tonight, he still wasn't going to put himself up randomly in some dive. He evaded one of the pestering women and turned to look at the big billboards on the square. They were left over from the summer season: one of them showed a striking girl in revealing clothes holding a bottle of something and grinning at the passers-by. The slogan was even more summery: 'Refreshing to the core'. Meng smiled involuntarily, which was when he noticed the guy from the van again. The man was smiling, too, smiling at him and waving the sign he held in his hands. His eyes motioned for Meng to read it, but Meng shook his head and said, 'I'm not a teacher.' Without a word, the man flipped the sign over. There was something else written on the other side: 'Everything you need: home-style comfort, colour TV. Air con, sauna/massage.'

The man's face seemed familiar to Meng, particularly the smile, which looked a little stiff. He concentrated and fixed his eyes on the man for a moment. Suddenly an odd term popped into his mind: atmospheric pressure. Meng was suddenly positive that the man was his high-school physics teacher. He wanted to call out to him by name, but once he'd opened his mouth, he realized that he had forgotten it. His surname was Di, or was it Ding? Or maybe even neither? Meng just couldn't call it to mind. Instead, he could only recall the nickname they had given him: Diesel. Meng felt a little sheepish although, whatever the look on his face, it must have given the man some grounds for hope, since Diesel – let that be his provisional name – winked at Meng and said, 'On a freezing day like this, what's the point of standing around here shivering? Why don't you come to our guesthouse. You won't regret it. We're a school-run guesthouse, and you can bet the people's teachers aren't out to cheat the people.'

Meng gave a little laugh at the sound of Diesel's voice – it was the sonorous kind people sometimes call a 'mallard voice'. Diesel looked Meng over before squatting down. A cotton-gloved hand came through the bars and started to drag Meng's travel bag away.

Diesel said, 'We have a special car for pick-ups and drop-offs. On a day as cold as today, I don't want to loiter around here either. If you come along with me, we'll head off immediately, OK? How does that sound?' Meng reflexively grabbed his bag, while a strange urge to apologize flustered him.

'Sorry. Sorry. I'm not accustomed to staying in guest-houses like yours.'

Diesel's eyes flashed. He stood up and, still wearing his stiff smile, looked right at Meng. 'Guesthouses like ours?' he said. 'Sir, I would suggest that you have no right to judge without having seen it. What makes you think the conditions will not be to your liking? Our hostel operates under the aegis of the ministry of education. We're not like these others; we don't take anyone for a ride. If it says central heating, there's central heating; if it says colour TV, there's colour TV; if it says hot water, there's hot water!'

This impatience reminded Meng of what physics class had been like long ago. 'Atmospheric. Pressure. Who's that talking? Whoever doesn't want to be here can bugger off right now!'

Meng had concluded that Diesel didn't have the faintest recollection of him, but it was for precisely that reason that his inner urge to apologize was even greater.

'That's not what I meant. I'm not a big fan of TV. Actually . . . actually, I'm only staying one night. The facilities don't really matter as long as it's clean.'

He saw a frosty smile play on the corner of Diesel's mouth, a smile just like the one he used to wear whenever he entered the classroom, their exercise books stacked under his arm.

'How do you know we're not clean? I'll have you know we're a model of hygiene.' Diesel looked a little angry now. 'You think I'm a cheat, do you? I was a people's teacher for thirty years; I sacrifice time in my declining years to do a little something for society, and you accuse me of coming down here just to con people. Is that it?'

Meng began to feel uncomfortable; the sense of desperation that Diesel used to provoke in physics class returned vividly. Meng had never been able to answer his questions correctly, and Diesel had had a special proclivity for asking him. Meng wondered why he had recognized Diesel at first glance, but still Diesel hadn't recognized him? The women outside the gates were exchanging confidential whispers; they shot reproachful glances at him which seemed to mean, How come you let him butt in? Meng blushed deeply and carried his luggage around for a moment inside the railing, then he glanced at Diesel, but Diesel wasn't looking at him; he was slapping his sign against the railing. You could tell that his teacherly anger had not yet cooled. Meng took another few tentative steps. Then, in the space of a moment, an uncharacteristic decision became reality. He walked up to Diesel and said, 'OK. I'll stay the night at your guesthouse.'

Absolutely everything about the city had changed. Development is a hard truth. The city had turned into an endless succession of construction sites and neon lights. He bumped around in the battered van for about half an hour, then it stopped and he heard Diesel say, 'We're here. I said it wasn't far, didn't I? This is the old town. In the thirties, this was the commercial hub of Tiancheng.'

Meng had no idea where he was. The whole city now consisted of indistinguishable demolition zones. The ground was covered in rubbish and broken bricks, and only a few reusable wooden doors and windows were tidily stacked. And when there are no longer any buildings or trees by which to tell your way, it's inevitable that you lose your orientation.

'Where the hell are we? Where the hell is this?'

He saw a three-storey building standing solitary in the rubble, with lights on only one floor. 'This is a waste-land.'

Diesel didn't respond, but wrested Meng's luggage from him and ran towards the building, shouting, 'Miss Zhang! A room!'

The guesthouse was filled with a raw, damp smell. A woman at reception was huddling against an electric heater, and she looked over at Meng with a glance neither defiant nor apologetic.

Meng stood hesitating at the counter: 'From the looks of things, you couldn't possibly have central heating here.'

The woman said, 'There's air conditioning.'

Meng said, 'What was all that about first-class facilities? From what I can see, you don't have any facilities here at all.'

The woman looked at Meng, then over at Diesel, then she puckered her lips into a smile.

Meng continued, 'They tore down all the other build-ings around here. How come they're not tearing yours down? This place looks illegal.'

Before he had even finished his sentence, he felt a hard shove on the shoulder. It was Diesel. Looking at him angrily he said, 'Is that any way to talk, sir? If you want a room, then fine, but if you don't, bugger off. But to come here and insult people! Illegal! What do you mean, illegal? What kind of people do you take us for, huh?'

Meng reflexively took a step backwards. 'I was just joking. There's no need to get all worked up.'

Diesel was still glaring. 'That's no way to joke with anybody. When you make a joke, you don't do it at the expense of other people's dignity, do you understand?'

Meng said mockingly, 'Yup. Got it. Got it, all right.'

Meng had already retreated to the exit and was looking out through the glass doors. It was pitch black outside and the little van had already left. He could not rid himself of the feeling that he had been taken for a fool, and this thought made him baulk. He stood by the window and scratched his head. The woman suddenly gave a cough and said, 'If you don't want to stay here, we're not going to force you. If you go out the door and walk four hundred metres, there's a hotel that's in a little better shape.'

Meng looked at her gratefully and asked, 'Do they have central heating there?' But before the woman could answer, Diesel glowered at him and shouted, 'This is Tiancheng, not Beijing. What the hell kind of central heating do you expect? You're lucky to have air con!' Meng shook his head. The sound of Diesel's voice still held an awesome power over him – 'Atmospheric pressure! If you can't do it, then that's that! Don't try to fake your way out of it!' he remembered.

Meng wondered what attitude Diesel would adopt if he recognized him. He gave the door a push and then quietly closed it again.

'It's really cold out. Why is Tiancheng so cold nowadays?'

Diesel rolled his eyes at him, which seemed to mean he wouldn't deign to respond to such stupid questions.

'I lived here for eight years; I went to school here,' Meng remarked.

He saw how Diesel's exceedingly hostile expression grew somewhat milder, then he gave a snort and said, 'Well, then, that's good. You're a native son returning from his travels. You ought to have some feelings for Tiancheng, so what's with the snooty airs? Complaining about this, that and the other.' Meng watched Diesel, hoping he would expound upon his theme, that he would ask him where he had lived and what high school he had gone to, but Diesel picked up a newspaper and seemed unwilling to continue the conversation. This, too, conformed to Meng's recollection of the man, for if memory served him right, he had never been eager to forgive a student who had crossed him. He was a person who made others feel awkward and that much hadn't changed. Meng scratched his head, still hesitating. In the end, it was the receptionist who tactfully convinced him. She said, 'It's late and awfully cold; I think it's best if you stay here the night.'

The room was as crude and dilapidated as Meng had

expected. The patterned sheets and cotton quilt were damp to the touch. There was a Peacock TV at least a dozen years old, and with the colours distorted so the female broadcaster acquired a green face and lips that looked like they had been smeared with blood, a horrifying shade of red. The only surprise was the presence of a balcony, and quite a sizeable one at that; a solitary luxury feature futilely fixed outside the window. Diesel turned the air-conditioning on with the remote, which he then slipped into his pocket. Noticing the surprised expression on his guest's face, he began to explain the guesthouse rules and regulations.

'I can't do anything about it. It's not that I don't trust you, but we've already lost four remotes.'

'Do you really think I'm going steal your remote?'

Diesel shook his head, 'Not that *you* would steal it. I just told you, didn't I? Those are our rules. After I turn on the air con, I have to take it with me.'

'You really don't trust me, do you? When all is said and done, what you're afraid of is that I'll run off with your remote.'

'Hmph! You, sir, have an unpleasant way with words. Everyone has to obey the regulations. I'm on duty today, and if the remote control gets lost, it's me who has to replace it.'

At this Meng laughed out loud. 'No matter how you put it, you're still afraid you'll have to replace it, right?' Meng's attitude seemed to amuse Diesel. Keeping a protective hand on his pocket, he walked self-consciously towards the door, as if to effect an escape. Meng, behind him, said, 'We should have a chat. Can I talk with you?' But Diesel didn't turn back; he just waved him off with his hand and said, 'No. You should rest.' Meng followed him out the door, but by that time his figure was already disappearing down the stairs; the little old man had made a break for it, just like a child. Meng could appreciate how he felt. Actually, he wasn't at all certain he wanted to chat with this one-time teacher, especially given that their student-teacher relationship had long since vanished, like mist in the morning. Nor did he have any clue what it was they should talk about.

Through the window, he could see that snow had fallen on the balcony. A mop was propped up in one corner; it even had a plastic bag over it. Meng paced around the room and considered giving his cousin a ring, but quickly discarded the idea. The air-conditioning was purring along. Meng put his hand in front of the air vent, but it was still blowing cold. The temperature in the room hadn't changed. He reflected that this was not fated to be an evening to enjoy; he was mentally prepared for further unpleasantness. Perhaps Diesel had been right: a native son returning from his travels should be generous in his judgements. Meng opened the door onto the balcony and a gust of cold wind blew in his face. He nearly abandoned the thought of going out, but then he realized that it looked out over a school or, to be more accurate, the

229

sports grounds of a school. And suddenly he felt he had seen it before.

The sports ground was only 20 metres away, and the fallen snow could not obscure the oval outline of a running track. In the nocturnal haze, you could also clearly make out the straight lines of horizontal and parallel bars. The school, too, was clearly on the demolition list, since already certain buildings were skeletal, the doors and windows removed. A very high flagpole stood loftily in the nightscape, but the flag had been struck, too. Meng followed the flagpole down with his eye. He could just make out the stairs leading up to the platform. They were covered in snow, and from a distance emitted a shimmering white light. Déjà vu. Meng turned his head to look out to the north-west, and it was then that he saw the black form of the brick Song Dynasty tower, facing the flagpole in the distance. Meng's orientation in the city suddenly returned, and he was certain that the school he was looking at was Eastern Wind High School, his own high school.

He could still remember that the length of the track at Eastern Wind was 375 metres, making it 25 metres shorter than the track and field standard. That was something his P.E. teacher had told him back then; he had been greatly impressed by the talent Meng had exhibited for the longer distances. Meng looked down on the snowy sports grounds and hazily made out a white-vested adolescent dashing along the track – 375 metres – four laps to make exactly 1500. That had been his best event. That was his former life. Meng shouted out in a strange voice at the abandoned sports grounds; they looked totally desolate in the night. Some concrete prefab slabs were piled where the sandpit was located. Someone had built a snowman on the pile, exacerbating the desolate look of the grounds. A native son returning from his travels. Meng suddenly contemplated the odd chance that led him to witness this unnatural scene. He laughed and thought, I'm not that kind of person. I won't bear the cold any longer just to indulge in nostalgia. Everything is coincidence. And what is coincidence? Why, coincidence is coincidence.

There had still been no change in the room temperature. Meng realized quickly that although the air con was blowing air, it hadn't been set to heat. He walked out into the corridor and called downstairs, 'Hey, you! There's a problem with the air con. Can you come up and have a look?' He was surprised at how he had addressed Diesel. No matter what, he shouldn't have just shouted 'hey, you'. There was the sound of languid steps on the staircase, then Diesel emerged in his sweater, holding the remote. He looked as though he had been sleeping.

'What's wrong with the air con?' he asked. 'Isn't it working? Why should there be a problem?' From his expression, Meng could see that he was in a mood to make himself unpleasant. He seemed to suspect Meng of making things up just to pick a fight.

The smile disappeared from Meng's face: 'Come see for yourself if there's a problem or not.'

Diesel was clearly only superficially acquainted with the air con. Meng watched as he pressed randomly at the buttons on the remote. The fan suddenly coughed and died. 'Crud,' Diesel shouted suddenly, 'Is it locked? It's locked, isn't it?'

Meng said, 'It's an air con machine, not a camera. It doesn't have an automatic lock.' He motioned for Diesel to hand him the remote, but was ignored. Diesel was still anxiously hitting the buttons, then he uttered, 'Young people think they know everything. Just because it's air con and not a camera it doesn't have an automatic lock. Is that a scientific way of thinking?' Meng gave a small laugh, 'Let me give it a try.' He held his palm open and asked, 'Do you think I could have a try?' He watched as Diesel's nostrils convulsed for a moment before he suddenly placed the remote in his hand. 'You want to try? OK, go ahead and try,' Diesel said. 'If I can't get it started, let's see you do it.'

His totally unnecessary anger reminded Meng once more of the long-ago physics class. It was with exactly that kind of annoyance that he had taught the principle of siphonage. The atmosphere. Pressure. Atmospheric pressure. Meng couldn't resist joshing him, and remarked, 'Maybe there isn't enough atmospheric pressure.'

But Diesel didn't take it as a joke and sniggered coolly, 'That's what young people are like today, throwing around concepts they know next to nothing about.'

Meng suddenly felt himself in a tight corner. Under Diesel's mocking eyes he pressed the remote control buttons but failed to reanimate the exasperating air con. It seemed to have given up the ghost. Scratching his head, he said, 'Could it be that it needs a new battery?'

Then he heard Diesel's pleased voice once again, 'Impossible.'

'And why is it impossible?'

Diesel grabbed the remote from Meng's hands and said, 'It's impossible because it's impossible. We put in a new battery just last week!'

Diesel's victorious expression irritated Meng. Sitting down on the bed, he looked on at Diesel with the remote in his hands. 'If there's no air con, how am I supposed to sleep? You said there was air con. But after all your talk, this air con is a piece of crap.' Diesel still energetically pressed the buttons on the remote, while at the same time motioning to Meng to be patient for a moment. 'Don't keep pressing them if you don't know what you're doing. It's definitely broken. Just give me a new room, OK?'

Diesel threw a glance at Meng and, seeing his gloomy expression, he said, 'This is the only room with air con. There's nothing I can do; you'll just have to put up with it.'

233

Meng gave a strange laugh and said, 'Great! Put up with a freezing room all night.'

Diesel turned and stared sternly at Meng, then gave a renunciatory smile. With a darting movement, he returned the remote to his pocket and walked out. 'We'll take off the fee for air con,' he said loudly, 'So I'll ask you not to regard me as a cheat, thank you very much.'

With that the door was flung heavily back. Meng sat on the bed, thoroughly dejected, not only because of his frosty room, but also because it seemed to him that the experiences of the evening were the wages of a journey conceived in error. He had plainly wanted to go south, but despite himself he had gone north. This was nothing like a reunion with a former teacher ought to be. Perhaps he should tell him the truth, but Meng doubted there was any point now in invoking their common past. No, it was definitely pointless. The reality staring Meng in the face was this: he was compelled to spend a night in this polar room. Only later could he allow this encounter to become a memory.

He entwined himself in the blankets to go to sleep. He was young and actually not all that easily affected by the cold. He had even imagined Diesel would say something to that effect: 'Young people can put up with a little cold; it won't kill you.' But Diesel hadn't said that; he was someone who made you feel awkward, but he wasn't harsh or rude. He had been that way in the past, and he was that way now. Meng soon fell asleep. Had he spent a dreamless night, then perhaps things wouldn't have happened as they did. But Meng dreamed of an exam, and in the dream he needed very badly to take a leak, so he pushed back the examination paper and stood up. He got out of bed and walked in a daze into the corridor, heading towards the bathroom door. Shivering and standing by the piss trough, he heard the sound of a door slamming in a gust of wind. The sound didn't register with him immediately, but when he got back to his room he found the door wouldn't open. There must have been a problem with the lock, because now he couldn't get back in. The night was transforming into a long series of tribulations. He was in his underwear and beginning to shiver in earnest. He hugged his shoulders and, facing down the stairs, yelled loudly, 'Hurry! Bring the key up! I'm locked out!'

After about a minute, Diesel appeared in the corridor, eyes heavy with sleep.

'What now? Why did you close the door when you went out? You should keep it open.'

Meng said, 'I didn't close it; the wind blew it shut. Everything in this place is broken. Even the door lock is broken!' Meng gave Diesel a sidelong glance, as if he intended some response, but he said nothing and instead dangled his keychain from his hand.

'Go to the duty room and put an overcoat on. Watch that you don't catch cold.'

Meng said, 'No need for that. Just hurry up and open

235

the door.' Then came the greatest surprise. Meng watched as Diesel kept passing back and forth through the keys; he couldn't seem to find the right one. 'What now?' Hugging both shoulders, Meng pressed in close in order to look at the keys. 'Tell me you haven't lost it.'

Diesel raised his head, and from his dismayed expression he could see that his guess had hit the mark. Diesel exclaimed, 'It's ridiculous! Ridiculous! What happened to the key?'

Meng almost leapt to his feet, 'Everything has to happen to me! What terrible luck! Enough bad luck to last me eight lifetimes!' He saw that Diesel's expression had become extremely disagreeable, but he was past caring. He rubbed his hands, stamped his feet and said, 'Enough bad luck to last me eight lifetimes!' Diesel stared blankly for a moment, then suddenly took off down the stairs, and as he ran he said, 'I'll get that overcoat for you first.' But Meng was enraged, and he screamed at Diesel's back, 'What good is an overcoat? I want to get into my room.' Shouting was not enough to cool his anger, though, so he delivered a flying kick to the door.

'They should close down hostels like this, and the sooner the better!'

It was very quiet in the hostel. Except for the sound of the wind outside, Meng could hear only the fragmentary, hectic sounds coming from the duty room. He lifted up his eyes and heaved a sigh heavy with resentment. Before long, a flustered Diesel was hurrying up the stairs carrying a padded army overcoat, which he tossed over to him, saying, 'Please don't shout. Shouting isn't going to help.' Meng wrapped the overcoat around his shoulders and found that it was still quite warm; Diesel had no doubt been using it as a blanket. Now that he had something to ward off the cold, Meng's mood took a slight turn for the better. Looking at the keys in Diesel's hand he said, 'That's fine. You made me come and stay here. First-class facilities. First-class service. I didn't realize you were going to make me stand in the hallway and shiver till dawn.' Meng saw that Diesel's head was beginning to sway back and forth and that his eyes were shooting out a dreadful, scorching fury, a fury far exceeding that of the remembered physics teacher. He began to regret his excessive words, but it was too late for regret, for all of a sudden Diesel hurled the keys to the ground. Then, dragging over a chair that stood in the corridor, he sprang on top of it. Meng realized now that he was planning to go through the window above the door; it hadn't occurred to him that Diesel might resort to such a method. As he watched Diesel clumsily push the window open, Meng felt he shouldn't let Diesel do such a thing for him, but strangely the words that came out of his mouth were something entirely different: 'I bet the window's locked tight, too.' Diesel's back, which was hanging in mid-air, trembled a moment, then he suddenly struck the window and it opened with a clatter. Diesel turned his head to shoot Meng a contemptuous glance. Meng evaded his look, turning away in embarrassment. In the periphery of his vision, however, he could see Diesel's head go through the window, then his legs and chubby torso all squeezed through while his feet kicked and swayed outside. Meng could see Diesel's old-fashioned, cotton-lined shoes, torn at the toe, and the worn-through nylon socks. Above him, he could hear his panting. Only now did Meng make a tardy gesture, grabbing Diesel's feet and protesting, 'Never mind. Don't go up there. I'll go through the window myself.' But Diesel's feet kicked free of his hands; Meng could feel the anger residing in them. Then he watched as they slowly disappeared through the window; Diesel's whole body had finally passed through the narrow window. At the same time, dust from the window frame and from Diesel's coat streamed onto the ground.

Diesel opened the door from the inside. Meng, standing outside, turned sideways, avoiding Diesel's eyes. Diesel opened his mouth wide to pant and said, 'Come in then. What are you standing outside for? Huh? I've opened the door, haven't I?'

Meng stood motionlessly. He saw Diesel rush at him, and suddenly fell prey to the illusion that the man would strike him, but Diesel just pushed him into the room. Then he began brushing the dust off his own clothes, saying, 'What were you standing out there for? You're the guest; I'm here to serve. You locked yourself out and I climbed through the window to let you in. What is it you're considering now? Do you want to swear at me some more?'

Meng grew hot in the face, and said haltingly, 'I didn't swear at you. Why would I swear at you?'

Diesel again gave Meng a hard push and said, 'Well, if you didn't swear at me then that's all right.' And then, 'Now, young man, get into bed and go to sleep.'

Diesel closed the door behind him. Meng heard him pick the keys up outside the door and move the chair back to its original position, then there was silence. Meng stood in the room and had a premonition that the affair would not conclude in silence; and indeed, Diesel's voice suddenly broke out in the corridor, a voice of suffering and complaint.

'Young man, let me tell you something. I'm sixty years old this year! You would let me crawl through the window, huh? You let me crawl through the window!'

Meng left the hostel soon after dawn. The woman at reception was only half awake. She showed understanding for his early departure and commented, 'I guess you didn't sleep too well. This place used to be quite all right, but they're about to knock it down and these last couple of business days have been a little chaotic.' Meng chuckled and said, 'It was only one night, in any case, it's over with now. I'll get a good sleep tonight.' In the duty room he saw a folding bed with Diesel's body underneath the overcoat. He couldn't see his face, though he could hear the light puff of his snoring. Indicating the bed with his mouth, he asked the woman, 'Is the old man's name Di?'

The woman said, 'No, it's Chen, C-H-E-N. Why? Was there something wrong with his attitude?'

Meng shook his head, 'That's not what I meant. Can I ask something? Did he used to teach physics at Eastern Wind High School?'

The woman responded, 'Well, he used to be a teacher, but whether it was at Eastern Wind, or if he taught physics, that I don't know.' The woman looked at him with curiosity. 'Were you his student? Wake him up and ask him, then you'll know for sure.'

Meng waved his hand and said, 'Never mind. I'm not sure myself. He might have been the physics teacher, then again he might not. I don't really remember.'

The woman seemed quite eager to clear up the identity of her co-worker, 'Wake him up. I'll wake him up myself.'

Meng stopped her with a cry that was almost one of fright, 'No, no!' he said, 'Let him sleep. I still have lots of things to see to. I should go.'

Meng opened the door of the guesthouse. Outside, the ground was a single stretch of mire – ice and snow – and the winter sunlight illuminated the city that he hadn't seen for so long. It was a place he had once lived, but to know whether any trace of him had remained in the disorder of the rubble, you would have had to ask the rubble itself. Meng didn't know. But in the morning Meng was as vigorous as the morning itself, and yesterday's moodiness was left behind with yesterday. He walked quickly towards the road, and discovered to his surprise that the sun, which shone so splendidly over the city, hung by some good fortune right over the famous Song Dynasty tower.

A Xiali taxi appeared out of nowhere and turned to approach Meng. The driver poked his head out the window and looked out at him. Meng took a few leisurely steps to the taxi window and asked, 'Do you have a meter?'

And this time he spoke in genuine Tiancheng dialect.

The Q of Hearts

There are some people whose thieving habits simply cannot be corrected. This kind of problem was especially serious in Mahogany Street, which is where I am from. If you broke your vigil for even a moment, your salted fish, cigarettes or even your broom might vanish from your home. So when I found I was missing the Q of Hearts from my deck of cards, I immediately assumed that someone had stolen it.

You don't know how I loved those cards. It was 1969, and they were my only toys. My brother and I often played a game called Lucky with them. When you play cards, you can't afford to be missing even a single one from the deck, and for exactly that reason I had written my name on the back of every card. I had thought that now no one would dare to steal them, but I was wrong. When I asked my brother about the whereabouts of my Q of Hearts he said, 'Who cares if you lose a card? Fat Man Li's kid from our school's lost and no one's looking for him, who the hell's going to help you look for a stupid old card?' But from his expression I could tell that there was something fishy going on. A few days before, he had asked me to lend him ten cents and I had ignored him. I suspected that he had stolen the Q of Hearts in spiteful revenge. Entertaining these suspicions, I extended my hand under his pillow. There was a drawer beneath the bedding, and I began to rummage in it. You should know that my brother has a bad temper and he suddenly cried out, 'You think I'm a frigging cow demon? You frigging looking through my things?' And as he spoke he aimed an angry kick at my bum.

After that we started wrestling. Of course I was the one who ended up bawling. My brother, seeing that the situation was beyond help, leaped out the window and landed on the street outside. Through the window, he said, 'Don't be a baby. What's the big deal about a card? It's just a Q of Hearts. I'll get you another one sometime, OK?'

My brother was the king of big talk, and even supposing he meant it, I didn't believe he could get his hands on that Q of Hearts. The year was 1969, and the city was going through some kind of weird revolution. People had abandoned all entertainment, the streets were empty and the shop doors were all left slightly ajar. You could have walked clear through the city without seeing a trace of a playing card. Imagine a day in the winter of 1969: the snow is falling fast and there is a child walking along Clothmarket Street – which was called Red Flag Street then – pausing frequently and pulling himself up to every counter along the way to gaze up at the goods on the shelves. The storekeeper says, 'Well now, what does the little comrade want?' To which the child replies, 'Playing cards.' Then the storekeeper frowns and says in an aggravated tone, 'As if we'd stock playing cards. Nothing of the kind.'

The reason I relate my search for the playing cards in such detail is that I want you to believe that everything I say really happened.

I went with my father to Shanghai for no other reason than to buy a new deck of cards. It took about two hours by train to get there from our home city. Though it was the first time in my life that I had been on a train, I have no recollection about how I felt. Besides, a trip of two hours was too short for to me remember anything apart from my father talking about rubber and steel or something to the man sitting next to him. They talked and talked until the train stopped, and then we were in Shanghai.

Shanghai in 1969 was a dusky, dead city. My saying that is actually mostly a literary deduction, since besides the tan buildings with the clocks and big domes, and the wooden rack for putting bean products on that I saw near the hotel, I have almost no recollection of the streets of Shanghai as I saw them on that trip. My father was on official business, and I followed him down the big streets, looking intently at the displays in the windows of every store we passed. It shouldn't surprise you that, although it was 1969, Shanghai's stores were more like *real* stores than the ones we had at home, with soap, toilet paper, sweets and cakes all neatly laid out on the shelves. A few times, I saw something that at first glance looked like the little cardboard boxes playing cards come in, but as soon as I ran over to take a better look, they would turn out to be either a package of pain-killing cream or cigarettes. Weren't there any playing cards in Shanghai, either? Shanghai had no playing cards, and this was a discovery that disappointed me through and through. I thought of how the women on Mahogany Street were always cawing and crowing about the things you could get in Shanghai. From the way they talked, Shanghai should have been a city stocked with everything anyone could want. Now it seemed it had been an outright lie.

As I said, my father was on official business, so he didn't have time to take me into the stores to look for cards; he had to finish up his affairs before everyone got off work for the day. In front of a large beige concrete building covered with hanging slogan banners, my father let go of my hand and pushed me up to the window of the registration room. To the middle-aged woman inside, he said, 'I have to go up to your revolutionary committee to see about some arrangements; look after my son while I'm gone.'

I saw the woman's detached glanced sweep over us and a snort issued from her nostrils. 'Taking your son with you on business! Is that any way to go about things?'

My father was in no mood to justify himself. Carrying his black briefcase, he sprinted up the stairs and left me alone in the strange concrete building, standing in a strange woman's cold glare.

I saw that there was a pot of water in the registration room giving off puffs of steam, and that the water was boiling over a little. The several red flags and the portrait of Mao Zedong on the wall seemed damp and hazy. Beneath her desk, the woman was making some kind of mechanical movement with both hands; occasionally she looked at me askance. I very much wanted to know what she was doing and so, supporting myself on the sill, I jumped up to see. One pale hand gripped a circular embroidery frame, while the other pale hand held a needle and thread. I even saw the red flower on the white silk; a large, half-finished red flower.

'What are you doing?' The woman had noticed my hop, and with an action that was almost fearful, she threw down the things in her hands. Then she stuck out one hand to grab me by the arm, but I managed to escape her. Something ferocious lit up in her eyes as she picked up a piece of chalk from her desk and threw it at me, and with great anger in her voice she said, 'You little spy! You little mole! Nasty brat! Get lost!'

I ran to the other side of the road. I thought the woman very weird: weird for secretly embroidering under the office desk and weird for her volcanic anger. What did I care what she was hiding her hands for? She was just embroidering a flower. Why did she have to do it on the sly? If I had known she was just embroidering, I wouldn't have taken the trouble to look. The problem was that she didn't know what I had had in mind. In fact, when I had lifted myself up to look at her hands, I had hoped to see a playing card; maybe even the Q of Hearts.

And so it was that the first time I went to Shanghai, I was filled with an immense sense of loss. My father took me by the hand and walked me angrily through the streets. He said, 'Playing cards! Playing cards! Don't you know that's the feudocapitalistic plaything of revisionists? A very bad thing!'

I am now certain that the hostel we stayed in on that occasion was near the Bund or the Huangpu River, because during the night I heard the great Customs House clock strike and the sound of whistles from the little steamboats and cargo ships. I also remember that there were three beds in the hostel, and over each bed was hung a tent-like mosquito net which would usually be for summer use. Besides my father and me, there was another man with a northern accent and a full beard as hard as hog bristles.

Initially, I slept by myself in one bed. The light was on, and outside my window, the wail of the city descended into darkness. I couldn't see anything outside; I could only see through the mosquito net to the wall of the room. The wall was off-white, and on it was a Patriotic

248

Hygiene Month propaganda drawing. It seemed to me that the man grasping a fly-swatter on the drawing looked a lot like Cathead from our street – Cathead might also have been connected with the stolen Q of Hearts, another likely suspect – and so I pondered the question of Cathead and the Q of Hearts. Then suddenly I saw the bloodstain. It was like a map that had been printed on the wall, right against the mosquito net and only a palm's width from the edge my pillow.

'There's blood on the wall!' I cried out loudly to my father, who was lying on the next bed over.

'What blood?' My father raised himself up slightly on his bed and gave it a cursory glance. 'It's mosquito blood,' he said. 'Someone killed the mosquitoes in summer and the blood stuck to the wall.'

'It's not mosquito blood.' I examined the bloodstain with no little fear. 'Who ever heard of so much blood coming from a mosquito?'

'Don't worry about it. Close your eyes and have a good sleep. They'll turn off the light in a second,' my father said.

I saw the hog-bristle man extract himself from the mosquito net. He ran over to my bed in a few steps and lifted the mosquito net up over my bed. 'You mean this bloodspot?' First he glanced at me, and then he directed his shining gaze at the bloodspot on the wall. I saw him make an alarming action: he put his index finger in his mouth and kept it there for a moment. Then, he cold-bloodedly extended it to scrape off some of the blood before returning it to his mouth. Next I saw him frown slightly and spit on the floor.

'It's human blood.' He jumped back into his own bed and chuckled from inside the net. 'Human blood. As soon as I saw it, I knew that's what it was.'

For a moment, the dread made my heart beat madly in my breast and I threw myself into my father's bed and said nothing, covering myself under his blankets.

'It must have spurted up from someone's head; I could tell as soon as I saw it,' the hog-bristle man said. 'If you use an awl to crack open someone's head, that's exactly what the blood looks like when it spatters on the wall. And if you swing your belt at someone it's about the same. I could tell as soon as I saw it. They must have detained somebody here.'

'Impossible. This is a hostel,' my father said.

'You think you can't detain people in hostels?' The hog-bristle man emitted another contemptuous laugh and said, 'I guess you haven't been around for much of all this. They detained someone in our unit's bathhouse, and the blood there isn't on the wall, it's on the ceiling. On the ceiling! Do you know how human blood gets on a ceiling? If you haven't seen it with your own eyes, you'll never guess.'

'Never mind that. I'm with my son.' My father said, interrupting his monologue. 'I'm with my son and kids are easily frightened.'

Then the man stopped speaking. The lights were turned off and the hostel rooms suddenly sank into darkness. Even the bloodspot on the wall fell into the oblivion. Except for an unclear whitish glare, I could see nothing on the walls now. I heard the hog-bristle man on the bed across from me snoring thickly, and then my father started snoring too.

Kids are easily frightened. The whole night I clasped my father's arm, imagining the events that had happened in the hostel, imagining one person bleeding and another one holding an awl or a belt. For a long while I couldn't fall asleep. I remember clearly being in Shanghai and hearing the midnight toll of a clock and thinking that it must be the sound of the famous clock on the Customs House.

The next day there was no sun in Shanghai, and the sky looked like a greyish iron sheet covering the tops of the high buildings and telephone poles. My father, grasping a slip of paper, took me back and forth through an enormous emporium. On the paper was a list of knitting wool, bedsheets, leather shoes including sizes, plus other such products – a list entrusted to my father by my neighbours, for him to make purchases on their behalf. In that building, which still held obvious traces of colonial taste, the people were as many and as jumbled as the goods for sale. At the leather shoes counter, I very nearly lost my father. I had gone up to the stationery counter, mistakenly thinking that a box of paper clips might contain playing cards. When I returned, crestfallen, to sit on the shoe-trial stool, I saw that the person sitting next to me was no longer my father, but a stranger in a blue woollen tunic suit.

At this point I opened my mouth wide, stood on the chair and wailed. My bewildered father rushed over, threw down what he was carrying and gave me a couple of spanks. He said, 'I told you not to run off, and what did you do? How many times have I told you? This is Shanghai. If you get lost, no one will find you.' I said that I hadn't run off, I had been looking for some cards. My father made no further recriminations, but took me by the hand, and in silence we set off towards the exit. 'There aren't any cards in Shanghai, either,' he said, as if to himself. 'Maybe you can get some in the little towns and villages. When I get sent to Jiangxi I'll take a look for you, OK?'

To cheer me up my father took me to the banks of the Huangpu River to look at the boats. When we reached the river, a slushy rain began to fall and there were few pedestrians along the Bund. We walked along the iron railings, and I saw for the first time the river heading out to sea. The water was a greyish yellow with ripples of oil; I was thoroughly disillusioned, for it was the complete opposite of what I had imagined. I also saw a great many gulls, with their slender, nimble wings; their cries were a hundred times more sonorous than those of the sparrows outside our eaves in the trees of Mahogany Street. It was the boats that excited the most profound excitement though, both those moored and those moving about the river; their masts, portholes, smokestacks, anchor posts, not to mention the colourful flags whistling in the wind. It seemed to me that they were no different from those I had drawn in my sketchbook.

After that, it was just rain and snow swirling down onto the Shanghai streets, all the way until my father climbed onto the short-distance train, which was the abrupt conclusion to my Shanghai trip. Also, the wretched weather made the afternoon darken prematurely, and my impressions of the road home are of gloom and cold.

The carriage was almost entirely empty, and every wooden seat seemed to exude its own chill. We started off sitting in the middle of the carriage, but one of the glass windows had been shattered and so my father led me to the back, near the bathroom, where the faint smell of piss could be detected, but it was warmer. I recall that when my father took off his blue woollen tunic suit to drape over me, I asked him, 'Isn't there anyone on the train? Just us two?' and my father said, 'The weather's bad today and it's a slow train, so there aren't so many people.'

Just as the train was about to depart, four men suddenly boarded. Carrying with them the outside chill they burst into the carriage; the three young men were wearing padded army overcoats, and only the old one, who was wearing a gauze mask, had on a blue cotton tunic suit like my father's. As soon as they came in I knew that it was snowing hard, for I saw that their hats and shoulders were covered in large flakes.

This is what I wanted to tell you about: these sudden arrivals, especially the man in the mask, who was constantly being pressed and jostled by the three others. They passed us and chose the seats in the middle of the carriage, where we had been sitting before; they didn't seem to mind the cold. I saw the old man sitting between two of his companions. He began to turn his head towards us, but before he could finish this movement his grey head was jerked back by something. Across two rows of seats, I could see his stiff back; one of the others took his hat off to shake the snow off, but that was all – I didn't hear them speak a single word.

'Who are they?' I asked my father.

'I don't know.' My father, too, watched detachedly, but he wouldn't let me stand up to have a closer look, just saying, 'Sit down. You're not allowed to walk over there; and don't stare.'

The train sped through the wind and snow of 1969, along open country. Outside the window was almost nocturnal darkness, and a thin cloth of snow already lay on the idle winter fields. My father told me to look at the snowy landscape outside, so I peered out of the window. Suddenly, I heard a sound in the car. It was the four of them standing up; the three wearing overcoats clustered around the old man in the mask. They walked into the aisle towards us and I quickly realized they were heading to the bathroom. What astonished me, however, was the man in the mask. He was being propped up and pushed forward and as he glanced from behind his companions' shoulders, he was staring at my father and me. I saw his tears clearly; the old man in the mask had eyes filled with tears!

Although my father pulled me forcefully towards the window, I nevertheless saw how three of them entered the bathroom, and that one of them was the masked old man. One of the young men stayed outside the door; he wasn't much older than my brother but he threw me a frosty glance that frightened me. I drew back my head and quietly told my father, 'They've gone into the bathroom.'

Three of them went into the bathroom, but the old man in the mask did not come back out, only the two young men. Then I heard the three men in overcoats whisper to one another as they stood by the carriage links. I couldn't help but turn my head towards them, and what I saw was how the three men in overcoats, one of whom was straightening out his collar to protect his ears, opened the door to the next carriage and disappeared from my field of vision.

I didn't know what had happened to the old man with the mask. I wanted to have a look in the bathroom, but my father wouldn't let me move a muscle, saying, 'Sit down. You can't go anywhere.' It seemed to me that my father's manner and voice were very nervous. I don't know how much time went by before the conductor led a cultural propaganda team into our carriage, carrying drums, gongs and copper cymbals. Only then did my father relax his grip on my hand, which he had been holding throughout. He sighed with relief and asked, 'You need to go to the bathroom? I'll take you.'

The bathroom door was unlocked and as we opened it a fierce gust made me shiver. With one glance, I saw that the little bathroom window was open and that wind and snow were blowing in. There was no one in the bathroom. There was no masked old man.

'The old man isn't here,' I cried out. 'Why isn't he in here?'

'Who's not here?' my father asked, avoiding my eyes. 'They went into another carriage.'

'The old man isn't here. He was in the bathroom,' I yelled. 'How come he isn't here?'

'He went into another carriage. Don't you have to pee?' my father said, looking at the swirling snow outside the window. 'It's so cold here; hurry up and take a pee, all right?'

I did have to pee, but suddenly I saw that on the wet, grimy floor was a playing card. If I tell you, no doubt you won't believe me, but it was a Q of Hearts. As soon as I saw it, I knew that it was a Q of Hearts, the very Q of

Hearts I had lost and been unable to find. I'm sure you can imagine what I did – I bent down and picked up that card from the ground or, to be more accurate, I scraped it up and wiped the muddy snow off it. I waved it at my father, 'The Q of Hearts! It's the Q of Hearts, the one I needed!' I remember how my father's expression altered rapidly – astonishment, confusion, shock and fear – but in the end it was nothing but fear; in the end my terrified father snatched the Q of Hearts out of my hand and threw it with one gesture out the window, yelling confusedly, 'Throw it out! Hurry! Don't just hold it, blood! There's blood on the card!'

I would wager that there wasn't one trace of blood on that card, but on the other hand, it isn't as if my father had been speaking deliriously, either.

That 1969 trip to Shanghai acquired in my memory a mysterious postscript – the old man in the mask, the Q of Hearts. Through my entire childhood, my father refused to discuss what happened on the train, and for that reason I've always believed that the man on the train must have been mute. Only a few years ago, when my father was able to talk about events now long in the past, did he correct this error in my memory. 'You were still a kid then, you couldn't tell,' he said. 'He wasn't mute. No way he was a mute. You didn't see it, but the mask was moving – his tongue, his tongue had been . . . they had . . . had . . .'

My father didn't finish his sentence. He couldn't; his eyes filled with tears. I didn't need to say anything more, either, and the truth is that I don't much like to dwell on these things any more than he does. Over the years I have often recalled the tears of the old man on the train, and when I recall those tears, I suffer.

In any case, the Q of Hearts was just a card. I still like to play poker with my cards, and every time I pick up a Q of Hearts, I feel like the card has some kind of singular import – no matter whether it's a good move or not, I don't let the card out of hand lightly. I don't know why, but I'm used to playing it last.

Home in May

Yongshan was taking her son back to Licheng to visit relatives, but when she reached her brother Yongqing's house, she discovered he had recently moved away.

Some of her relatives had passed on, others had left the city, and yet more had simply grown distant. Her younger brother was the last of her close relatives in Licheng, so as you can imagine, his disappearance deeply embarrassed Yongshan in front of her son. Her brother's home was totally empty – Yongshan could see that through the round hole where the lock had been. The narrow parlour was quite dark and the only thing that could be clearly seen was a broken white toilet; perhaps it had broken when they'd attempted to take it out, so her brother had left it there, a shining white ring. Out of sheer disappointment or fury, Yongshan beat heavily on the door. But a few knocks was not enough to calm her frustration, so she switched hands and beat the door even more. Her son let go of the rolling suitcase and sat down on it.

'They've moved out. What's the point of knocking?' he said, looking calmly at his mother. 'Don't your hands hurt when you go at it like that?'

A neighbouring couple came out of their apartment, obviously confused about the connection between these two people and their former neighbour. The man asked her, 'Are you related to him?'

'I'm his sister,' she answered.

The woman standing behind her husband looked Yongshan over and said, 'You mean cousin? On which side?'

Yongshan, understanding the meaning of the couple's doubtful looks, answered quietly, 'Not cousin. I'm his older sister.' She blushed as soon as she finished speaking, for she knew her tone made it sound like she was lying. The neighbours asked no further questions, but suggested to Yongshan that she should call her brother's cell phone. Her answer was, 'I called the number, but it's out of service. Maybe I wrote it down wrong.' The woman then suggested that Yongshan enquire at the gas company, because if she remembered correctly that was where he had worked. Yongshan smiled confidently and corrected her, 'Not the gas company; the water company. I know that. My brother called me back in January to wish me a happy new year.'

Then they went downstairs. Her son took the suitcase and walked behind his mother, but rather than rolling it properly he began to drag it so that it grated against the cement steps. 'You don't have to take it out on the suitcase!' Yongshan shouted, looking behind her, 'It's new!'

Her son said, 'Oh, so now I'm taking it out on the suitcase? You're the one getting all worked up, not me.'

'Me? Worked up? About what?' Her son looked as though he would no longer bother to reply, so she explained, 'Your uncle holds a grudge against me. He didn't tell me on purpose – on purpose, I know it.'

Her son and the suitcase were standing crookedly on the steps when he said, 'Do you call this a family visit? So what are we going to do? Are we going to look for Uncle Yongqing, or what?'

Yongshan stood still, not answering; she had stopped by the window on the third floor landing and looked outside. 'This used to be the countryside. Something Commune . . . "Victory Commune".' She went on, 'I used to take Yongqing here to watch the open-air movies; we would walk along the paths at night, beside the pitch-dark paddies, and there were vegetable patches, too, where you could hear the frogs croak in the flooded fields, and there were fireflies sparkling back and forth.'

Her son wasn't interested in hearing about her endless reminiscences, and said, 'A family visit, you said. Well, might I trouble you to produce the family?'

Yongshan turned round to rebuke him, 'Shut up. Who said anything about a family visit? I haven't been to Licheng in six years; I've just come here to pay my hometown a visit, if that's all right with you.'

Her son looked at her a little afraid, and his taunting turned to lamentation: 'So, now we're going to drag our suitcase around the streets. People will think we're migrant workers.'

Yongshan twisted away, still looking out of the window. 'There's nothing wrong with coming back for a visit,' she said and seemed to have settled on this idea. 'We can go and see your uncle, or we can just forget it. We'll stay in a hotel if we have to; it won't break the bank.'

It was an afternoon in May, and the sun was very fine. They were on the north side of Licheng and the air was seasoned with the foul smell of dust and a faint, unidentifiable floral scent. The two travellers crossed the little square inside the gates of the housing complex; it was a crude, cramped little square, featuring concrete grapevine trellises, and though there were no grapevines on them, there were flowerbeds filled with roses and peonies. The sun lit up the faces of a few strangers here and there, making them look golden from a distance. They stopped for a moment in the square and her son went to the store to buy a Coke, and when he came back he saw that Yongshan had sat down to chat with a woman who was knitting on the flower terrace – so he went off to watch two men playing chess. Soon Yongshan lifted up her suitcase and said, 'Hurry up! What are you watching the chess game for?'

Her son ran up to her, 'I thought you'd met someone

262

you knew. What on earth were you chatting about if you don't know her?'

Yongshan said, 'Can't I talk to someone I don't know if I want to? I thought she was someone else – Huang Meijuan, a girl who went to elementary school with me, that's who I thought she was.'

She looked forlorn for a moment before turning back to look once again at the knitting woman, who had her head bowed as she worked in the sunlight. The yarn was a garish shade of peach, so she remarked casually, 'What a tacky colour. I wonder who would wear it?' Then she heaved a sigh and said, 'Strange. It's not as if Licheng is all that big, but I haven't met anyone I know since I got here.'

Her son took a sip of Coke and tilted his head to look at the greyish-blue May sky. He pondered a moment, then said something that sounded as though he'd learnt it from a TV series. He must have been a good mimic, for it struck his mother speechless.

'It's a shame you still remember Licheng,' he said, 'because Licheng forgot about you a long time ago.'

They took the public bus to Cabbage Market; the trip was Yongshan's decision.

'No matter what, we must go to Cabbage Market to take a look at the old house. We have to go this time, because next time there'll be nothing left to see.' She tried to push her son onto the bus, but he wouldn't let her touch him and shrugged her hands off.

'Don't grab me. What is this? A kidnapping?' he said. 'I'll visit whatever you make me visit – we can tour the outhouses for all I care.' He had likened the old house to an outhouse. He regretted the comment as soon as it left his lips. He stuck out his tongue, not daring to look at his mother. Fortunately for him, Yongshan was trying to find seats and had paid no attention to her son's mumbling. She claimed a seat and told him to sit down, but when he refused Yongshan took the seat herself.

She turned her head slightly to look at the streets outside the window, and said, 'I remember. There used to be a cemetery here, too, we walked past here when we went to the open-air movies. We were always too scared to look this way – the cemetery was to the left of the road – so we all kept our eyes fixed right and ran for all we were worth.' Her son wasn't paying any attention, and his indifference contained a message for Yongshan: 'Don't count on me co-operating. I'm completely uninterested in this city.' For a moment, Yongshan's eyes wandered between the road outside the window and her son, then finally they fixed on her son's suitcase.

'Actually, I know why your uncle's put off.' Her line of thought had jumped suddenly to the question of her brother. 'I know he's avoiding me on purpose. They got some money from knocking the old house down and he's worried I'm going to ask him for my share.'

Her son snorted and said, 'Well, are you?'

Yongshan stared at her son and said nothing, then all

the way to their stop she remained silent. He could see turmoil in his mother's eyes, like brewing storm clouds, but due to his tender age, he didn't realize what his mother was thinking about. Yongshan was silent and so was her son. He followed her off the bus and waited for her to lead the way, but she was standing beneath the bus stop sign and looking all around her. Suddenly she said, 'Where are we?'

Yongshan was lost. She was on her way home, but she was lost. The water tower at the soap factory must have been pulled down at some point, and without the water tower, Yongshan couldn't find the way to Cabbage Market. How could so much be gone? Yongshan watched the crowds of people and the buildings on both sides with something approaching dread. She said, 'I walked this road for dozens of years. How come I don't recognize anything? Do I really need to ask for directions to get to my own home?'

In fact, it was the same as everywhere else; the city of Licheng had been transformed through the efforts of various government departments. The narrow, winding roads characteristic of the old city had been resolutely straightened and widened, but it was more than a physical change – they had also forced people to abandon their old, unscientific sense of orientation. Many women now lost their way on the streets because, without a certain corner store, postbox or water tower, they could no longer find the associated street. Yongshan was just one of those disoriented women. She grumbled for a moment, then abandoned her attempts to find the tower. Finally, she asked directions from an old man selling fruit by the roadside, who immediately gave her the information she needed. The old man pointed to a great expanse of ruins to the north and said 'That's the way you'll want to be going; where the buildings have all been half torn down. That's Cabbage Market.'

Yongshan hadn't expected that her return home after seven years would consist of an itinerary of ruins. Looking down at the broken bricks and tiles covering the ground she said, 'How are we supposed to get across this?'

Her son behind her said, 'If you can't get across it, then let's forget it. We could say we've paid our respects to the old place, right?' But Yongshan had already walked over to pick up the suitcase. 'We'll have to carry the suitcase,' she said. 'Be careful where you put your feet; there's broken glass.'

And so it was that the ruins of Cabbage Market welcomed back Yongshan and her son so many years after their departure. Late Qing dynasty, Republican era and socialist wood and bricks mixed together and mourned in the May sun for their vanished ways of life, and now the tranquillity of their mourning had been disturbed by their last visitor. Perhaps every brick and tile in the ruin remembered Yongshan, remembered that girl of many years ago, scampering back and forth between Cabbage

Market and the cultural centre with an accordion on her back. Perhaps they were saying, 'Yongshan! Hello. How's that accordion practice going?' But Yongshan couldn't hear them. All Yongshan heard was the rumble of a bulldozer rolling in a construction site nearby, mixed in with the 'lalala' of a female rock singer coming from a nearby music store. Besides, Yongshan was now the mother of a thirteen-year-old and had long ago abandoned the accordion. With difficulty, Yongshan and her son were making the way back home. Neither one looked very happy. The rubble itself engendered their resentment, since it was impossible to roll a suitcase through it. And so, despite their hostile mood, they were compelled to carry the heavy suitcase between them. Mother and son puffed with fatigue, and every now and then the boy viciously kicked a glass bottle or crushed an innocent tile fragment. Meanwhile, Yongshan cursed the havoc and disorder of the rubble, but, as anyone knows, rubble is never tidy, and so her complaints were somewhat unreasonable. A rat in the rubble seemed to want to warn the visitors about something, for it suddenly popped out of a pile of bricks and tiles, frightening Yongshan.

'That scared me!' she said, covering her mouth. 'What's a rat doing here? And such a big one!'

Her son said, 'Of course there are rats in trash heaps. Where else are you going to find rats, if not in trash heaps?'

Yongshan frowned and took a look around. Towards

the west, a parasol tree was still standing, albeit with great difficulty, among the piles of bricks, and towards the east, the façade of a brick-and-wood house had survived the wreckage, standing lofty and solitary like a stage set. By the eaves, a line of writing could still be clearly read: 'Watch and Clock Repair While You Wait'.

Yongshan's eyes suddenly lit up: 'I know this place. This was Mr Kang's place. You remember him. Mr Kang – ugly as sin but great with his hands – he fixed watches.' She looked to the left side of the rubble, searching for something. 'The well was right here. I used to come to the well every day to do the washing, clean the rice, and rinse out the mop,' Yongshan said. 'How strange. Why can't I find the well?'

'It'd be strange if you could,' said her son. 'It must be under the garbage.'

Yongshan's eyes paused on the tree. 'Let's go and have a look.' She sounded quite excited. 'When I graduated from elementary school, I carved my name on that tree, and when I came back from the countryside it was still there. I grew up with that tree. I wonder if my name is still on it.'

'I'm not going,' her son said. 'Go and have a look yourself if you want to.'

Yongshan glared at her son and went over to the tree by herself. She walked, her back slightly bent, over the pile of bricks, and made two turns around the tree. What she saw was a cracked and battered tree trunk, on

268

whose coarse bark someone had written a line in red paint: 'Piss here and you're a dog!' accompanied by a very rude drawing. Yongshan couldn't find her name, so she lowered her head, reflecting, and sullenly walked down from the brick pile. Her son had taken a seat on the suitcase; he must have guessed the result, for he looked at his mother with eyes filled with ridicule. She tried to smooth her disappointment over and said, 'It's good that it's gone. Who knows what kind of people rub up against that tree. Disgusting!'

The sky suddenly began to grow dark. They had reached the depths of the Cabbage Market rubble and the orange sunlight had vanished from the scene of devastation. They were a stone's throw away from their old home when Yongshan loosened her grip on the suitcase. 'Let's put it down,' she said to her son. 'If I didn't tell you that behind this wall is our old house, would you have recognized the place?'

'No,' her son said. 'Who can remember stuff like that?'

Yongshan stared at the half wall still standing. She looked for the roof, but there was none. Nor was there a door. She saw the cement steps that led up to the front door, but they were swallowed in the debris. Yongshan looked and looked, and suddenly she was angry with her son. 'You can't remember anything? Your grandma looked after you here till you were three. Right up until her heart attack, when she had to go to the hospital, she was the one who cared for you. Don't you remember that either? You don't recognize this, you can't remember that – you're not human, you're a pig!'

Her son discovered, to his surprise, that his mother's eyes were shining with the glow of furious overreaction. 'I remember grandma, but that doesn't mean I remember the house,' he uttered quietly in his defence, then he said nothing more; for though he understood that he had provoked his mother's wrath, he felt guiltless. And it really was true that he had no recollection whatsoever of Licheng, or of the old house in Cabbage Market.

Besides Yongshan and her son, the vast rubble of Cabbage Market was completely empty. Sunset glowed over the main street not far away, and the sound of people and cars would occasionally subside, then a fragmentary, hardly discernible, rustling would drift across the rubble, a sound like a subterranean sigh. A pigeon flew in the face of dusk towards the rubble and circled over mother and son for a while. Then, panicking, it flew to the parasol tree. It was probably somebody's domestic pigeon, lost a long time ago, and now that it had finally found the way back to its shed, both shed and owner had vanished.

There was only half a wall left of the old house, and in it half a window. Yongshan walked up to it. The window-frame had had many layers of red paint, and the long years of sunlight and rain had given the surface stripy wrinkles, like the wrinkles on an old man's body. The glass was broken, but the frame was still firmly set into the broken wall. Yongshan stretched out her hand to give the window a push, and it opened with a creak. Something fell down off the windowsill. Yongshan looked in and found that it was an ink bottle, which had fallen into the debris inside without breaking.

'It's your grandfather's ink bottle,' said Yongshan. 'He used it to correct his students' homework. He liked to keep it on the windowsill.'

Her son, standing behind her, peered inside; perhaps he was trying to remember the brief time he had spent in this house as a child. Maybe he couldn't recall, or maybe he wasn't trying, but he said, 'It's like an earthquake zone. It's as if we're earthquake victims.'

Yongshan touched the window; the greasy frame was covered in a layer of dust which came off on her hand. 'When I was small, I liked to stand by this window and play the accordion,' she said. 'Your grandpa could read music, and sometimes before recitals he would make me practice, then he'd stand next to me and turn the pages.'

'I never knew you played the accordion,' her son said. 'What happened to it?'

'I gave it to your uncle,' she said. 'Your grandpa wanted him to learn it, but he didn't take to it. Your uncle's a good-for-nothing; later your grandma told me he sold the accordion to a scrap collector for twenty bucks.'

The pigeon on the pagoda tree flew back towards them, so low they could see its grey feathers, which looked as if they'd been dipped in water. The pigeon stopped on the remaining wall of the old house, paused for a moment and flew off again.

'That pigeon can't find its way home,' Yongshan said.

'Maybe it's a homing pigeon?' Pigeons were something her son was interested in and his eyes brightened. He followed the pigeon's flight path with his eyes and said, 'A homing pigeon can fly five hundred kilometres and come back home. A homing pigeon can find its way back home no matter how far it goes.'

'Even people can't find their way back home these days. How can a pigeon?' said Yongshan.

She stopped following the pigeon with her eyes and bowed her head to look for something. 'Let me see,' she said. 'Maybe I can find your grandma's flowerpots. We could take one home as a memento. Do you remember how grandma made a flower terrace outside the door? She planted lots of flowers and the pots were all made from Yixing clay. They were very good pots.'

'What's the use of bringing pots home? You never plant flowers.'

'We don't have to plant flowers. It would be a memento, don't you see?'

It was obvious that her son was trying to suppress his irritation; he picked up a tile fragment and threw it far away. It happened to land on a piece of glass, which made a crisp and resonant bang.

'Can't you behave like a decent human being?'

Yongshan said. 'How old are you, anyway? It's time you grew up.'

'If you take me to a trash heap, how can I behave decently? Do you have some master plan or something? It'll be totally dark in a second. Are we going to look for Uncle Yongqing or not?'

Yongshan looked blank for a moment, then turned to look inside the house, supporting herself on the windowsill. It was obvious that she had been avoiding this question. While Yongshan had been pondering the old home in the dusk, her heart, too, had sunk into the shadows. 'I'll take you there in a moment. Don't worry, Licheng is my hometown; I won't make you sleep on the street no matter what.' She spoke to her son, then suddenly craned her neck to look into a corner. Her son assumed that this was her final glance and was surprised when Yongshan called out loudly, 'The cabinet. Our five-drawer cabinet's still here!'

Only half believing her, her son quickly climbed in through the window, and there against the broken wall was indeed a cabinet, covered in plastic film and a few newspapers, standing crookedly in the rubble. It was a style of cabinet that had been popular in the south in the seventies, and though it didn't have five drawers, that's what it was called. In any case, it looked like it might serve as a small wardrobe. Carved, symmetrical wood-work was inlaid in the dark red drawers.

The sight of the cabinet made Yongshan nostalgic. Her

son was prepared for this, and having helped her through the window, he kept his peace. He sat on an abandoned plastic stool, and looked up at the dusky sky over the rubble of Cabbage Market, remembering, no doubt, the graphics from some computer game. He gave a giggle and said, 'It's like I'm in the Infinite Magic Castle. Do you know what that is? You go into the castle and forget everything, but you have all these powers, so you can walk with your brain, or talk through your nostrils!'

Yongshan tried to open the cabinet door, but saw that somebody had hung a little lock on it, so the door could not be opened. Yongshan went over the wood carvings with her hands and said, 'I'm sure you don't remember this cabinet, but I used it every day. I had to put the clean clothes in it and take out the stamps to buy rice and oil. You couldn't possibly understand those things; you don't know anything about what it was like.'

'What good would it be if I did?' her son said. 'What's the problem, as long as you know yourself?'

'I wonder who put the lock on. Must be your uncle. How could he have forgotten to take the cabinet with him?' Yongshan held the lock in her fingers, then contradicted herself, 'Maybe it's not your uncle. He's a good-for-nothing; he'd throw it out or sell it. Maybe some scrap collector locked it. If we hadn't come, he would have sold it.'

'So let him. It's not new and it's not antique. Who would want it in their home?'

'You're a good-for-nothing, too.' She gave her son a vicious glance and said, 'When you grow up, you'll be even more useless than your uncle.'

Forced back into silence, her son gazed around the rubble and saw that the lights of evening were turning on in Licheng. He looked past the ruins of the house and saw an even greater expanse of rubble, hazy with dust, shrouded by the colours of the gloaming. This was his mother's city, his mother's rubble, and her son didn't feel any close connection to it. He felt exhausted and, bending down to hug his knees, he curled up like a cat. He spoke to his mother in an attitude of great passivity, 'Just call me when you've seen enough, and you're tired of wallowing in the past. I'm going to have a nap.'

Her son heard her rustling about, doing something with the cabinet; he didn't even lift his head, which meant, 'Go ahead, do what you want, it's nothing to do with me.'

But Yongshan suddenly shouted at him, 'Get up, quick! Help me carry the cabinet out.'

She had the cabinet bound with hemp rope and several packing strings, so that it resembled a piece of luggage. There was even a length of rope by which to haul it along. Who knows where Yongshan had found the ropes. She stood by the cabinet and looked at her son with some pride. 'It's all properly tied together. I've tried it; it's not heavy at all. We can take it away.'

'Are you mad?' said her son. 'Why on earth would you

drag this old thing off? Maybe you've gone mad, but I haven't. And I'm not going to take it.'

'I don't care if you want to or not; you have to.' Yongshan's voice became sharp, and there was also a tremor in it. 'You really make my blood boil sometimes. Don't you have any feelings at all? This is the last memento we have of your grandparents. I can't just leave it here!'

Her son stood up, but turned away. He didn't move, but there was the sound of snorting. They stood like that, in a stalemate, for about two minutes, and then he heard his mother stamp her foot. She said, 'If you're not going to help me, I can do it without you. I'll take it out myself!'

On that May Licheng evening, Yongshan and son, having returned for a family visit, were walking down the street. Yongshan was in front, rolling a suitcase, but the thing her son was dragging along puzzled the passers-by: it seemed to be a piece of furniture. Everyone looked back to examine it as it chafed against the road surface, emitting occasional piercing sounds, creaks and groans. People of a certain age recognized it as a five-drawer cabinet, which had been popular in the seventies, and there were some who called out, 'Look! A five-drawer cabinet!'

They had still failed to meet anyone Yongshan knew. The last time she had returned, seven years earlier, she had encountered old neighbours and elementary school classmates on the streets of Cabbage Market, and even run into someone who had played the accordion with her in the Children's Palace, but this time she hadn't seen a soul. Yongshan led her son along the streets of Licheng, and it was as if they were in an unfamiliar city. The cabinet had, to a large extent, relieved her helpless, distressed mood. Every now and then she looked back at her son and the cabinet he dragged behind him. 'Watch out; don't let the string break,' she said. 'Don't pull that long-suffering face at me. There's nothing wrong with a boy of your age getting a little exercise. Hang in a little longer; you just have to take it to your auntie's on Mahogany Street.'

Her son didn't take great care at all. When he heard one of the packing strings snap, he said nothing; soon afterwards another packing string snapped and he heard the clatter of the lock. Then, just as he had hoped, the cabinet refused to budge. He stopped and said in an almost delighted tone, 'It's snapped. They've all snapped. I told you the strings would snap!'

Not only had the string snapped, but the cabinet door had broken from the shock, and two of the drawers creaked to be let out. Yongshan ran over and smacked her son on the head. 'You did it on purpose,' she said. 'I knew you wouldn't do a good job of it. If you won't take it, then I will.'

One of the drawers fell out of the cabinet. It was empty and exuded the smell of mothballs. The newspapers that covered the bottom were from 1984. Yongshan squatted down and looked at what was written in the newspaper. 'Eighty-four,' she said to her son. 'You weren't even around yet, then.'

He looked at his mother and said, 'Just when I thought it couldn't get any more embarrassing! Can't you see that people are staring?'

Yongshan ignored his complaints. 'Your grandma used to like to put the residence permit and grain stamps underneath,' she said as she removed the old newspapers. A photo abruptly appeared before their eyes. It was a family photo of four people – a man, a woman, a boy and a girl – sitting in two rows. All of them were wearing army uniforms and, except for the little boy, who looked miserable, the other three were smiling stiffly. The background could be instantly identified as a painted curtain; it depicted Tiananmen Square in Beijing.

The photo from the past century tickled him: 'A photo like this is cool, man.' He tried to take it out of his mother's hand, but she threw the photo back into the cabinet as if it had scalded her.

Her expression was very strange. She said, 'I made a mistake. This photo isn't of our family.'

He couldn't absorb this information right away and, lifting the photo up to have a look, he said, 'No wonder. I didn't think the girl looked like you.'

Yongshan's lips were trembling, as if she were afraid she might burst into tears. Suddenly she covered her face.

'I've made a mistake,' she said. 'How could this be? This isn't our cabinet.'

All at once, her son realized the full extent of the injustice he had suffered transporting the cabinet and shouted, 'And so after all that, you were making me lug somebody else's stuff around town! You've got to be kidding, right?'

'How could this be?' she squatted down and looked vacantly in the direction of Cabbage Market saying, 'I wonder who left the cabinet there? It was in our house, and it looks just like the one we had.'

Her son produced some derisive hooting noises. Having thus finished mocking his mother, he relaxed and took a closer look at the strangers' family photo. 'Whose picture is this? It must be some neighbour's. Man, do they look lame; so lame, it's almost cute. Do you know these people?'

Yongshan scanned the photo blankly. 'No,' she said. 'I left here a long time ago. They might be people who moved to Cabbage Market later; I don't know them.'

Now that he'd been relieved of his onerous burden, her son joyfully dragged the cabinet to the side of the road. He put it next to a ceramic garbage can that was about half the size of a person, with a tiger's head and a huge mouth to throw the garbage in. Once he'd finished this bit of business, he took a step back and examined how the garbage can and the cabinet stood, so to speak, shoulder to shoulder: an old piece of furniture with an unknown owner and a majestic garbage can. Underneath the pale light of the street lamps, the garbage can looked like a bodyguard protecting the cabinet. The son looked at his mother who was squatting on the ground and seemed to tacitly agree to the disposal of the cabinet. Her son was very pleased with himself, and giving himself a clap he said, 'Cool, man! Modern art!'

Yongshan didn't look at the cabinet again. She stood up slowly and, as she rose, her eyes welled up with tears. The lights were on in the windows of Licheng, and the newly paved road glimmered with an orange and white glow that seemed to flow like a river. Yes, her eyes welled up with tears, for she felt that she had now truly left her native city far behind, and it her. Besides some memories, the city had left her nothing, and she knew in her heart that she had bequeathed it no part of herself. Yongshan fished out her handkerchief and wiped away the tears. She heard her son say, 'Where are we going to go now?'

She hesitated and, looking back at him, she began to feel the stirrings of a guilty conscience. 'Where do you want to go?' she asked.

He looked at her doubtfully and said, 'I dunno. I'm going where you're going. Didn't you want to go and see your cousin?'

Yongshan bent down to brush some dust off the suitcase and said, 'Suppose we didn't go?' It seemed like she was soliciting her son's advice. 'I haven't seen her in seven years.' Her son said nothing, and a kind of pity, and lenience, began to emerge in his eyes as he looked at her.

'Whatever.' Then he joked, 'You're the boss; I'm just staff. I'll go wherever you're going.'

Night-time Licheng was nothing like it used to be. After seven o'clock the streets looked splendid all lit up, and Yongshan took her son to a famous local restaurant. They ate Licheng's famous crab dumplings, noodles with congealed duck's blood and fried wontons. After stuffing themselves with a filling meal, both of them felt their strength return, so Yongshan took her son to a large department store, where they walked around and rode up and down in the lift. Yongshan bought some of Licheng's famous silk, as well as some other local specialities, for gifts. She got a pure wool sweater for her husband, and even bought her son some brand-name sneakers, which were on sale; he picked them out himself. Then they rolled their suitcase to the train station, one in front of the other, as before, except that now Yongshan was carrying a few shopping bags. One was an ordinary white plastic bag, but the other was a red bag with an elaborate design, covered in countless white pear blossoms.[14]

On the way to the station, Yongshan saw her son furtively take something out of his pocket and stick it into the suitcase's inner lining. He had always enjoyed collecting, and he must have found the picture very

[14]Licheng means 'Pear City'.

amusing: four strangers in a family picture. Well then, let him keep it. Yongshan didn't stop him. She was leaning on a lamp post, waiting for her son, when she took a deep breath and smelled something. 'The air in Licheng is better than at home,' she said, 'I wonder what flower that is. Lovely smell. The air here is best in April and May.'

Then they walked with their luggage to the train station, looking very much like tourists who had come for the day on an organized trip. Yongshan was a very thrifty woman; they had walked all day and yet still she couldn't bring herself to hail a taxi. She told her son, 'We can rest once we're on the train. Why should we pay for something we don't need?'

The Giant Baby

The town doctor took a piece of bread out of his basket. Even this simple lunch had been delayed again and again on account of the sheer number of his patients: childless women who came to him looking for a cure to their infertility. To make matters worse, the bread was a few days old and already quite stale. Just as he was taking his army canteen off the wall to take a sip of water, footsteps sounded. They were followed by the appearance of a woman's shadow swaying back and forth on the bamboo curtain before stopping by a very small window that had once been used to dispense medicine. Through it, the doctor could see a white blouse with red flowers, and underneath it the slight bulge of the woman's breasts, though he couldn't see her face.

'Come in,' said the doctor, biting off a mouthful of bread, 'I can hardly examine you if you're standing out there.'

'Out here will be fine.' The woman's voice was very low, as if she feared that passers-by might hear her. Then she said, 'Just give me some medicine, doctor. That'll be enough. I have to rush home, so please hurry.'

The doctor laughed and took a swig of water from his canteen. 'That's a new one. How am I supposed to give you medicine without examining you? And what medicine do you need, anyway?'

'The childbearing soup,' she said in an even quieter voice. 'Everyone says it works. But please hurry up, doctor, I have to get home straight away.'

Something about this woman was very odd, and so the doctor decided to go outside and get a good look at her from the steps of the clinic. She was wearing a straw hat with cotton cloth wound around it that covered her face. Because of the cloth, he couldn't tell who she was or whether he knew her.

He decided to ignore this furtive woman, and instead he sat down, opened up his logbook and wrote down the date. Then, all the while loudly chewing his bread, he informed the woman outside, 'I'm a doctor, not a temple god. My medicine might work well enough, but it's not some kind of Taoist cure-all. I don't know where you get your ideas from!'

At some point the woman had come inside. The doctor heard the creaking of the stool behind him, and at the same time he noticed a powerful, acrid smell of sweat. He looked behind him to find her sitting stiffly on the stool.

'I won't take off my pants,' the woman said.

'Nobody asked you to,' the doctor replied, a little annoyed. 'Is that why you think I became a doctor? Now just hold out your hand so I can take your pulse.'

Hesitantly, she did as she was told. Irritated as he was, the doctor pressed her hand roughly down on the table and took her pulse. Meanwhile, he occupied himself by staring at the profuse grime that had accumulated under her fingernails. Her hand emitted the slightly nauseating smell of chicken shit.

'I suppose there is a man?' the doctor asked casually. He knew that wasn't the proper way to ask such a thing; but for some reason he felt thoroughly malicious towards this woman.

She hung her head and didn't respond. He noticed that she had sweat stains all over her straw hat, just like a man. She also had a silver necklace on, which was the kind of old jewellery women in the town had long ago stopped wearing. She must be from the mountains, up by Wangbao, he thought, for that was the only area where women still wore necklaces like that.

'Are you from the mountains? From Wangbao?' The doctor listened carefully to the woman's pulse, but her long silence aroused his suspicions, so he asked, 'What is this, anyway? Do you mean to tell me there isn't a man? Are you even married?' The doctor stared at the cloth hanging from the straw hat and was suddenly seized by the desire to tear it off, but her reflexes were quick and she managed to dodge his lunging hand. The doctor scoffed at her, saying, 'You're nuts, do you know that? Do you want to get pregnant without a man? You can drink childbearing soup till hell freezes over before that happens!'

The woman's body twisted on the stool, and her breathing became more rapid. Then the doctor heard the sound of her muffled sobbing. All of a sudden, she was down on her knees embracing the doctor's leg and crying 'Save me, doctor, give me a child, give me a son, so I can take revenge.'

Automatically, the doctor jumped up to free himself. His arm knocked off her hat, and she gave a sharp cry. At that moment the doctor saw the world's most hideous face, the face of a severe burn victim. Apart from her unscathed eyes, the skin of her face resembled nothing more than blackened pine bark.

What happened next seemed to the doctor to be part of some kind of dream. He recalled that the woman picked up her hat and ran out, while he sat petrified by shock in front of the window. He thought she had left, but a moment later her filthy, grime-fingered hand thrust through the window and the woman said, 'I beg you, give me the soup. Give me the soup, so I can take my revenge.'

In shock, the doctor picked up a pile of medicine packets and passed them to her, accidentally brushing her hand in the process. At this touch, he was seized by a sensation of intense dread, and grabbing at the woman's fingers he said, 'Revenge! Revenge for what?' She freed her hand and said, 'Wait till I have a son and you'll find out.'

It was a summer afternoon and the weather was oppressive. The doctor remembered rushing out after her to see which direction she would take, and even then he had the premonition that this woman would one day become the subject of much tongue-wagging. He was about to call out to the people from the barber's across the street, or from the cooperative next door, so that they too could come out and see the woman, but the ingrained idlers were all dozing behind their counters. Thus, the hideous mountain woman passed through the cobblestone streets of the town as if she were a normal farmer's wife, without attracting anybody's attention. The doctor watched as she turned off and disappeared into the cornfields, following the paths up to the mountains.

The matter preoccupied the doctor for the entire afternoon, and at about four o'clock he heard a terrible thunderclap from the horizon, so sharp and resounding that both he and the few women in the room had to cover their ears. For some reason the doctor thought immediately of the woman. He supposed she must still be on her way up the mountain, hurrying on amidst the lightning flashes and rumbling thunder. An invention of his mind's eye disquieted him: the dim image of a blue bolt of lightning hitting the woman's straw hat, the paper medicine packets in her hand torn and the black herbs within leaking into the mire of the mountain trail.

It was rare for the people from around Wangbao to come down from their mountain village. They grew corn, sweet potatoes and apples to bring to market, while they themselves ate only the simplest fare. As a result, they enjoyed sturdier health than the relatively affluent townspeople below, and rarely went down the mountain for medical attention. For a long time the doctor took pleasure in discussing the woman from Wangbao with his patients, but nobody knew who she was; nor did anyone recall a woman with a straw hat. No one was very interested in his story, so when the doctor began to speak again about the vengeful, child-hungry woman, they all repeated the same sentence: 'She must be crazy!'

Then, in the spring, when the cooperative's itinerant wagon was sent up to Wangbao, it returned with sensational news: a virgin birth had occurred there. And there was more: the girl's labour had lasted three days and three nights and the newborn was enormous. According to their account, he weighed 9 kilograms and looked like a little boy of three, with swarthy skin and a powerful voice, but only four fingers on his right hand. The most baffling part of his anatomy was his willy, which the people from the cooperative said was like a 'top-notch carrot'. One of the clerks who had seen him said, her eyes popping with astonishment,

'Cross my heart, I swear there's even a ring of hair around it!'

The doctor, who happened to be buying cigarettes in the cooperative at the time and who commanded respect in medical matters, berated the women: 'Are you really that brainless? Do you believe every half-baked rumour?'

But one of them responded, 'You're the brainless one! And it's not a rumour. We saw the baby ourselves.'

The doctor asked, 'And how do you know it's a newborn? People from those parts are backward and superstitious. Who knows, maybe the kid was three years old!'

The woman gave him a reproachful glance and raised her voice: 'We saw her give birth with our own eyes. We even gave her cotton blankets and quilts. It was with our own eyes that we saw it, right in front of us. Her face is so badly burnt that no one wants to marry her; she's an old maid. The whole village stood around outside, watching her give birth.' Someone nearby snickered and said, 'What I'd like to know is, if this immaculate virgin wasn't sneaking around with *someone*, then how did she get pregnant?'

The clerk, her eyes still glowing excitedly, said, 'Exactly. That's what's so strange. Everyone in the village says she's never been with anyone. They're saying it's the thunder god's son. I mean, how else can you explain a giant baby like that?'

At this, the doctor realized something. For a moment he was bewildered, but then he said, 'The medicine!' and ran directly to his clinic. His thoughts in disarray, he began searching through the previous year's logbook until he found the entry he was looking for. He saw the woman's name: Ju Chunhua. Next to it, he saw the question marks he had drawn in the columns designated for 'marital status' and 'reasons for infertility'.

He had given her six packets, he remembered. The formula for this medicine was something that had been handed down in his family for generations, but unexpectedly he was overcome by a kind of horror. Rather than the theory of conception-by-thunder-god, he had to admit that this preternatural birth was more likely to be a consequence of his own fertility treatment.

In the spring, the doctor quietly raised the price of his childbearing soup. Though some patients complained, he refrained from mentioning Ju Chunhua's pregnancy to them as justification. He realized that if he tried to capitalize too brazenly on his success with her, he risked provoking the opposite reaction: they would say that a miracle was a miracle and write him off as a quack. What he did instead was to leave the logbook open on the relevant page, with a note beside it written in ballpoint pen: 'Ju Chunhua from Wangbao got her medicine here.' Any time a patient saw the entry, her face would light up with the same expression of enthusiasm, and she would exclaim, 'I always said it wasn't the thunder god who got her pregnant, didn't I? I don't care what anyone says, I'll bet it was your medicine.'

In response, the doctor would laugh coolly and say, 'You know, my medicine's strong stuff, so you get what you pay for.'

One day a group of panic-stricken women appeared on the streets of Liushui carrying their children; their silver necklaces marked them out as Wangbao people. The cries of the women and children alarmed the townspeople as the mothers clumsily held up their children's right hands, bound in bloodstained rags and cotton wadding. One of the Wangbao women showed her son's hand, and in her distressed tale Ju Chunhua's name came up once again: 'That's not a child that Ju Chunhua gave birth to it, it's vermin! The little wolf cub bit my son's thumb off!'

Weeping and pushing one another, they pressed into the clinic. The doctor, who had never encountered such a situation, became flustered. When he finally began to examine their injuries, he discovered that the thumb on the right hand of each child looked like it had been crushed by a combine harvester, and hung from the hand like a mown-down plant. The doctor, who knew exactly how to deal with infertile women, broke out in cold sweat at the sight of these little thumbs. He found the merchurocrome and absorbent cotton and asked urgently, 'What happened? Is there a rabid dog loose in Wangbao?'

This provoked another round of wailing from the mothers of Wangbao: 'It's not a rabid dog, it's that miscarriage of Ju Chunhua's. He runs around everywhere biting the fingers off the other children.'

The doctor asked, 'Nonsense. He's only six months old; he won't even have all his teeth yet.' But the mothers of Wangbao said, 'Doctor, he's got all his teeth already! And he bites worse than a wolf.'

'That's impossible. A six-month-old baby can't even walk.'

'It's not a normal child, doctor, it's a demon! He was running around when he was eight days old, suckling at everybody's nipples. We all gave him our milk, because he was so strong that it was no use trying to push him away.'

The doctor stared in alarm and said, 'How can that be? His mother, Ju Chunhua, doesn't she look after him?'

The women began to yell altogether, 'That's what you don't understand, doctor! She *wants* him to do it! When her son bites off someone's thumb she's right next to him, looking on. She even smiles.'

As the women were speaking, Ju Chunhua's burnt and hideous face flashed before his mind's eye. He muttered to himself for a moment before asking, 'This woman, Ju Chunhua: why does she want revenge?'

Immediately, the Wangbao women fell silent, and traces of remorse and self-accusation appeared on their faces. One of them said, 'It's true we didn't treat her very well, but you can't blame us, the way she looks.' Another one said, 'She must hold it against us that we wouldn't let the children see her. You know how children are easily frightened: we thought she would scare them. But she just isn't human; if she had to take revenge then it should have been on us. Why did she have to take it out on the children?'

The doctor began to nod, since he had begun to grasp something of what lay behind the matter. 'I understand', he said, 'why the giant baby goes for the thumbs. She wants her child to be the same as yours: four-fingered.'

The women all agreed with his deduction and one of them said, 'That woman! I wouldn't give a pile of wolf-shit for her conscience.'

There were seven children with seven little thumbs, and the doctor wrapped them all in gauze bandages the way you might set saplings in soil. Knowing this would do little to solve the problem, he advised the mothers to hitch a ride with the tractor to the district hospital where operations could be performed on them.

While the women made ready to leave, picking their children up to go and wait for the tractor, the doctor asked them some questions about Ju Chunhua. Of course, the first thing he asked was about the huge burn covering her face. Their answers surprised him: they said she was like that as soon as she came out of her mum's stomach, and that no one was to blame. At this, the doctor went silent for a moment, but then he asked the question closest to his heart: 'Did Ju Chunhua . . .' his eyes glistened as he looked at the anxious women. 'Did Ju Chunhua tell you that she got the childbearing soup here?' The women all looked at him in stupefaction; they clearly had no idea what he meant. Then one of them asked, 'What "childbearing soup"? We all know the truth of it now. It wasn't any soup, and it wasn't the thunder god! She did it with a wolf, otherwise she wouldn't have whelped a wolf cub!'

Another woman added, 'It stands to reason: the men all stayed away from her, but I guess the wolves didn't.'

The doctor realized that in the face of the extreme grief and anger of these women, it would be useless to ask for any further facts concerning Ju Chunhua. If he wanted to find out the truth about this seemingly fantastic occurrence, and about his family's hereditary medicine, he would have to take a trip to Wangbao himself.

The day for his trip to Wangbao was overcast, so he brought an umbrella in case of rain. The path was not a good one, and he was soaked through by the time he was halfway up the mountain. From that vantage point he could see the yellow mud huts of Wangbao on the slope of the mountain, with their famous giant apples hanging abundantly on the trees. Just outside the village, the doctor saw a girl picking apples and asked her how to find Ju Chunhua's home. The girl looked at him curiously and replied with a question, 'Are you the police? Are you coming to take the wolf cub away?' Before the doctor answered, the girl took out her right hand and showed it to him.

'The wolf cub bit me, too, but I pulled back quick, so all I got were his tooth marks.' For whatever reason, the doctor didn't approve of the way the girl referred to the giant baby.

He spoke to her kindly though, 'It's not nice to call someone a wolf cub. He's a child, the same as you. It's just that he's developing too quickly.' The girl's clear, innocent gaze made him unwillingly divulge his secret. He said, 'You know, the giant baby's mother got her medicine from me.'

The girl led him into the village. Once there, the doctor became aware of the nervous, strange atmosphere. Many of the villagers were carrying hoes or iron harrows and hurrying towards an earthen structure at the foot of a pagoda tree. The faces of the adults were grim, but the children were delighted, as if attending a festival. There was already a dense crowd of people gathered at the foot of the tree, so he asked the girl, 'What's going on?'

'They want to drive Ju Chunhua and her son out of the village, so the wolf cub can't bite anyone any more.'

The doctor walked forward quickly, pushing people out of his way. This attracted the attention of the villagers and they turned towards him.

'Who are you?' they asked.

The girl shouted out from behind, 'He's the district police who's come to put the wolf cub in gaol!'

But the doctor, who was in a great rush to see the giant baby, was in no mood to explain himself. The townspeople gave way to him without really understanding what was going on, and let him push open Ju Chunhua's unlatched door, nearly striking her in the process as she was nursing the infant. The scene not only startled the doctor, but set the crowd outside in an uproar: no one had expected the two of them to be enjoying such a tender moment at a time like this. The doctor took one step backwards and watched as Ju Chunhua slowly put her boy down. Now he could see that the baby really was gigantic. He looked as if he was already seven or eight years old and his skin was as black as charcoal, though his features were regular. The boy looked at the doctor curiously and asked, 'Are you the police? Why do you want to catch me?'

The doctor started walking backwards, shaking his head at the giant baby and at the same time shouting to Ju Chunhua, 'I'm the doctor from Liushui, don't you remember? You took some of my medicine.'

Over the giant baby's gigantic skull, he saw Ju Chunhua tip her straw hat. Her face was still hidden under the shadows of the brim and the cloth in front of it, but he could sense her indifference. He watched as she patted the giant baby on the head, her hoarse but quiet voice striking the doctor like lightning.

'Your daddy has come. Say "daddy" to him, son,' Ju Chunhua told the giant baby.

The doctor was petrified by shock as he stood there, listening to the drone of the crowd outside.

The giant baby's four-fingered right hand, which was neither large nor small, reached out to him impatiently. His bright eyes gazed at the doctor and his smooth red lips were already open, on the cusp of pronouncing that simple but resonant word: daddy. Finally, the doctor let out a wild cry.

'No, I'm not. I'm not!' He dropped the umbrella he was carrying and pushed past the villagers to escape. He could feel that there were people behind him, chasing him, shouting something, but immense fear had caused the doctor to lose any sense of sound. All he could hear was something resembling the whistling of the wind in the open fields.

Throughout autumn and winter, the doctor in Liushui was somewhat out of sorts; he even spent a period of time bedridden. The people in town had not learned of his visit to Wangbao, so that when he reappeared at the clinic, they asked him what illness he had been suffering from. He carefully concealed the story and claimed to have had nothing more than a cold brought on by exposure to wind.

As soon as the clinic reopened, the infertile women of the town came flooding back. They were disappointed, however, for they found the doctor a changed man: he treated them coldly, and prescribed puny amounts of medicine. Some of them complained, asking, 'But Dr

Zhang, what happened? We're happy to give more money, if that's what you're on about, but you're prescribing medicine like it's arsenic! What could this small amount possibly be good for?'

The doctor made a grimace of irritation and laughed at them coldly. 'You don't want to have a giant baby, do you?' he said, 'If you want a normal child, this much is plenty.'

In winter, the doctor would often sit in the sun with the barber from across the road. He was particularly alert when anyone went in or out of town, and asked the barber to warn him if he should ever see a woman wearing a straw hat. Of course, the barber was curious about what lay behind such a mysterious instruction. The doctor, however, though he had been on the point of telling him several times, simply told him that someone held a grudge against him and that sooner or later she was bound to come calling.

Towards the end of the year, a woman with a straw hat did indeed appear on the town's street, leading a boy of a little over ten. Both were dressed in rags and seemed worn out by the journey. People quite naturally connected their arrival with the floods south of the mountains, since quite a few victims of the disaster had already come to beg in the wealthy area around Liushui.

As they passed by a noodle shop, the well-meaning owner ran out after them with a bowl of noodles that someone had left unfinished and handed it to the boy.

Much to her shock, he glared fiercely at her and heaved the bowl back in her face. With a cry, she brushed off the spilt noodles, then she turned on the woman with the straw hat, swearing at her, 'Damn you! Damn you! What kind of mother are you? Is that how you raise your son?' She saw the woman incline her head and suddenly lift off the cloth covering her face to reveal her burnt and gruesome countenance. 'This is the kind of mother I am, and this is how I raise my son,' she said.

The noodle shop wasn't far from the clinic, and the doctor heard the owner's sharp cry of surprise from inside. By the time he went out to see what had happened, Ju Chunhua and the giant baby were already standing on the steps. The doctor saw that in his hands the baby was holding the umbrella he had left that day in Wangbao. His mind went completely blank and he mumbled, 'So you've come. I knew you would. But I don't want anything to do with the two of you.'

Ju Chunhua looked at him from under her straw hat. Against the sunlight, you could see dust drifting slowly up from her hat and clothes. As if she hadn't heard his muttering, she pushed the giant baby forward and said, 'Give daddy his umbrella back.'

The giant baby grinned at him, revealing a row of pitch-black, much-worn teeth. He squeezed the umbrella into the doctor's hand and then used his right hand to tug at the doctor's beard. The four fingers on the baby's hand were perfectly round but very coarse, and they moved wantonly on the doctor's chin. Under the caresses of the giant baby, the doctor trembled from head to toe. He felt as if he had suddenly shrunk to the size of an infant. The giant baby, with his breath of garlic mixed with tobacco smoke, reminded him of his own childhood. It was an awful smell, the smell of nightmares, and he realized that it was absolutely identical to that of his father and grandfather. Fear and disgust filled his heart. He gripped the baby's wrists and said, 'Don't do that. I'm not your father.'

The baby turned back to look at his mother. The doctor, too, gave her a pleading look and said, 'You shouldn't lie to a child about a thing like that. Who is his father anyway? You can't just make up whatever you like.'

Ju Chunhua, standing on the sunlit stairs, suddenly belched. 'If he says he isn't your daddy, then he isn't your daddy. And if he's not your daddy, then he's our enemy. Revenge, child! Revenge!'

Then the doctor received a slap on the face that made his bones smart. The baby was brandishing his four-fingered fist, screaming, 'Revenge, revenge!' The doctor fell down the steps, not only because he had received such a fierce blow, but also because it felt like he had experienced a proverbial bolt from the blue, a bolt that had struck him on the cheek. The doctor forgot his pain and allowed the tears of panic to flow freely.

*   *   *

The year was nearing its end, and there were already children around setting off premature firecrackers. In the spot where Ju Chunhua had disappeared with the baby, there was now a man selling holiday goods and flirting with a group of women. Through the pain, the doctor regarded the town as it prepared for the festival. These oblivious people, he thought. They don't know the giant baby has come. They're still in the dark. They don't know the baby is walking through this town with his mother right now. They don't realize that this year vengeful blows will replace the bangers and firecrackers. Blows coming like bolts from the sky, striking every person once on the face.

And, oh, will it hurt.

ISHQ & MUSHQ
Priya Basil

'AN ENTICING DEBUT NOVEL BY A MUCH-VAUNTED
YOUNG NOVELIST'
Glasgow Herald

When Sarna Singh leaves the lustrous green hills of Uganda
for England, rows of cramped old houses were not what she
was expecting. Husband Karam has brought her to Clapham
Common, hoping that the greenery will remind her of
Kampala. But Sarna is convinced they have moved to England
so he can visit his secret London lady friends. She has a
devastating secret of her own. How long before Sarna's web of
deceit destroys her own family?

Against a backdrop that spans Partition from India,
Elizabeth II's Coronation and Churchill's funeral, to the
present day, Priya Basil's explosive family drama
is passionate and moving.

'WITH A VERVE FOR THE COLOUR OF LIFE, THIS BOOK
. . . SURPRISES WITH ITS UNDERLYING WISDOM'
Good Housekeeping's 6 Great Reads

'BRILLIANTLY WOVEN . . . CLEVER AND OFTEN FUNNY'
Candis

'THE PRODUCT OF A DEFT HAND THAT MIXES
ENGROSSING NARRATIVE WITH UNEXPECTED
DASHES OF MAGICAL REALISM'
India Today

9780552773843

BLACK SWAN